Passion & Hope: A Lesbian Love Story

ISBN

Paperback	978-1-68547-228-3
Hardcover	978-1-68547-229-0
eBook	978-1-68547-230-6
Library of Congress Control Number:	2023907662

Printed in the United States of America

101 Foundry Dr,
West Lafayette, IN, 47906, USA
www.wordhousebp.com
+1-800-646-8124

PASSION &HOPE

A Lesbian Love Story

R.L. ATKINS

Table of Contents

CHAPTER ONE

Tricia's Odyssey

Tricia Flick left her home at Lake Rumford when she was twenty nine. She had lived there her whole life. Her Father was the head of a major Law Firm and very successful. He had several teams of attorneys that worked for him. That success came with a price.

That price was not being able to spend quality time with his two children. His wife died when they were small and they had a series of Nanny's as they were growing up.

Trish was the eldest and Tommy was five years younger. For the most part they had everything that a Kid could want, except for the love that only a Parent can give.

Thomas Sr. never chose to remarry after the death of his young wife and so with his Law practice he was not able to be with them during their formative years. Trish did not get along well with the nanny's and they didn't stay long.

There was one who she did get along with and that was Betty

Ruth. She was a twenty something college dropout who decided that she could make her way as a nanny. She applied for a position with a placement firm that specialized in hiring help for professional people that have no parent in the home during the day and into the evening.

When she came into Tricia's life, Trish was thirteen at the time and they hit it off right away.

Her father was pleased to see someone who his daughter could get along with. Betty Ruth was a live in nanny and had a room of her own in the house.

She was an attractive woman with red hair that she wore in a single braid that hung down her back. She was five foot six and weighed one hundred thirty pounds.

She was able to make friends with both of the children right away when she started to work there

Tommy Jr. was seven at the time and just fell in love with her.

Trish was fascinated by her braid and wanted to wear her hair the same way. She had a manner about her that made the children comfortable.

When their father was home he enjoyed her company. He needed to have a relief from his stressful daily life.

Once or twice a week he would enter her bedroom after the kids were asleep and they would have sex. For this he gave her a bonus in cash.

She was quite talented in the bedroom. She was able to show him ways of making love that his wife never would have dreamed of. They were both virgins when they married and had no experience in the ways of making love.

He and his wife only knew that the man laid on top of the woman and that's how it was done.

Betty Ruth taught him a lot of different positions to have

intercourse.

And then there was the oral sex. He had no idea that it could feel so good. She taught him how to give her pleasure as well.

She stayed with the Flick Family for five years.

When Tricia was seventeen Betty Ruth took her aside one day and told her,

"You are a full grown woman now and you need to know the ways of love."

"What do you mean by that?" Trish asked.

"I mean the ways to make love, you know fucking."

Trish got red in the face and sat in silence.

Betty Ruth asked her,

"Have you ever felt an urge in your panties to have someone touch your private places?"

Trish knew what she was referring to. Yes, she had those urges and she had been doing more than just touching herself.

"I do have those urges that you are talking about. What should I do about 'em?" She asked.

Betty Ruth smiled and said,

"Follow me." She showed Tricia to her bedroom and opened a box. In the box were several sex toys. Betty Ruth said,

"When you get those urges come on in here and you can use one of these."

Tricia looked at them with interest. She had never seen any before.

"May I touch one?" She asked.

Betty Ruth said,

"Sure you can, go ahead and pick one up." Tricia reached in the box and picked up one of the smaller toys and held it in her hand. It was soft yet hard at the same time. It was six inches in length.

Betty Ruth said,

"Now watch I will show you what you can do with it.

Pull your pants down and drop your panties."

Tricia had a strange feeling come over her as this woman who she had been around for five years was asking, no, telling her to make her girl parts naked in front of her. She did what she was told to do in spite of her mind telling her that it was somehow wrong.

Betty Ruth then told her

"Take it and stick it inside your pussy. There is a switch on the end that starts a vibrator. When you turn on the vibrator you will get some sensations that you have not felt before."

Tricia pushed the toy into her vagina that had started to get wet. It went in about half way and she turned on the vibrator. The feelings that she felt were pleasant and she enjoyed it.

Betty Ruth said,

"Now push it in and out and see how that feels. Any time you want to use one of these you are welcome to come in and get one. I just ask that when you are finished with it wash it off and return it to the box, OK?"

Tricia nodded her head as she continued to use the toy on herself. Then Betty Ruth said,

"Lay down on my bed and use it. You can pull your legs up and get it in deeper. When you get to where you are feeling your muscles tighten and relax and then tighten again and again that is when you are having your climax. You can have these many times with this toy. It can do what a man's cock can do and more with the motor in it."

Tricia started to feel what Betty Ruth was telling her. Then it happened and she pulled the toy out and then pushed it back in.

Betty Ruth asked,

"How was that?"

Tricia smiled at her and said,

"Thank you for showing me this. It will work well when I can't sleep."

"That's why I have it." Betty Ruth told her. "I know that you will soon be thinking about getting fucked by some boy. It will not be as good as this, trust me."

Tricia wondered if she was right. Was this why she never heard Betty Ruth talk about a boy friend? She kept him in a box.

A week later Tricia asked her brother Tommy if he would like to see something in her room. Tommy replied,

"Sure what is it?"

"Come in here and I will show you." She said.

Tommy went in her room and she closed the door. When he came back out he had a strange look about him. He couldn't believe what he had just seen and done.

Tricia said,

"Don't tell anyone what just happened and I will owe you one, OK?"

Tommy smiled and replied,

"You sure do owe me one. And sometime I will collect on it."

Sure enough the time came when he would collect on that debt. It was five years later when he brought Vicky Steel to the house one night.

"Trish, I want you to meet Vicky."

"Hi Vicky how are you?"

Tommy said,

"Vicky here would like to kiss a girl and I thought of you."

Trish said,

"If this is a joke or some kind of initiation or your buddies are watching the answer is no."

She turned to Vicky and said,

"You're a pretty girl and if I wanted too, I'd kiss you. No question."

Vicky told Trish,

"You're a very pretty girl and I would love to kiss you too."

The girls kissed and made love after Tommy left. This was not the first time Trish kissed a girl. She had had several girlfriends while in high school and then when she was in college. They all were casual affairs and Trish never formed a bond with any of them.

She liked Vicky and they paled around while Vicky was staying at her cousin's house for a few weeks that summer. She was a nice distraction for Trish who had no steady boyfriends, or girlfriends for that matter.

When Vicky went back home Trish told her brother,

"You can bring a girl like her home to me anytime, and she was such a sweetie."

Tommy replied,

"She sure is, I think I will marry her someday."

Trish laughed and said,

"Good one Bro, you'll still be playing the field until you are forty."

"No," said Tommy, "I'm not like you. I want to have a family someday and I want Vicky to have my babies."

Trish laughed and replied,

"Then I want to wish Vicky and you the best."

Trish had gone to college to study Journalism. She hoped to become a TV news personality. If not then she would just travel the world in search of her destiny.

After Vicky was gone from her life Trish picked up with another one of Tommy's friends called "Peaches". It was not her real name, but hated that which was Mildred.

Peaches suited her personality and she stole Tricia's heart the first time they met.

She was a dainty little girl who was barely ninety pounds and was four foot five inches tall. She had long blond hair that flowed down over her shoulders like a cascade of gold. It had a shine in the sunlight and Trish could not keep her hands off of it. Peaches had a light complexion and blue eyes. She too was drawn to Trish. They shared their first kiss while sitting on the porch swing looking out over the lake. She had shaved her pussy hair and looked almost childlike. Trish thought while they made love,

'How lucky am I to have this Doll here in my arms.'

Peaches loved Trish too and they were inseparable when tragedy struck. Peaches was coming back from town after doing some shopping and she was going too fast for the wet road. Her car slid off the Highway and struck a tree. She lived long enough in the Hospital for Trish to get there and say good bye.

Trish was broken hearted and went into a dark depression after the death of Peaches. She had considered suicide. The Doctor put her on a powerful anti-depressant and in a few months she was back to her old self.

She just took an attitude of,

"Loves found, loves lost, move on".

One day she met a man named David Strong. He was tall dark and handsome as the cliché goes. He had a full head of brown hair that he wore brushed back on the sides and over the top. He had a short beard, a quick smile and a happy laugh. They met at a Coffee Shop that Trish went to when she was in town.

David worked as a Real Estate salesman. He knew every inch of the county as he had listings everywhere. He was very good at what he did and was very successful at it.

He took her to dinner that evening and after they ate Trish invited him up to her house. When they arrived he was impressed. He said,

"You have one of the best homes in the area and you have it decorated very nicely."

"Thank you, "Trish said, "Would you like a drink?"

"I'm not much of a drinker since College. I did my share there."

"So did I", Trish responded. "Let's sit out on the porch and talk a while."

David followed her out and they sat on the swing.

"You have a beautiful view of the lake from here. If you ever decide to sell it let me know, I can get you a fortune for it."

"I'm not in a hurry to leave here like you say the view is perfect."

David looked to her and smiled,

"So are you Trish, may I kiss you?" Trish melted in his arms.

After a while he said,

"I sure would like to see the layout of the house, especially where your bedroom is located."

Trish thought,

'Is this really happening, of course it is that's why you brought this delicious hunk of man here.'

"Right this way." She said.

He took her by the hand and they walked thru the house to her bedroom. He kissed her again as she took off her shirt and then her jeans. He did the same.

Trish laid on the bed and David ran his hands over her body. He asked her to turn onto her belly. She complied and he continued to caress her back and down her butt and down her legs.

"You are a beautiful woman and I want to make love to you but only if you want me too."

Trish rolled on to her back again and spread her legs apart.

"I'm ready if you are."

She whispered with her eyes closed just enjoying his touch. He kissed her feet and up her legs, one and then the other. This is how Trish liked the fore play to commence. He continued up to her crotch where he gently licked her lady parts. She took a deep breath and pushed his head into her so that she could feel his tongue working its magic on her.

"Oh David that feels so good, I don't want you to stop." She felt an orgasm starting and she knew it was not going to stop.

"Put it in me now!" she begged.

He moved up and kissed her on the mouth as he slid his cock into her.

They had a good relationship going for a year when he started with a strange cough. He went to see his Doctor and found that he had stage four lung cancer and had only a month at best to live.

Trish stayed at his house until he passed. With tears in her eyes she thought,

'Am I ever going to have a lover that I don't lose?'

Trish was feeling sorry for herself when she found Daisy.

Trish was working for the local daily newspaper when she walked in. Daisy was fresh out of College and full of enthusiasm at the prospect of her first real job. She looked like a school girl with an outfit that was right off the cover of "Seventeen".

She had red hair like Betty Ruth and it reminded Trish of the first time she explored her sexuality with her.

Betty Ruth seduced her when she was seventeen. She remembered how she learned about sex toys and then one night when her father was away on business Betty Ruth came into her bedroom and asked Trish to take off her pajamas that she wanted to show her some more things. She began,

"I don't know if you will ever have an interest in another girl, but

I want to teach you how to pleasure her."

As Trish laid there on her bed she felt Betty Ruth put her hands on her breasts and rub them with her palms while touching her nipples between her fingers.

She felt her tongue go into her crack. She felt it in her vagina. Betty Ruth continued to lick and suck on Trish's pussy parts until Trish felt an orgasm hitting. Her legs and stomach muscles twitched as her body screamed in pleasure. Betty Ruth laid on her bed beside her and said,

"Now do it to me so I know that you have learned how to do it."

Trish was still feeling the afterglow of her own climax when she pleasured Betty Ruth.

"You are a quick learner Trish, you will be able to make any girl happy."

* * *

The Newspaper hired Daisy and they assigned her to work with Trish. Daisy was excited to be working with someone who knew as much as Trish and was easy on the eyes.

They spent the next week together as Daisy learned the job she was to do. She would bump up against Daisy whenever it seemed natural to do it. After a while Daisy bumped back and smiled at Trish.

"I know what you are doing, and I like it." Daisy said with a coy look.

Trish smiled and replied,

"Would you like to come up to my place sometime? It overlooks the lake."

She looked at Trish and asked,

"Can I come up there this weekend? Can we go swimming in the lake?"

Trish replied,

"Sure, bring a suit and I have a friend who has a dock that we can use."

The women went about their work smiling the whole time waiting for Friday.

* * *

Friday came and Trish showed Daisy on a map where her house was.

"I know where that is, the house on the hill, right?" "That's it, I'll see you when you get there." Trish acknowledged.

It was after seven when Daisy arrived. Trish greeted her with a smile and said,

"Come on out on the porch I am about to put a couple of steaks on the grill, that's what we do here."

Daisy inquired,

"Where do we sleep?"

Trish looked at her and replied,

"There's five bedrooms here so you can have your pick, my brother Tommy sleeps in an upstairs bedroom."

Daisy asked,

"Where do you sleep?"

Trish relied,

"I sleep on the first floor back the hallway."

Daisy smiled and said,

"That's where I want to sleep too."

Trish smiled at her and said,

"There's plenty of room."

They sat at the table on the porch and ate their steaks and looked out over the lake. The sunset was beautiful. Trish smiled and felt happy.

$$* \quad * \quad *$$

They went in the house and Trish offered,

"There is a bathroom with a shower stall back the hallway to my room if you would like to take a nice shower before bed. I often do because it helps me relax."

Daisy asked,

"If I do will you wash my back?"

Trish teased,

"Only if you wash my front!"

Daisy shed her clothes as she walked back to the bathroom. By the time she got there she was naked. Trish admired her body as she went into the shower stall. It was a full sized bath area with three shower heads. One on the side of the wall and two overhead. The one head could be taken in your hand and used to rinse off the private parts. It felt good.

Trish joined Daisy in the shower and as promised they washed each other while sharing a kiss. When they finished they went to Trish's bedroom and dried off before laying down on the silk sheets that covered the bed. They were so soft and smooth compared to the plain old cotton sheets that Daisy had. She thought,

'I could get used to this.'

As Trish expected Daisy made the first move.

"I love to feel your mouth on mine and the feel of your body next to me." Daisy said as she kissed Trish and their hands found places to explore on each other.

She laid on her back as Daisy placed her hands on her breasts. She was gentle and soft in her touch.

Trish could tell that this girl had been around before. "When's the first time you made love to a girl Daisy?"

"It was in High School and then in College."

"You sure seem hungry for some good lovn' tonight."

"I sure am and I hope you are hungry too. I can't wait until I can get down on your sweet pussy." Daisy said as she was gently holding Trish's pubic mound.

She slipped her middle finger into Trish's crack and could feel the wetness starting to flow. She sucked on Trish's nipples that had gotten hard from the touching that Daisy had done.

Daisy found Trish's opening and her finger went in smoothly. She was getting wet too and then she moved down to Trish's soft, wet pussy. She sucked and licked her clit while she continued to move her two fingers in and out and then Trish had her first orgasm of the night.

Daisy turned around and put her pussy in Trish's face so that she could continue to pleasure her and vice versa.

Trish put her hands on Daisy's beautiful ass cheeks and squeezed them as she sucked and licked Daisy to her climax.

Daisy got up and told her

"Get up on your knees now and I will give you another thrill."

Trish had an idea of what Daisy wanted to do, she was right.

Daisy got behind Trish and spread her ass cheeks apart and licked her anus. Her tongue worked around and in it while she stuck a finger back in Trish's pussy hole. It was not long before Trish felt another orgasm coming. Daisy continued to finger fuck Trish's pussy while licking her ass.

Then Trish said,

"It's my turn now."

Daisy moved over on the bed and assumed the position with her knees on the bed and her magnificent white ass was there for the taking.

Trish ran her hands over it and held it tight while she parted Daisy's cheeks. She started at the top of her crack and worked slowly down to her puckered hole. Trish worked her tongue around it and lapped it over the pucker. She continued to go down her crack until she could lick and taste Daisy's pussy.

They pleasured one another until very late in the night. Then they embraced and kissed for the last time before falling asleep.

* * *

The next day they went over to the cottage where Jeff lived. Trish knew that they could use the dock to swim. She knocked on the door when she got there. Jeff opened the door and was pleasantly surprised to see two women in thong swimming suits standing in front of him.

"Hi Trish, who's your fiend?"

"This is Daisy, she works with me at the Paper. Can we go out to the platform to swim?"

Jeff smiled and said,

"Sure, no problem, I'll get my suit too and join you."

Trish looked at Daisy and smiled. Daisy knew she was going to get fucked today.

* * *

The two women walked down to the dock and swam out to the platform. They were sitting on it when Jeff came down to join them. He swam out to the platform and grabbed onto Daisy's legs and pulled her into the water. She hollered and grabbed onto Jeff around his back as he put his arm around her.

She wrapped her legs around his waist and they held onto the side of the platform.

Trish was watching from above. She could imagine what they were doing. Jeff had fucked Vicky right here and now he was fucking Daisy. Trish jumped in the water and swam over to them. She said,

"Is it my turn yet?"

Jeff replied,

"I'll take care of you later." Trish asked,

"Is that a promise?" Jeff laughed as he continued to fuck Daisy and then he said,

"We can go back up to the house, give me a half hour to recover. And then she can watch".

Trish asked,

"Do you still have some KY?"

Jeff smiled and said,

"I don't go anywhere without it."

Daisy looked at Jeff and asked,

"What are you going to do to Trish?"

* * *

They went back to the Cottage and Jeff led them back to his bedroom. Then Trish asked Daisy,

"Did you ever get it in your ass hole?"

Daisy replied."

No, I haven't done that. Probably the only thing I haven't done."

Trish said,

"Well Jeff did me one time and he knows what he is doing. Do you want to try it or just watch?"

Jeff said,

"I can be very gentle, ask Trish."

Daisy said,

"Can I watch and then maybe try it."

"That will be OK with me." Trish told Daisy. Trish took the thong suit off and laid on Jeff's bed. He went to his dresser and got the tube of lube and a condom.

He told Daisy,

"Watch how she puts it on my cock."

Trish put the condom in her mouth and then on second though handed it to Daisy.

"Here you can put it on."

Daisy asked,

"OK, can you tell me how to do it?"

"It's easy, just put it in your mouth and when he puts his cock in you just unroll it as he goes in."

Jeff asked Trish,

"You asked if it can be done when you are on your back, well let's try it and see."

Trish replied,

"I'm game lets go."

She put her legs up over her head and was able to present her ass hole just fine. Jeff lubed it up good and lubed the condom as well. He was able to insert with ease the first time he pushed. She had really learned to relax.

In this position she could play with her clit while Jeff was pumping slowly in and out. He had an idea and pulled out of Trish.

He asked Daisy,

"Would you like to try it now?"

She looked to Trish for guidance and she smiled at Daisy and said,

"Try it, Jeff is just the right size and he is ready to go."

"Oh, alright, I'll do it but it better be good."

Jeff gave the tube of KY to Trish and said,

"You're her friend, you do it."

Trish took the tube and put some on Daisy's puckered anus and pushed some in with her finger. She moved it around for a while like Jeff does.

"Now just relax and let it happen."

Daisy chose to do it with her knees under her. Jeff started to put his cock in her and she tightened up.

"You have to relax or it can't go in.'

"I'll try." Daisy said.

Jeff continued to press in and finally he felt her relax enough that he could get about four inches in. He was able to pump enough to give her a good feeling and he left his load in the condom.

"There, was that so bad?" Trish asked.

Daisy replied,

"It gets tight and I'm glad he had the lube but you are right, it does feel good after a while."

Trish told her,

"The more you do it the better it will feel, just stay with men who have small cocks. Or a girl with a magic tongue."

When they returned to work on Monday there was a tension between them that Trish sensed.

"Daisy, what's the problem today? You seem upset or something."

Daisy told, her,

"After that crazy weekend I just need time to recover."

Trish said,

"I thought we had a good time with each other and with Jeff too."

Daisy had a tear in her eye and told Trish that she would like to take a couple days off to get her head on straight.

Trish said,

"Well I guess that you can use some vacation days for that. You are coming back?"

Daisy replied,

"I don't know. You are the best lover that I ever had and that is something to come back for."

Trish told her,

"I hope you do, I need your help here and you are welcome at my home anytime."

Daisy left that afternoon and never did come back.

Trish was again on the losing end of the short relationship with Daisy. She thought that she should just move on. She had no equity in the hill top house. Her father still had ownership of it. So she didn't have a lot of money to do anything too radical.

She thought about just getting a small motor home and traveling all around the country. She had no money to buy one. Her depression was coming back and she felt trapped here.

Then came the tragic news that she and Tommy's dad had died of a heart attack. The woman that he was living with called to tell them about it. They had no idea of their father's wealth just that he had a successful Law firm.

They went to the firm's office and sat down with one of the partners who explained their father's last will that he had drawn up. If not a perfect parent after his wife died, he at least tried to provide a substitute in the form of a nanny for the years while the siblings were growing up.

He wanted his common law wife to be taken care of and had set up a trust that would provide her a monthly income. He left the bulk of his estate to his children, Tricia and Tommy Jr... It consisted of the hill top house and several dozen rental properties that would continue to be taken care of by a property management company and the profits from the rentals would go to the siblings with a fee paid to the management co. The attorney said,

"You have suffered a loss, but your father has provided well for you. There is a trust fund that will pay each of you eight thousand dollars each month. He wanted the firm to continue after his passing so he had met with all the partners and among them they chose a new senior partner who would manage the firm. A price was arrived at for the value of the firm at the time of his death and the partners agreed to purchase it from the estate. The value of your fathers' share of the firm was determined to be six million dollars."

Tommy and Tricia were numb as they tried to come to terms with what was going to happen to their lives.

Trish thought about the motor home that she wanted to get, now she could. She also didn't have to worry about money. She would have more then she could ever spend. Tommy was happy to have the house and now he made plans to find Vicky and bring her there to live with him.

*   *   *

Trish stopped at several motor home dealers and finally picked the one that suited her needs. It was not a huge bus, but just the right size for a future peripatetic, vagabond, wanderer looking to see the world. It was twenty five feet long. It was perfect for one person to travel. It had a silver and blue paint job that she liked.

When she arrived back at the house Tommy was there. She said,

"Well I am going to pack up some things and then I will be heading out. Tell Vicky that I love her and think about her often."

Tommy said,

"Tell her yourself, she's here."

Trish turned around and there stood Vicky.

"Come here you," Vicky said as she put her arms out and Trish ran over to hug and kiss her.

Vicky asked,

"Where are you going to go with that little house on wheels?"

Trish said,

"I don't know, where ever the wind blows. Maybe to Texas or up to Maine for Lobster. I want to see the desserts and the mountains. I want to meet new people along the way. You never know what's around the corner."

Tommy said,

"Keep in touch so we know you are alright, I love you sister and I am going to miss you not being here with me."

Trish had tears in her eyes as she said her good byes to Vicky and her brother. She got in her new motor home and started down the road.

She drove out around the Lake and went past Jeff's house. He had moved away last year when he and Kate Springer got married.

She remembered the crazy things that she did with Vicky and him and with Daisy. Jeff was some kind of good stud alright and she was going to miss him.

The money from her father's estate was deposited into a Bank account. All she had to do when she needed any was just go to an ATM and punch in her numbers and the money just kept coming.

She headed up into New England and went to Bar Harbor Maine as she said she would. She sat on a dock by the Harbor and ate her fill of Lobster Tails. That was always a treat that she longed for.

While she sat there a young woman came up and sat down beside her.

"Hello, my name is Kitty, that's short for Katherine what's yours?" She asked.

Trish looked up, smiled at her and said,

"I'm Trish, that's short for Tricia."

Kitty smiled back and looked at the pile of Lobster tails that were on Trish's plate and said,

"Wow, you sure do like Lobster!"

Trish replied,

"It is something that I always wanted to do, eat as much as I wanted."

"It looks like you did, they sure are good aren't they?" Kitty asked. "You aren't from around here are you?"

Trish told her,

"No, I'm just passing thru."

Kitty asked,

"Where are you from and where are you going?"

Trish told her,

"I am from New York State and I am going where ever the road takes me, I am a free bird."

Kitty confided,

"I am too, I am on the run from my crazy ex, I ran away from him to keep from being beat up all the time. When he gets drunk he does bad stuff. I had enough. I want to start over."

Trish said,

"I 'm sorry to hear that, you don't deserve to get beat up like that."

She could see the bruising on Kitty's arm.

Then Trish had an idea,

"Would you like to come along with me? I have a small motor home, but it's big enough for two."

Kitty's eyes lit up and then she said,

"I have no money to help with expenses."

Trish replied,

"I can get my hands on more cash than you can imagine."

Kitty asked,

"You didn't rob a bank did you?"

Trish replied,

"No, I am a Trust fund brat. You know the ones who have a huge pile of money that they never earned."

Kitty said,

"That's nice, I never had a pot to piss in or a window to throw it out. When we were growing up, the five of us, three girls and the two boys, we would wear our brothers or sisters' shoes as they out grew them. We were poor enough to get government surplus cheese and stuff. It's not easy being raised by a single mom who struggled to keep us fed."

Trish thought about her own life of privilege growing up. She didn't have a mother, but she had a nanny. Her father was mostly an absentee dad. He made it home for weekends. Now she was talking to a person who she could not really relate to but felt a bond growing. They were both damaged goods.

Kitty with growing up dirt poor and then having a savage man for a boyfriend. Trish asked Kitty,

"Would you like to get a lobster tail? They have some nice ones, my treat."

Kitty was hungry because when she ran away from her boyfriend she had no money and no food.

"Can I really? Oh, Trish, you are so generous. How am I ever going to repay you for your kindness?" Kitty asked.

Trish smiled and said,

"Getting you away from here and to safety is going to be my payment."

Kitty finished her Lobster and the two of them headed over to Trish's "Home on wheels" as she called it.

They got in and started out along the high way and Kitty asked, "Where are we headed now?" Trish came back with, "Take a look at that map and you tell me where to go."

"There is a town called Bethel up in the other side of the state, looks like a nice place with a lake." Trish told her,

"I grew up living in a house overlooking a lake, when the moon was full it reflected on the water. It was beautiful."

Kitty saw a tear in her eye and asked her,

"You miss it don't you?"

"I do, but I just needed to get away for a while."

Kitty asked,

"Did you have a boyfriend or husband there?"

Trish told Kitty,

"The truth is I had a girlfriend that left me. I really thought that I had found the one."

Kitty said, "I had a girlfriend too long ago. I miss her too. She drowned in a boating accident. She didn't have a life jacket on and the boat hit a log in the water at high speed and she was thrown out of the boat. The boat was damaged so badly that it sank along with the other girl who also drowned. She was only sixteen."

Trish thought about Peaches and how she died in her car. "You know Kitty, we have some things that we have both suffered thru. I lost a girlfriend too. She died when her car hit a tree. I was able to get to the hospital just before she was gone. I kissed her as she died."

Kitty saw the tears streaming down Trish's face and took a tissue and wiped them away.

She said,

"You poor girl, we do have a lot in common."

Trish continued to drive until they got to Bethel. There was a nice camp ground there and she pulled in for the night.

Trish lit up the gas stove and heated up some baked beans with bacon and they sat at the table eating.

When a couple who were in the camper next to hers came to the door and gave a shout.

"Hi neighbor, could you drink a beer?"

Bill and Ruth Casey were retired and had sold their home in Iowa and decided to spend the rest of their days on the road. They had been on the road for the past two years and had been in all of the lower forty-eight states.

Ruth had been a school teacher and Bill worked as a mechanic at the Des Moines Airport. He worked on the airplanes for thirty years and had prepared well for their retirement.

Ruth had a pension from the school and she also started an IRA plan on top of that.

∗   ∗   ∗

Their camper was a fifth wheel model and they had a big Dodge pickup that they pulled it with. Next to Trish's it looked huge. It had three bedrooms with a double bed, a full bath, a sitting room and a nice kitchen.

Trish had one bedroom, a small bathroom with a shower and a kitchen.

Kitty was the first to reply to Bill's offer.

"Sure I can drink a beer with you."

Bill stepped inside the camper and looked around. Being use to his he could really see the difference between them. He said,

"Kind of looks like compact living. Come over and see the inside of ours."

Trish piped up and said,

"OK, let's go over to your place and drink some of your beer."

They finished their supper and then they went to see Bill's Camper.

Ruth met them at the door and showed them in. Bill took some cold beer from the refrigerator and passed it around.

She asked,

"Where are you girls from?"

Trish replied,

"I am from New York and Kitty is from Maine. We got together at Bar Harbor and decided to see the country and meet some people. So here we are meeting people."

Bill asked,

"How long is your vacation?"

Trish replied,

"I am a permanent Road Bum. I am pushing thirty and have come into an actual fortune that has allowed me to retire early. So I guess that I still have another thirty or more years of vacation."

Ruth looked at Kitty and asked,

"How do you fit into this arrangement? Are you just friends or are you in a relationship?"

Kitty said, "We are just friends who met and decided to take a ride. How long a ride? I don't know. I do know that I can't go back or I will die."

Trish came in with,

"You never know what may happen along the way. Kitty is a sweet girl who was in a terrible, abusive relationship. You can see the bruises on her arms where he beat her."

Ruth looked at Bill and then he told about how their daughter was in the same situation. She didn't leave and he finally killed her. He said,

"She even had a restraining order on him that he ignored. After all that's just a piece of paper. He had a knife."

Tears came to Ruth's eyes and she left the sitting room and went back to the bedroom. Trish heard her sobbing and went back to try to comfort her. She put her arms around her and held her.

"I know your loss. I have lost several people that I loved who died too young. But I can't feel the same pain that the loss of a child can bring."

Ruth stopped crying and told Trish,

"Thank you, it has been just over two years ago that we lost her. That's when we took to the road. We needed to distance ourselves from where it happened."

They went back and joined Bill and Kitty. Bill asked, "Where are you planning to go from here?"

Trish said,

"Where ever the wheels take us. Probably go over to Vermont from here. Then head down the coast on route one and skip the Interstates."

"Good idea that way you will be able to see the charm of New England and everywhere else you go."

Trish and Kitty went back to her small motor home for the night. They decided to both sleep in the double bed. They got undressed down to their underwear and crawled into the bed.

Trish fell asleep and Kitty was still thinking about Ruth and Bill's daughter and how she was murdered. When she did fall asleep she had a nightmare where her boyfriend was chasing her with a machete. He was gaining on her and her legs wouldn't move any faster. Then just as he swung it at her head she woke up with a scream. She sat up in bed and started to cry.

Trish woke up and asked,

"What's the matter Kitty?"

"He was chasing me and trying to kill me." She replied with tears flowing down her check. Trish put her arms around her and told her,

"You're safe here now with me, I will protect you."

Kitty felt the warmth of Trish against her body and it stirred an urge in her.

"Kiss me Trish." She said.

Trish hugged her harder and kissed her on the lips. Kitty felt like she was melting.

The heat of their bodies touching in the darkness was making her bolder. She held Trish in her arms and let her hand go down to Trish's bare belly. She rubbed it slowly and moved it down to her mound.

Trish responded by parting her legs so that Kitty could reach her crotch. Her own hands were moving on Kitty's body too. She put her hands on Kitty's soft butt and squeezed it gently while the two of them shared a deep kiss.

Kitty slid her hand inside Trish's panties and felt her crack. She ran her finger up and down until she opened up enough to let her finger enter her vagina. With her finger wet from Trish's juice she pulled it out and rubbed it on her clit. Trish had sex with a lot of women but there was something about Kitty that was different.

She continued to rub Trish's parts, inside and out when Trish began to reciprocate. She pulled Kitty up so that her crotch was at her face. Kitty had slipped her panties off and her hairy pussy was already wet when she pressed it against Trish's mouth.

Her tongue was eager to probe Kitty's open vagina. Kitty turned around and took the sixty-nine position and started to lick Trish's clit and down her crack. She sucked on her labia pulling them into her mouth. Trish did the same. They continued to pleasure each other the same way until they both had a beautiful release.

They fell asleep and when Trish woke up it was already ten o'clock. She could smell bacon and was surprised to see Kitty standing at the stove making breakfast.

"Rise and shine sleepy head." Kitty teased.

Trish got up and went over to Kitty and said,

"Does this make us more than friends?"

She stood behind her and cupped her breasts. Kitty looked up and replied,

"I think so, I know I am ready to be more than friends."

She turned off the stove and turned to kiss Trish.

"We better eat breakfast before it gets cold."

Trish looked at a map and chose their next destination.

"It looks like we can easily get over to Lake Champlain. I'm sure there's some camp grounds along there."

They headed off for Vermont. They found a small camp ground where they stayed the night. It was very peaceful and quiet. After making love that evening they both went to sleep and Kitty did not have the night mare.

The next morning they got up and took a walk around a small pond that was on the camp ground. They had breakfast and then got on the road by ten.

They headed south into New York State and decided to go to the Catskill Mountains. After several hours on the road they came to the town of Roscoe. There they found a nice camp ground that even had hot showers.

They decide to stay there for another day before leaving. There was a camp store there that they could pick up some snacks and fresh eggs. The fridge in Trish's rig was not too reliable. If they could hook up to electricity it was good. But going down the road she had to watch for spoilage of things when they thawed.

They met a couple of other women that were on vacation together. They left their families behind so that they could just have a long weekend of girl talk.

Trish asked the one woman,

"Where are you gals from?" She answered,

"We live in Connecticut and we come over here every year to get away from all the stress at home."

She asked in turn,

"Where are you from? I see New York tags on your motor home, so I guess you are from NY."

Trish replied,

"Yes, I lived over near Lake Rumford. Now I am on a lifetime trip with my lady here."

And she put her arm around Kitty's waist and hugged her.

The other woman said,

"Oh I see, you two are a couple, right?"

Kitty looked at Trish and then replied,

"We sure are, I think it was love at first kiss."

One of the women said,

"Yes, we are too, but our families don't have a clue. We started seeing each other on the down low when our kids were in grade school. After a PTA meeting one night we decided to stop for a drink and one thing led to another and here we are."

Trish smiled and replied,

"Yeah, you just never know when it can happen. I have had several relationships, but they didn't work out. I hope this one does."

Kitty smiled and said,

"Me too, she's helped me change my life. She may have even

saved my life."

The first woman said,

"I should introduce us, my name is Lois and this is Silvia. We were both 'Stay at home Moms' and have had enough of the stress of raising kids and then going to bed with men who don't care about us and our needs."

Silvia said,

"I have even tried to teach my husband how to please me but he is just an ignorant slob. All he wants to do is watch sports on the damn TV."

Then Lois added,

"Yeah, mine is the same way. How do you get a man to go down on you? It isn't that hard to do. Silvia and I do it every chance we get."

Trish laughed and replied,

"Only a few know how to get the job finished. I have had some good teachers, but now I am happy with this pretty girl." She looked at Kitty touched her hair and smiled.

Kitty said,

"We haven't been together for long but I think it could be forever." She smiled at Trish.

Lois asked,

"Have either of you been married?" Trish told her,

"No, but I have had some relationships that failed. There was a man who I did love, but he died. Then I had a sweet girl who died in a car wreck. Then I had one that just left me, and I don't know why. So I hope that Kitty and I can make it. We are set financially. I am as I told her, a trust fund brat. My brother and I received a huge inheritance when our dad died and we couldn't spend it in a lifetime. "

Lois said,

"I am happy for you. We are stuck with a frustrating situation in our beds and kids who are old enough to take care of themselves but don't move out."

Then Trish had an idea,

"How would you girls like to accompany us on our endless journey?"

Lois and Silvia looked at each other and then laughed. "How could you ever have the four of us in your tiny motor home?"

Trish replied,

"We couldn't do it in yours either. So it's time to get a REAL motor home." Silvia asked,

"Do you know how much they cost?"

"I do and I can pay cash." She said.

✳ ✳ ✳

The next day the four women piled into Silvia's car and they headed to the largest town in the area in search of a motor home. They found a dealer outside of town who had some real nice, large models.

Trish walked along with the other three and looked at what was there. The owner of the lot came out of his office.

"How are you ladies today? Are you interested in a great way to see the U S A?"

Trish said,

"Yes we are looking for one that all of us would be comfortable in and has a GOOD refrigerator."

The dealer said, "You came to the right place, what price range are you looking at." Trish replied, "Show me what you have."

The man walked along with them and pointed out the amenities of each as they walked by.

Trish was getting frustrated listening to him so she asked, "Which one is the top of the fucking line, that's the one I want."

He looked at her and said, sarcastically,

"You can't afford that one."

"Try me," She replied.

"OK, you see that Silver one with the Gold trim that is parked up by my office?"

"Yes, how much?"

He replied, "One hundred and seventy thousand dollars. I guess you have a piece of shit trade in for me to take some off, well I am firm on the price. It even has a satellite disc."

"Where is the nearest bank or ATM? She asked.

He smiled and said "There is a lot of banks in town. And there is an ATM at the convenience store gas station."

Trish replied,

"Thanks we'll be right back."

They got in the car and headed for town. They stopped at the first Bank they came to and went in.

The Teller asked,

"What can I do for you today?"

Trish showed her the card that she had in her wallet and the woman checked the balance in that account and turned to Trish and asked, "How much do you like to have?"

"I am getting a motorhome from the Idiot down the road, do you know if he insults all his potential customers? Give me a cashier's check for one hundred seventy thousand dollars. Do you think there are taxes on that amount as well?" She hit her computer and came up the additional amount. Trish said, Just make it for that whole amount, I want that motor home today."

She turned and looked at the other three who couldn't believe that she could do this so easily. When they had the check Trish went to the ATM outside and withdrew another thousand dollars for some WAM, 'Walk around money'. They returned to the dealers Lot and went into his office.

"Well I see your back, what now?"

Trish showed him the check and said,

"Now give me the fuckn' keys and title so we can get on our way".

He had never sold one for cash before and couldn't believe this young girl had the means to do it. He called the bank to verify it was their check and not a counterfeit. When he got off the phone he handed Trish the keys.

"Have a nice trip ladies."

When they got back to the camp ground Trish went to the manager and told him that he could keep hers and sell it or give it away. She handed him the signed off title. Lois and Silvia decided to take theirs back to Connecticut and park it in the driveway and leave with Kitty and Trish. They were two fifty somethings ready for adventure.

From Roscoe they headed across the Delaware River into Pennsylvania. Trish got on and followed the Interstate south into Maryland and then into West Virginia. They parked for the night in a Walmart parking lot.

Lois and Silvia sat with Kitty in the spacious lounge area and chatted. Silvia asked Kitty,

"How did you and Trish meet?"

Kitty replied, "We met in Bar Harbor Maine. I saw this beauty sitting alone eating Lobster. So I sat down and we started to talk. I showed her my bruises and told her my story of abuse. She invited me to come along with her and escape my abuser. So here we are."

Lois asked,

"When did you figure out that you liked each other?

Kitty smiled and said,

"We first made love in Maine at a camp ground there. I kind of started it when we were in bed together. How about you guys?"

Silvia recalled, "Our kids went to school together and Lois and I met at a PTA meeting. We just knew that we clicked and started seeing each other in the afternoon when we had my house to ourselves."

"Yes," Lois added, "We got to be intimate friends and we shared each other's secrets regarding our love life. We discovered that we had both married selfish, boring men who were only interested in their own satisfaction and not ours."

Silvia said, "That was when we decided to take care of each other's needs sexually so that we got what we needed."

Kitty felt sorry for the two women and yet was happy for them. She said,

"I had a girlfriend in high school who died in a boating accident. She was the first girl that I ever kissed. Trish has lost a girlfriend too."

Lois said,

"I'm sorry for your loss and I am happy for you that you met Trish, She is so sweet and generous that I can't believe that we ran into her. It's as if it was meant to be."

Trish had been in the store getting some things for them to eat. "We can stay here for the night and then head for Tennessee in the morning." She told them.

"So pick a bed and get some sleep or get some loven' if you want. I know I do."

The women all laughed and went to their separate rooms.

Silvia and Lois got undressed and Lois said,

"I'm going to take a shower, will you join me?"

Silvia grinned and said,

"I hoped you would ask." They headed for the bathroom and enjoyed a nice hot shower. They returned to bed and Lois laid down on the bed and Silvia laid down beside her.

"Nice bed isn't it?" Silvia remarked.

"Yes it is now kiss me." Lois whispered.

Silvia turned and met Lois's lips. She got on top of her and Lois's hands moved down to Silvia's ass. She ran her hands along the smoothness of it and then she took each cheek in her hands and pulled them apart. She put a finger in Silvia's butthole. Silvia pushed back and let it slid inside. Lois wiggled her finger while they kissed. Their tongues meeting in a warm embrace. They lingered for a while until Silvia moved down to Lois's breasts. She squeezed, kissed and sucked each one.

Lois gently pushed her head down to her pussy. Silvia knew just what Lois wanted her to do.

She licked on her clit until it became engorged and looked like a small penis. Silvia started to suck it in while she put two fingers inside her vagina and rubbed her G spot. This always brought Lois to an orgasm and tonight was no different except for not being in Connecticut.

Silvia turned around so that Lois could suck her clit while she continued to lick Lois's pussy.

Trish and Kitty were likewise engaged in mutual satisfaction.

After they each had several orgasms they fell asleep.

The next morning they got up and Trish announced,

"Today we are going to visit Dollywood, I hope you like Country and Bluegrass music. Silvia said,

"I can listen to anything and find some good in it."

Kitty said,

"Before my dad died he use to play the mandolin and mom would sing along to the songs that he played. So I kind of grew up listening to Blue Grass as a kid."

Trish added,

"My dad hated it and I didn't get to hear much of it. So I decided to head down south where it is the main sound that is heard. I love to hear a Fiddle and a Banjo and a Mandolin playing together. It sends a chill up my spine."

Lois smiled at Silvia and said,

"You can send a chill up my spine with your tongue."

They all laughed and Tricia pulled onto the Interstate heading south.

They arrived at Dollywood in the early afternoon and visited a number of different venues there. They feature up and coming musicians along with some major headliners. The park has a train that they rode and along the way it is ambushed by robbers. They spent a pleasant day enjoying all the music, food and rides. They located a nearby motor home park for the night.

In the morning after they had breakfast they met a couple who had pulled in beside them. They were in there mid fifty's.

Trish spoke first,

"Good morning folks. How was your night?" The man whose name was Dan Holt and his wife Ellen, replied,

"Good morning to you ladies. We slept well, it's a nice park here isn't it?"

Trish said,

"Yes it is, we usually just find a Walmart to stop for the night, but they frown on dumping gray water on their lot."

He laughed and replied,

"For sure, these places are good for taking care of all our needs. They have a good camp store here too. We have stayed here before."

Kitty asked, "Where are you folks from?"

Ellen replied," We are free to roam. We sold our house in Texas and bought this rig. Ain't it a Beauty?"

Trish replied, "It sure is." Dan looked hers over and said, "Yours ain't no slouch either. You don't see many like that one. Ours cost a hundred grand. I'll bet you didn't get yours for that did you?"

Trish replied,

"No, it was a bit salty, but it is big enough for the four of us."

Ellen was curious and asked,

"How are you girls related?" Lois answered,

"We are not blood related, we're just sexual relations."

Dan and Ellen smiled at that and Dan said,

"To each their own. But we just believe that sex should only be between a man and a woman. Anything else is a sin, good bye." And they walked away.

The four women looked at each other and Lois said,

"I can tell they're from Texas alright. But I'll bet if we gave Ellen three glasses of wine she would be all over Kitty here."

* * *

Silvia added,

"I know I would be. " As she smiled at Kitty.

Trish said to Silvia,

"You're not bad for an "Old woman" either. I'd bang you if I got the chance."

They all looked at each other and Kitty said,

"OH, what the hell. Would you guys like to switch partners tonight? I have never been with an older woman before."

Lois said, "What's this with bringing up age? How old are you Kitty?"

She replied,

"I just turned nineteen."

Trish added, "But she is soon going to be sixty-nine,"

The all laughed and Kitty's face got red.

"I will be thirty in June." Trish told them.

Lois replied,

"I guess that I am the old lady here, I am fifty three and Silvia is fifty-one."

Silvia offered,

"I'm game for a switch, tonight I will take Kitty and Lois, you take Trish."

Trish replied,

"If it's OK with Kitty and Lois. I don't want to come between your deal."

Lois responded,

"I don't know if you can handle her, she's a mouthful."

Kitty smiled and said,

"I have the mouth for it." As she opened wide. They laughed and then Trish said,

"OK, tonight we can switch and then tomorrow we can switch again. Sound like fun?"

* * *

Silvia stroked Kitty hair and held her close as they laid on the bed. Kitty had her hand on Silvia's back and rubbed it softly. Kitty remarked, "Your tits are nice and soft, mine are tight and hard." Silvia smiled and said, "Some day when you are fifty-one your tits will be soft and flabby too."

"No, no I didn't mean that it's a bad thing. I like them and I want to just snuggle my face in between them."

Silvia leaned back and pushed Kitty's head down to her breasts. It felt good to have this young woman on her and to feel her licking her hard nipples and sucking on them. She had nursed her two children the first year of their lives. It was a sensation that only a mother can understand.

Kitty slowly worked her way down Silvia's' belly. She licked all around her navel and prodded her tongue into it. Silvia relaxed and just let Kitty continue to pleasure her.

Silvia had a full natural bush and this was something that Kitty had not encountered before as her first was only sixteen and had little pubic hair.

Trish was clean shaven and smooth. Kitty took a mouthful of hair in her mouth and shook it like a dog growling as she did it. It made Silvia jump and gasp at the same time.

"That's something different. No one ever did that before. Stick your finger in me and do it again."

Kitty stuck her finger into Silvia and gave her another growl and shake.

"Wow, I thought about shaving, but now I am going to rethink that. You showed me why I have that much hair. Now you can go ahead and lick my pussy."

Kitty spread Silvia's labia apart with her fingers and licked them while running her tongue all the way from her vagina to her clit. She wiggled it into her as far as she could. Silvia was in a state of ecstasy as this young girl was quickly bringing her to her first of three orgasms while Kitty was between her legs.

She said, "It's my turn now to pleasure you."

Kitty laid down on her back and Silvia started by kissing her and sucking on her tongue. That same tongue that had just given her so much pleasure.

She fondled Kitty's small breasts and ran her thumb over the hardening nipples. She licked and sucked on each of them. The whole while she had her hand on Kitty's pussy.

Kitty spread her legs apart so that Silvia could reach her vagina. Silvia reached her pubic mound and she saw that Kitty had some bush like her, so she tried to shake it in her mouth like Kitty had done. But Kitty's was to fine and short for her to get a bite on it.

Kitty said, "Just bite on me."

Silvia took Kitty's mound in her mouth and gently bit it in a series of little bites. Kitty sighed and said,

"That feels good, now go to the main event."

Silvia slid down between her open legs and started to lick Kitty's legs and worked from her knees up to her crotch.

She parted her outer lips and licked the folds of Kitty's labia. They were short but she could still get her mouth on each one and gently suck on them. She licked the opening of Kitty's vagina.

Silvia held her clit between her thumb and first finger. She rubbed and tugged at it as it got hard. She ran her tongue across it and sucked it into her lips. She rolled it between her lips and gently put her teeth on it and bit it.

Kitty let out a squeal and quickly covered her mouth. She watched as Silvia continued to give her several orgasms in a short time. She had not even entered her vagina yet.

Kitty said,

"Put your fingers in me now."

Silvia said,

"Wait here."

Kitty didn't know where she was going until she returned with a Toy. It was about as real looking as it could be.

"This is what Lois and I brought along in case we needed a cock for some reason. OK if I use it on you?"

Kitty looked at the toy and said,

"Go slow, I am really tight down there."

Silvia put the end of it in her mouth and got it wet with saliva before she inserted it into Kitty's vagina.

'She's right, she is tight,' Silvia thought. Kitty relaxed and let it slid in.

Silvia put it in slowly so that her opening could stretch to accept it. When she had it in about four inches she pressed the button to start the vibrator.

This was a new feeling for Kitty as she had never had anyone use one on her before. She laid there and just enjoyed the feelings that it provided. Silvia continued to lick Kitty's clit while the toy was doing its work.

Kitty enjoyed another series of intense orgasms. Silvia said, "Now it's my turn."

* * *

They stopped at Graceland to pay Homage to the "King". They went to the Peabody Hotel to see the famous Mallard ducks that are paraded thru the lobby twice a day. In the morning when they are brought down from the roof top pen to swim in the lobby pool. Then they are paraded back to the elevator for their return to the roof for the night.

They entered into the State of Louisiana late the next afternoon. They found a Walmart outside of New Orleans and spent the night. Per their agreement, they switched partners again. This time Kitty was with Lois and Trish with Silvia. They called for an Uber to come to the Walmart and pick them up and take them to a fine restaurant for dinner. He took them to an upscale place with a Cajun band playing and of course the finest of Cajun food. From Gumbo and Frog Legs to "Mud Bugs", that's Crayfish, or Crawdad's.

Trish ordered a rack of ribs to share with Kitty and the others tried some items on the menu that they had never heard of.

With the music playing and the fine meal and after several rounds of drinks they called for their Uber driver to come take them back to the Walmart.

When they went inside the Motor Home Trish said, "I guess it's us tonight Silvia, are you ready for this?"

Silvia replied, "I hope you are as good as Kitty, that's some girl, don't let her get away."

"Trish smiled and said, "I hope you are as good as the Old woman was last night, my toes are still curled." Silvia said,

"Well let's hop in the sack and find out."

Lois and Kitty went into the other bedroom and Kitty asked Lois, "Are you really as good as Trish says you are? I know I can curl your toes for you."

Lois smiled and replied," Get your clothes off girl and find out."

Kitty jumped up and down and twerked her ass as she playfully stripped. Lois, smiled at her antics and said,

"I think you had too much to drink kiddo. Let's get those panties off and see what you got." Lois said with a wink.

Kitty stood on the bed and leaned against Lois. She put her arms around her and bent down to kiss her. Then she pushed her head between her tits. Lois licked them as Kitty moved from side to side. She laid down on her back. Lois said,

"Turn over now and show me that sweet ass."

Kitty smiled and turned over. Lois said,

"Now get up on your knees."

Kitty pulled her knees up under her and Lois got behind her and started to lick all around her asshole. Kitty found herself relaxing her entire body as she felt something that she never had felt before.

"You are curling my toes and it feels so good."

Lois replied,

"I hope you are enjoying this because it will soon be your turn to pleasure me."

Lois then put her fingers in Kitty's vagina. She could feel how wet she was getting and wanted to feel that wetness on her face.

Lois laid down and told Kitty,

"Sit on my face now so I can taste your girl juices."

Kitty got up and straddled Lois's head with her face right at her pussy.

Lois started to lick her all over her pubic area. From her clit to her anus. Kitty continued to sit on Lois's face until she had another orgasm. This time it happened while Lois had her finger in Kitty's asshole.

Lois said, "Now it's your turn to get me off."

She got on her knees and said, "You know what to do, curl my toes girl."

Kitty had never done this before so she approached Lois's backside with trepidation. When she got up close Lois said softly,

"I can feel your warm breath on me. Now I want to feel your wet tongue on me. Run the tip around the opening and then up and down the crack. When you are ready to do it, just put the tip in my hole. Then wiggle it around."

Kitty followed her instructions perfectly. She kept up her ministrations on Lois until she heard her take a gasp and then tighten and relax as Lois felt her orgasm happening.

Kitty went down her crack to Lois's vagina and licked it and then inserted two fingers in as far as she could and started to curl her fingers to run over the G spot. It was not long before Lois had another orgasm. Finally they laid down and went to sleep.

✳ ✳ ✳

The next day they made pan cakes for breakfast and got on Rt. 10 and headed for Texas. When they got to Huston they stopped at a western wear shop and got some shirts and boots and of course. Cowgirl hats. Trish reasoned that this would not make them look like lesbians.

It was rodeo season and they decided to take in a rodeo. There were girl barrel racers, bronc riders, steer wrestlers and bull riders the most dangerous of the rodeo events. It was always the last event of the day. They got seats in the middle of the crowd and blended in pretty well.

During the day a young cowboy who was seated behind Kitty started talking to her. She ignored him at first but he got more persistent.

"What's the matter pretty girl, ain't I handsome enough for you? Or is that your wife there with you? If you would like me to I can get a couple of my buddies here to … Before he could finish his sentence. Lois turned around and said sharply,

"Leave her alone please, my daughter here just lost her husband in a motorcycle accident and we thought coming here would help get her mind off it."

Tricia turned to him and teased,

"I'm available cowboy if you are a good rider."

He looked at Trish and smiled,

"You're a cute one. What's your deal sweetie?"

Trish told him,

"After the bull rides are over is when the cowgirl rides begin right?"

He smiled and replied,

"I can meet you out in the parking lot after the rodeo."

"You can just follow me out to my vehicle, OK?"

He was still smiling when he agreed to do that.

"By the way, my name is Tex." Trish held out her hand and said,

"Howdy Tex, mine is Sweet Pea." He replied,

"I'll bet you are a Sweet Pea. Is this your mother too?" Trish said,

"No, she is my aunt and her sister."

He then said,

"I want to apologize for being a jerk before. I didn't want to look like I was hitting on you, but I am."

Trish flirted,

"You're handsome enough for me cowboy Tex. If you would like to we can leave now before the bull riding."

"No, a friend of mine is riding tonight and he has drawn the worst bull in the line to ride. I just hope he doesn't get hurt or killed." Trish said, "I understand. We can wait until after he rides."

✳ ✳ ✳

Rob Harris had been riding bulls since he was in junior rodeo as a teen ager. He was a pretty good rider. But tonight was going to be different for him. None of the bulls that he had ridden successfully were of the caliber of "Bone Crusher".

This bull had not been ridden in five years. He was a huge animal that stood over six feet tall and weighed over a thousand pounds. He is so dangerous that there was a purse offered to the first man to ride him of TEN THOUSAND Dollars. He had crippled and nearly killed the last four cowboys who attempted to stay on his back.

Rob really thought that he could ride him and he really wanted the money.

He was the last rider of the night and everyone was waiting to see what Bone Crusher would do.

Rob was six foot six and weighs two hundred thirty pounds. He works out with weights every day and is very strong. His black hair and brown eyes reflected his native heritage. His mother was from the Hopi tribe. His father was white and his grandfather started the ranch in the early twentieth century during the dust bowl days when land was cheap.

* * *

Would he be strong enough to stay on Bone crusher for the eight seconds?

Bone Crusher was moved into the holding stall and Rob lowered himself down onto his back. The massive beast made an ominous growl that moved from his throat out to his mouth and the sound was felt in Rob's backside. He gripped the rope in his hands and indicated to the handlers that he was ready.

* * *

The next instant the gate swung open and the mighty bull seemed to explode into the air. It looked like he was launched from a rocket of some kind and Rob held on as its front feet hit the ground and the rear feet kicked into the sky. The bull turned its head to the right and then to the left as it attempted to toss Rob into the air. It rose again into the air as it kicked itself up with its powerful hind legs.

The time was only three seconds, five to go to ten thousand dollars.

Rob felt like his entire body was going to break when the bull spun around and jumped at the same time.

Two more seconds ticked off. Only three more agonizing seconds to hang on.

Rob could feel the rope start to get lose in his hand and he squeezed harder to hold on.

The giant bovine put its head down the kicked one more time into the air as Rob heard the buzzer sound indicating that he was now in the money.

He timed his release so that he would be able to get clear of Bone Crushers deadly horns and hooves when he hit the ground.

The rodeo clowns job is to divert the bulls' attention away so they don't attack the cowboy when he is down.

Rob hit the ground and was back on his feet with his brown Stetson waving triumphantly in his hand.

* * *

Tex was jumping up and down as he watched his friend defeat this notorious Bull.

Trish was with him and was excited to see Rob, who she didn't know yet, ride this creature.

She looked up at Tex and said,

"WOW that was exciting. Can we go see Rob?"

Tex told her that the Sports Writers would want to interview him first and then he would be able to talk.

A half hour later they were finally able to get Robs attention and Tex asked him,

"Well Buddy, how does it feel to be ten grand richer?"

Rob smiled and said,

"That was the longest eight seconds of my life."

Then he looked at Trish and asked,

"So, who is this bit of sunshine?"

Tex looked at Trish and said,

"This lil' gal's name is Trish and she has some girl friends with her that want to meet a real live bull rider."

Rob offered,

"Why don't you bring them over to the ranch later and we can have a victory party."

Trish said, "Show us the way cowboy. We like a party."

She and Tex went over to where Kitty, Lois and Silvia were seated in the stands and told them that they were all invited to a party out at Robs ranch, The "Acken back Akers".

It was located about thirty miles west of Huston and was comprised of five thousand acres of grassland. It was the home of some of the finest Black Angus beef cattle in the State of Texas.

Trish rode with Tex and the rest followed them in Trish's motor home.

When they arrived it was eight o'clock and Rob's ranch hands had prepared a fine supper for their returning Rodeo Hero.

Trish and her friends had never seen so many rib eye steaks lined up by the outside barbeque grills. There were also some Red Snapper that had been brought in from the Gulf. They looked at each other and smiled. They knew they were going to eat good that evening.

A uniformed waiter brought around some wine and beer and other spirits for their enjoyment.

There was a western band playing off to the side and Rob was retelling the story of his ride to his friends who were at the rodeo and saw it firsthand but liked to hear about it from the man himself.

After everyone had eaten their fill and had danced till they dropped the guests started to leave. Rob told the women that they could stay the night in the motor home or come inside the house and sleep in real beds. They were welcome to stay the next day and go ride horses or ATV's.

"That sounds like fun." Trish said, "Staying and riding, I have never been on a horse before."

Lois said, "I rode when I was a teenager, but that's been a while.

If you haven't guessed."

Kitty said, "The ATV's sounds more my style."

Silvia agreed with Kitty. "I think I can control an ATV better than a horse."

"OK then, I will see you in the morning and after we have breakfast I will show you around the place." Rob said,

Tex escorted the women into the house and showed them where the bedrooms were located. Trish told them "You gals can sleep where ever you want to. I am going to sleep where ever Tex wants me to."

They all laughed and headed to several rooms. Tex and Trish entered a first floor bedroom that had its own full bathroom with a walk in shower stall. Trish said to Tex, "I want a nice warm shower to get the rodeo and road dust washed off before we go to bed."

Tex agreed that he too would like a shower and he would like to wash her back.

Trish smiled and cooed, "I'll let you wash anything you want to wash, cowboy." She blinked her eyes seductively.

He had already kicked his boots off and had his trousers half way down before she had the words out of her mouth.

They walked into the shower and turned the water on so that the water was just above warm but not hot.

They lathered each other up and with the soft water the soap made a lot of warm foam that ran down over their bodies.

Tex admired Trish's firm boobs and soft ass cheeks. He held her close to him and she could feel his hard cock between her legs. She raised up and wrapped her legs around him and he slid it into her wet pussy.

They kissed long and gently with their tongues lapping into each other's mouth. Trish asked, "Have you ever done it from behind?"

Tex replied, "You mean like doggy?"

"No," Trish said, "I mean in the back hole."

Tex smiled and said, "Oh, I know what you mean. No, I haven't done that yet."

Trish looked up at him and asked,

"Would you like to try it?"

Tex said, "Whatever you want to do is fine with me."

She said, "Since we have all this nice soap bubbles we don't need any other lubrication do we?"

Tex looked at her backside when she turned it towards him. He stood with the water hitting him on the back and he took a large pile of the soap bubbles and let it slid down over her ass crack. Then he stuck his middle finger in her anus and felt her relax.

He inserted his cock into her and she pushed back while leaning forward.

He could feel her open and close on him and he started to move in and out while she pushed back against his hard stomach muscles.

She could feel it building in her legs and in her stomach and it was not long before she had her climax.

Tex was also nearing his peak of sensation. It felt good to release inside her.

He continued to stroke in and out until at last his cock fell limp and she squeezed it out of her.

Tex said, "Thank you for letting me do that. I have never done it before, but I hope that I can find a girlfriend that will let me do it with her someday."

Trish smiled as she turned around and said,

"I'll tell you what to say to her, Show her what you got and then ask, can you shit a turd as big or bigger then this? It she says yes, then you should be able to enter her without much pain, even the first time."

Tex thought to himself, "I am not going to ask any girl that." Trish then said,

"And don't forget to carry some KY Lube along with you at all times."

Tex asked curiously, "How do you know so much about 'Fanny fucken' anyways?"

Trish confided, "The first time I did it was with the cousin of a girl I had met. She and her cousin had done it and then they showed me how to do it. I like it as good as a pussy fuck sometimes. AND, you don't get knocked up."

Tex just smiled again and shook his head. They rinsed off and went to bed.

Kitty had taken a bed by herself after the party and the other two shared another room.

Around two a. m. Rob opened the door to where Kitty laid sleeping. She was nude and with just a thin sheet over her. He stood beside her bed and admired her perfect body. He had been watching her earlier in the evening and hoped that she would be alone.

He reached down and touched her hair. It was soft and he bent down to smell it. When he did she somehow sensed it and woke up. She looked at Rob with her 'bedroom eyes' and he kissed her.

Now she was fully awake and was aware that a man was there. At first she was in a panic because Rob reminded her of her boyfriend in Maine who had beaten her up and was the reason she had left with Trish.

Then she remembered where she was and who this man was. She moved over in the bed and Rob laid down beside her.

She crawled on top of him and let the warmth of their body's mingle. He put his arms around her and held her. Now she was fully awake and wanted to feel this beautiful man inside her.

She put her hand down on his cock and could feel it getting hard. It had been a while since she had been with a man and right now she craved it. She was a virgin when she met Joey and had never been with any other man until now. She was ready.

She spread her legs apart and allowed it to penetrate her vagina. She was wet enough that it slipped in with ease. She rocked back and forth and moved her hips in a nice even rhythm.

Then Rob asked, "Are you sure you want to ride an ATV tomorrow? I think you would do just fine on a horse." Kitty smiled and said,

"You're the only horse that I'm riding tonight."

With that she picked up the pace and moved up and down on his hard cock. It wasn't long before Rob clenched his jaw and holding her ass in his hands he shot his load into her. He kissed her and held her close. She smiled and went to sleep.

* * *

In the morning they were all up and ready for breakfast. The cook had made Busquets and sausage gravy, or omelets of their choice with grits. Steak and eggs was the other option available.

They all ate a hardy meal and then headed out to the horse stable.

Rob picked out a pair of gentle animals for the women to ride and then Tex readied a couple of Polaris ATV's for Kitty and Silvia.

He and Rob each rode horses and showed their guests the trails that went all over the ranch. They spent the morning enjoying themselves out on the rangeland where they saw herds of Angus cattle and saw some large White Tail Deer that stopped eating to watch the riders as they passed by then went back to eating.

* * *

They got back to the ranch house at noon. After their horse and ATV rides they were ready for lunch.

There were several Reporters there to talk with Rob about his monumental bull ride. It seems that when someone can ride a bull that has not been ridden for five years it is big news.

They took a lot of pictures of Rob and then they asked the four women to stand behind and beside him with their arms around him.

Trish thought 'What the hell, it's all in fun. "Say CHEESE." Said the Photographer as he snapped several pictures.

The women left the Ranch later in the afternoon and headed west. Their destination was the four corners. That is where Utah, Colorado, Arizona and New Mexico come together.

They arrived the next day in the morning. It is a pretty desolate area and with only a marker that shows the four States coming together.

Trish said, "Let's get a picture of each of us in a different State and holding hands. " There were several other Tourists there that were happy to take Trish's camera and snap several pictures of them.

They stopped along the way at a place called Sand Creek. They were told there were some Indian pictographs there on some rocks. When they found them they also saw a hand written sign that said,

"Vandals, SNIPER ON DUTY".

Kitty said, "That's one way to discourage Idiots who would destroy these ancient works of art."

Back in Bar Harbor Maine, Joey Burke was glancing thru the Sports pages of the Portland newspaper when he saw a picture of some bull rider in Texas who had ridden a bull named "Bone Crusher". He got ten thousand dollars for his eight second ride. He thought 'That's over a thousand dollars a second.' As he looked at the picture of the man he saw that he was flanked by four women. He looked closer and saw Kitty's face. He came up off his chair and shouted, "I'm going to fucken Texas and kill that Bitch."

✳ ✳ ✳

The Aspin trees were turning yellow when Trish and company arrived in the Rocky Mountains of Colorado. It was the first time they had seen anything like it. They could hear the bugling of the bull elk as they vied for some cows to breed.

At night they could hear the howls of coyotes calling to each other as their way of communicating. Kitty had heard the coyotes back home and heard the Bull Moose bellowing like the elk did here. But this was different, she had Trish and she felt safe.

Some of the highest mountains had snow on the tops. It could have been there from last year at that elevation. Or it could be new snow as it starts early up there.

Trish parked the motor home at a scenic overlook and they made supper. She announced,

"Tomorrow we are going to head up towards the Dakotas. We can visit Mount Rushmore and then go over to Crazy Horse. He was one of the Indians who attacked General Custer at Little Big Horn. The monument to him is on the other side of the mountain from Rushmore.

One of the men who worked on Rushmore started the tribute to Crazy Horse and his children and grandchildren are still working on it. They will be for a long time to come. It is a popular Tourist stop and they take in a lot of money each year to finance the project. They bring in so much that they started a scholarship program for Indian children to go to college.

Not one dime of Government money has ever come into this project. All by donations.

* * *

Back in Maine Joey Burke had packed enough cloths for a week and had also taken his shot gun and deer rifle along. He got in his truck and headed for the Interstate and went south. He drove like a man possessed. He couldn't stand the thought of that bull rider with his woman. In his mind there was only one thing to do. Kill both of them. In three days he was in Texas. The background information he had on Rob Harris was that he had a cattle ranch west of Huston.

He stopped by the rodeo grounds outside Huston and asked a man there if he knew a Rob Harris.

The man answered, "Why sure, everyone knows Rob. He rode the rankest bull in all of Texas."

Joey asked, "Do you know where his place is?"

The man replied, "Yes, Acken Back Acres is west of Huston about thirty miles or so. Can't miss it. Big sign by the road with a big bull on it with a cowboy on its back."

Joey thanked the man and left. He stopped along the way at a gun shop and purchased a cheap .38 caliber revolver and a box of bullets.

He traveled west until he found the road leading to the ranch. He turned and followed it to the main house. Joey looked around and saw one of the hands near the stables. He drove over to him and rolled the window down and asked,

"Where can I find Rob Harris?"

The man looked at him and then asked,

"What do you want with him?"

Joey said, "I hear he is some kind of a bull rider. And I wanted to talk to him about his experiences doing that. I want to wright a book about rodeoin' and stuff about the west."

The man came back,

"He ain't here right now. He went into Huston to check on some upcoming Bull Riding events. He travels around the circuit looking for some fun." Joey said,

"Riding a damn bull don't sound like something I would call fun, more like dangerous and stupid?"

"Well, Mr. Rob earned a lot of money on top of bulls, and had some bones broke too."

Then Joey cut to the chase and showed the man a picture of Kitty.

"You see this woman around here with Rob? I saw her picture in the news with him when he rode that big bull."

The man looked at the picture and said, "Yeah, she was here for a day or so. She was with three others. One young and the other two were older, in their fifty's I guess. All were good looking. They were traveling in a big silver motor home with gold trim. Had New York tags on it. One of the nicest ones I have seen."

Joey asked, "Where did they go? How long ago did they leave?"

The man answered, "They left a week ago and said something about just going west to see the country."

This puzzled Joey because he knew that Kitty had no money to be traveling like this. He thought they must be whoring or something to make money along the way.

He decided to head west and check at campgrounds along the way to see if anyone had seen a large silver and gold motorhome at any of them.

* * *

Trish and her "posse" left Crazy Horse and headed up to Sturgis South Dakota. They had just missed the huge motorcycle gathering and the town was getting back to normal. Every year thousands of bikers descend upon the town for a week and drink and race and have biker fun. There are always some bikers that stop by all year long just to get a Tee shirt that says "Sturgis" on it. The girls did too.

* * *

Back in Connecticut Silvia and Lois's husbands had notified the police that their wives had disappeared after a week end in the Catskills. The camper that they had used was returned and they had just left. No note or message of any kind.

Because kidnapping was a possibility they notified the FBI. Pictures were sent out over the country and they were described as possible runaways or kidnap victims. The campground that they usually stayed at was called and the owner said the women had left with two younger women who had a large silver and gold motorhome that the one younger woman had just purchased and left the title to the smaller camper that she had with him to sell and keep the money.

He told the FBI Agent,

"She must have been a rich girl because I found out that she paid cash for the motor home. That doesn't happen every day."

"Do you have her name somewhere?" The Agent asked. "Yes, it's here in the roster."

After looking back to the time that Trish was there he found it, "Here it is, Tricia Flick from over Rumford way."

"Thank you." The agent said.

"They all seemed to be having a good time when they left here." The campground owner said.

With this information he was able to in a few minutes find out everything there was to know about Trish. Including the information about her inheritance. When he knew this the story started to develop in his mind that the women from Connecticut had not been abducted, but rather just decided to run away with this rich girl and take advantage of her generosity.

Just to be on the safe side he decided to issue a BOLO (be on lookout) nationwide for the motor home. When it was found they could check to see if there is a problem or not.

* * *

Joey had checked at a number of campgrounds with no luck. Then he asked at one near route 10 that the owner of it remembered it well.

"We don't see a lot of that model around here. Top of the line home. There were four ladies in it. I think they were lezzys, if you know what I mean. They said something about going to the four corners from here."

Joey jumped in his truck and headed north toward the four

corners. They were a week ahead of him and he had no idea of where they may go next.

They left Sturgis and headed west to Yellowstone National Park. None of them had ever been on a trip like this before and the sights that they were seeing for the first time were exciting.

They traveled thru the park seeing wildlife that they had never seen before. Bison, Wolves, Bighorn Sheep, Mule Deer and Elk. They stopped to watch a Coyote hunting for Mice in the grass. He would cock his head to the side to listen and then he would jump into the air and pounce on the rodent with his front paws.

They traveled thru the park and down to Jackson Hole. The sight of the Grand Teton Mountains were breath taking. They stopped for supper in Jackson and then in the morning they headed into Idaho and then north to Montana.

Joey Burke decided to go back to Maine and give up for now of finding Kitty. He thought that eventually she would show up back there as she still had siblings that lived there. None of them had a good thought about Joey as they all knew what he had done to their sister.

He made a plan to contact a friend of her brother, Jack, and have that friend ask Jack if he had heard from Kitty. Perhaps he could find out from him where Kitty and her friends were located.

He left Colorado and headed for home. Along the way he stopped outside of Indianapolis for the night and went to a local bar for a drink. He saw a young woman that he decided to strike up a conversation with.

She wore her red hair in two pony tails. Her skin was pale and she had blue eyes. Her name was Bethanie Jean Reynolds, she was twenty two. Joey asked,

"Can I buy you a drink?"

She looked him up and down and smiled, "Sure soldier, if you got the money, I got the time. Where are you from?"

Joey sat down beside her and said, "Maine. But I am on a road trip right now. Be going back in a few days. Are you from around here?" She replied,

"No, I am from Wisconsin and I am headed for Nashville. I am a song writer."

The Bartender served their drinks and left them to talk. "What do you do?" She asked. Joey replied,

"I have a Lobster Boat out of Bar Harbor." She said,

"Too bad you don't have any Lobsters with you I love lobster." He shot her a sly smile and replied,

"No, I don't have any lobsters, but I do have some "Trouser Trout" if you are interested." Bethanie chuckled and said,

"I'll bet you do."

He came back as he inched over closer to her,

"Would you be interested in some Trout this evening? We can go over to the motel and see what's cooking."

She put her hand on his knee and purred,

"Let's finish our drinks first."

Joey looked around the bar and then picked up his glass and said, "Cheers, bottoms up."

She followed him to his motel room and after they entered the room joey closed the door and took her jacket and hung it up. Then he approached her and took her by the arm and led her to the edge of the bed.

She smiled and he bent down and kissed her. He ran his hand up the back of her shirt and unsnapped her bra. She unbuttoned her shirt and then unbuckled her belt. She slipped her jeans off and then laid down on the bed.

Joey had not been with a woman since Kitty left and was eager to feel his cock inside of her. He removed his cloths and laid down on top of her with his hairy chest above her snowy breasts. She could feel his cock as it laid on her belly. He moved up and down savoring the softness of her skin on him. Slowly he lifted up his hips and then put the tip inside her. She took a deep breath and released it as he moved into her vagina.

She had not had such a large cock inside her for some time. As he slowly pushed in she lifted her hips to meet his thrusts. When he was all the way in she started to contract and relax her pelvic muscles until she could start to feel the beginnings of an orgasm.

Joey could feel his ejaculation coming too and in the next minute they both felt the release of their tension.

She kissed Joey and asked,

"Will you lick me clean? I will if you will."

Joey was not going to do this as he never had and wasn't going to start. "I don't think so bitch, I 'm not a pussy licker to start with and especially not one that I just shot a load in. If you want to lick my cock you can go ahead, but it ain't no two way street. Understand?"

Bethanie pushed him off of her and said,

"That's OK you son of a bitch. I thought we could fuck all night, but I see you are just a boy and not a real man."

Joey wasn't sure what happened next. He just saw red and grabbed her by the throat and shook her until she stopped moving.

He looked outside and saw nobody in the parking lot of the motel. He picked her limp body up and placed her on the bed of his pickup and closed the rear window of the cap so that she could not be seen.

After he took a shower and got dressed he left the motel and headed east on Route 70. Somewhere in Ohio he pulled off the road and tossed her into a River.

Joey returned to Bar Harbor the next day. He found his friend Don Billows at their favorite bar and approached him.

"Hey, Donnie how you been?" Joey asked. Don looked up and smiled.

"Where the fuck have you been lately?" Joey replied, "Out looking for my no-good girlfriend. You haven't seen her have you?"

"No, but I haven't been looking." Joey then asked, "You know her brother Jack pretty well don't you?"

"Yes, we go way back."

"Could you ask him if he has heard anything of her, I am getting worried about her." Joey said with a worried look on his face.

"I'll ask him if he knows where she is."

"Good, tell me what he says, will you?"

Don replied, No problem buddy."

❊ ❊ ❊

Kitty and Trish woke up in the morning along the Pacific Ocean somewhere in Oregon. Silvia and Lois were still sleeping so the younger women laid in bed and fondled each other's bodies while looking into each other's eyes.

Trish said, "I think I am falling in love with you sweetie." Kitty grinned and replied,

"I know I am."

They kissed and ran their hands down between each other's legs. Trish touched Kitty's clit with her middle finger and felt her swing her hip up so that Trish's finger slid down into her wet crack.

She continued to move her finger into Kitty's crack until she opened up so that Trish could run her finger inside her vagina.

Kitty raised and lowered her hips so that the finger went in and out ever so slowly. She liked to feel Trish doing this to her while they shared their warm tongues.

Trish took Kitty's hand and put it between her legs and rubbed it on her pubic mound and between her legs. Kitty responded by putting her fingers inside of Trish. They fingered each other for a half hour before taking the sixty-nine position and bringing each to a sweet orgasm.

They got up and started breakfast while the others got cleaned up for the day.

Lois asked, "Where to today girls?"

Trish said, "Today we will go down into California and visit the Redwood National Forest."

Silvia replied, "I have seen pictures of those trees but have never actually seen one."

Trish said, "Well today you will."

They stopped near the ocean and went into the water just to be able to say that they were there.

Kitty noted, "It doesn't feel any different than the Atlantic." Lois said, "The difference is Japan is over there and England is over there back home."

They laughed and played in the water splashing each other and acting like teenagers. Not a worry in the world as the wind was gentle and the sun was shining.

Kitty was the youngest and was getting homesick for her sisters and brothers. She asked Trish,

"Can we stop somewhere so I can check in back home? I am sure they are getting worried about me."

They stopped just inside the California border and Kitty called her brother Jack, who is the oldest of her siblings.

"Jack? It's Kitty."

"Where the hell are you we haven't seen or heard from you for weeks now?"

"Don't worry, I am in a good place with good friends. We just entered California."

Jack hollered, "CALIFORNIA? What are you doing there?"

"I have found a very good friend who has a motor home and she invited me to go on an extended road trip with her. We have two other ladies with us from Connecticut and we are having a ball."

Jack asked, "When are you coming back home? Donnie Billows asked about you. Said he hasn't seen you for a while."

Kitty looked at Trish and told him,

"I don't know, maybe never. I am in love, and she loves me too."

Jack just sat there in silence trying to absorb what his sister had just told him. Then he said,

"Kitty, we love you too and want you to be happy. If it's with another woman, then so be it. Just remember that if anything happens you are still welcome here."

A tear came to Kitty's eye and she replied,

"I know big brother, I will always love you guys too. But for now I am happy and I don't see anything that will change my mind. Tell the others that you and I have talked. I will call you again along the way. Bye for now. Kiss, kiss."

Kitty hung up.

Jack knew that Don was concerned about Kitty so he called him to let him know she was OK and in California.

When Joey found out from Don her location he was livid and decided to take the next flight he could get on and head out there to find her.

When he got there he would buy a cheap car to drive. He knew what the motor home looked like and so he would go on the hunt again. Seeking out campgrounds along the way asking about the big silver and gold vehicle.

＊　＊　＊

The FBI got a hit on the location of Trish's motor home. The California Highway patrol found them while they were on the road to Yosemite Park.

Trish wondered why she was being pulled over by the police.

The officer came up to the front door and smiled at her and asked,

"Are you Tricia Flick?"

"Yes officer. What's the problem?" She asked.

"May I come in?"

Trish looking bewildered said, "Of course you may."

He entered and looked around. He saw the others and asked,

"Are you ladies from Connecticut?" Lois and Silvia looked at each other and replied together,

"Yes, what's happened?" The Officer replied,

"The whole country has been looking for you since you left home. Your Husbands thought you were kidnapped or worse since you just left without any notes or messages." He asked Kitty,

"What is your name and where are you from?"

She froze and words wouldn't come out. Then she started to cry. Trish put her arms around her and comforted her. Then Trish told the officer,

"She is with me and she is fleeing from a dangerous relationship and she is fearful that he will kill her. So she doesn't want to disclose her identity as she's afraid that it would jeopardize her safety. She has done nothing wrong officer so please don't make things worse for her."

He said,

"If she doesn't want to give me her ID, I will have to take her in and find out the hard way who she is. How do I know standing here that she is not some killer that I should be arresting?"

Finally Kitty relented and told the officer who she was and the circumstances for her to run away. He understood because he had a sister who was in a bad situation himself.

"OK, you ladies need to make contact with your families and let them know you are not in danger at this time. I will report this back to the FBI who instigated the search for you. Meanwhile you have a nice trip. Wish I could go along."

He left and they all sat and looked at each other.

Trish said, "How is this not an adventure?

The FBI looking for us.

The Highway Patrol stopping us.

What will happen next?

And let's not forget the Bull Rider!"

Joey arrived at LAX airport at seven thirty after taking a night flight that started at Portland Maine and then to Newark and then to Los Angeles.

He took a Taxi from the airport to a small town outside the city. Because of the strict gun laws in California he was not able to buy a gun so he opted to get a heavy hunting knife.

He figured if he got close enough to shoot her he could get close enough to cut her throat. There he also found a ten year old Ford 150 pickup that he bought and he headed for the Interstate to look for the motor home. He had driven four hours going north when he saw the silver with gold trim motor home going south. At the next cross over he went to the south bound lane and followed them from a half mile behind.

He knew that he had found Kitty and she was not going to get away this time. All he had to do was wait for them to stop somewhere and then he would attack.

✳ ✳ ✳

As Trish drove along the highway the others conversed about the places that they had been and the sights that they had seen.

Near Bakersfield she found a nice campground that they could stay the night.

Trish said,

"Tomorrow we will go across the Mojave Desert to see Las Vegas. I will get some more cash at an ATM and we can spend the day gambling. Won't that be fun?"

Lois cocked her head and asked,

"Are you going to trust us with your money at a black jack table?"

Trish replied,

"Well I expect you to win some and then you can repay me." Lois asked, "But what if I lose?"

Trish told her, "Then you will have to go to bed with me again. So either way we both win, OK?"

She gave them all five hundred dollars to play with when they got to the casino. Kitty liked to play poker as her brother Jack had showed her how to play the game.

Lois and Silvia sat at the dollar slots and kept feeding the one armed bandits. The machine that Lois was playing paid off for a thousand dollars. She laughed and said,

"OH, darn now I won't be able to sleep with Trish tonight."

Silvia laughed and put another coin in the slot and pulled the lever. She got a hundred dollar payoff. Happily they danced around and Silvia said,

"Let's go see if you can lose all that. I want you to fuck Trish tonight and I will get the Kid."

Trish played Roulette and lost her five hundred in less than an hour. She walked over to see how Kitty was doing. She left the poker table and was now at a black jack table. She was up two hundred from the poker game and now she was kicking the houses ass at black jack. She even played split hands and won.

The pile of chips that were piling up in front of her was exciting and she was starting to show it. Trish asked,

"How long are you going to play?"

"I don't know, the house still has some money that I haven't won yet." Kitty replied. Trish stood back and looked at the pile of chips and then told Kitty,

"One more hand and we go."

There was over fifteen thousand dollars' worth of chips to cash in on the table.

Kitty decided to bet half of her winnings on the next hand. The cards started to fall, first an Ace. Kitty flipped over her card and it was a King. Trish said,

"Now can we go?

They pried the other two from the 'One armed Bandits' and went out to their motor home.

✳ ✳ ✳

Joey was waiting in the parking lot and watched as they all came back and started to get in.

When he saw Kitty was the last one in line he approached quickly and hollered,

"DIE YOU BITCH."

He had the knife in his right hand and it was over his head as he came at her.

Kitty screamed,

"NO JOEY, NO."

Trish was at the top of the steps and she reached inside a pocket alongside of the driver's seat.

She pulled out the 40 Glock that her Father had given her when she was 18.

She did a lot of target practice with it back at the lake house and she became very proficient with it.

Kitty had grabbed Joey's arm that held the knife and he started to beat her with his left hand.

She kicked him and he kicked back.

Meanwhile Trish came out of the motor home with the Glock held with both hands and shouted,

"DROP THE KNIFE, DROP IT NOW OR DIE!"

She could see Kitty was losing the battle for the knife.

Trish aimed for his head and then the shot shattered the night.

The bullet found its mark and Joey dropped like a sack of rocks.

Kitty had a knife cut on her right arm that was bleeding. Lois grabbed a shirt and wrapped it around Kitty's arm as a tourniquet.

The blood stopped and by now the Security Police had arrived on the scene and had the gun in their position. Trish gladly gave it to them.

They covered Joey's body and the women hugged each other as they wept with Kitty.

Her nightmare had come true.

But now it was over for good.

They all gave a statement to the police when they arrived and when they decided that it was a domestic situation that went bad and it was plain and simple self-defense.

When everything was wrapped up Lois said,

"Trish, I am ready to go home. You are just too exciting for an old woman."

Silvia said,

"I guess that I have had enough too. You have been a lot of fun to do a road trip with and I wish you and Kitty a long and happy life together."

She hugged Trish and smiled as she gave her a kiss on the check.

Trish said, "I want to see you two happy as well in the future, so let me set you up out here on the coast. We can find a nice little house and set up a trust fund for you to live off."

Lois and Silvia both hugged Trish and thanked her for thinking of them but maybe they should just go back home.

* * *

After Trish and Kitty put them on the plane back to Connecticut they walked back to the motor home and got in.

They looked at each other and then Kitty asked,

"Where to now Love? Thank you for saving my life."

Trish told her,

"I would walk thru fire for you. Let's get married."

Kitty hugged Trish and asked,

"Can we have Kids?"

"Sure we can, we're young enough to make our own or we can adopt some."

Trish smiled at Kitty and started up the engine and headed down the road.

Kitty's baby bump had not started to show but she will never forget Texas.

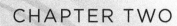

CHAPTER TWO

Tricia & Kitty

When we last saw Trish and Kitty they were in Las Vegas airport seeing off the ladies from Connecticut, Silvia and Lois, who had been along with Trish and Kitty on their road trip across the United States.

After the plane took off they stood for a moment and looked at each other. Kitty asked,

"Where to now love? And thanks for saving my life."

Trish told her,

"I would walk thru fire for you. Want to get married?"

Kitty hugged Trish and asked,

"Can we have kids?"

"Sure we can, we're young enough to make some of our own or we can adopt some."

Trish smiled at Kitty and started up the engine and headed down the road.

Kitty's baby bump had not started to show but she will never forget Texas.

Before they left Las Vegas they stopped at a Wedding Chapel along the way and got married.

They headed into New Mexico and decided that the States motto, "Land of Enchantment" was true. They decided to settle somewhere in the mountains in the middle of the State. With the help of a local Real Estate office they found their perfect location. It was 30 acres with frontage on a lake just like Trisha had grown up on.

The Realtor raised his eye brows when Trish signed a check for the entire amount. He smiled at Trish and said," We don't have that happen too often. May I ask how you acquired so much at a young age?" Trish said, "Good genes, I inherited it from my Father just like my perfect smile." With that they left the office and went down the road to see their new property.

They hired a contractor to build a house for them from Trish and Kitty's sketches and ideas. It was a six bedroom, four bath house of about 4,000 square feet.

Kitty decided to go to College to get a teaching certificate. Trish told her,

"You don't have to work, you know that, right?

Kitty told Trish,

"Yes, I know that, the reason I want to be able to teach legally is for when we have our kids we can home school 'em as we are a long way to a school for 'em." Trish thought about it and agreed.

While their home was being built they lived in the Motor Home. It was large enough for four people to live comfortably. They had no problem when they came across country with the others, Lois and Sylvia, in fact they enjoyed the time they spent with the older women. Kitty was a little shocked at how things went. It was fun to switch partners along the way.

She giggled when she recalled shaking Silvia's full pussy bush. Trish asked,

"What's so funny?" Kitty replied,

"Oh I was just thinking about when we played swap while on the trip. It was fun having those two along to have them get us off." Trish smiled and said,

"Yes they were a couple of horny girls weren't they?"

Trish was standing behind Kitty as she reminisced about what they did with Lois and Sylvia. She reached down in Kitty's blouse and felt her breasts. The nipples were getting hard when she rubbed her thumbs over them. Kitty looked up and asked,

"Want to make out? I do." Trish smiled and took Kitty by the hand and led her to the master bedroom in the back of the motor home. There she removed Kitty's cloths and they kissed as only true lovers can kiss.

Kitty could feel herself getting wet down there and longing for Trish's touch on her body. It was not slow in coming.

As Kitty laid on the silk sheets Trish laid down beside her and began to run her fingers up and down Kitty's belly. They went lower each time with her finger tips finding Kitty's clit. Kitty moaned softly as Trish continued to tease her with her hands. Trish's fingers were getting wet from running them up and down Kitty's crack. She put them in her mouth and loved the taste of Kitty's pussy.

Kitty rubbed Trish's back gently as she went down to lick Kitty's clit and beyond. After Kitty had a series of orgasm's she indicated to Trish that she wanted to reciprocate.

Trish smiled at Kitty and assumed the 69 position so they could continue to pleasure each other.

It was getting dark when they decided to break up the love making and move on to other topics.

The house was completed except for a few "Punch" list items. A paint touch up here and there, a door that needed to be adjusted. That was all the things the contractor had to do to make their house ready to be a home.

Kitty's pregnancy went along fine and no problems. When it was time for her to deliver they headed for the city where they would have a proper birth in a Hospital. She had told Rob Harris that he was going to be a Daddy.

He was excited and wanted her to come and stay at the ranch. She declined his offer and assured him that he was not going to get hit for support. He said that he would provide anything she wanted for the baby.

When the time came she delivered an 8 pound 6 oz. baby boy. She named him Rob after his father. She had asked him if she could name him Harris as well. Rob was positively excited to know that he was a father and his son was to carry his name.

Trish had wanted to get some foster kids to shelter and care for. A tragedy hit an Indian family when the parents of three kids were killed in a collision with a large truck. The Father went thru a stop sign and was broad sided by the truck. His blood alcohol was .26, well above the limit to be driving. His wife also died in the accident. Her blood level was also above the limit. They had been to a pre wedding party for some friends. They left behind three children. Two boys and a girl. Because the Mother was Irish and the Dad Apache the people on the reservation wanted nothing to do with the half breed kids. The parents had met in an Army Hospital where he was a patient. He had been in Afghanistan when he stepped on a land mine. He was an Army Ranger and intended to stay in the Army. He was 25 when they met. She was a Nurse at the Hospital where he was brought in. He had lost his left foot and received a medical discharge from the Army.

Trish petitioned the Children's Court to give them to her and Kitty to foster with intent to adopt. Since the people on the

Reservation had turned them away because their mother was white.

They had no family to take them so the Court had no problem assigning the Children to Trish and Kitty. The oldest boy was Evan. He was 9 years old at the time. Brother Buddy was 7 and their sister Patty was 5.

Rob Harris came to visit Kitty and the baby a week after the birth. He brought all sorts of baby furnishings and toys. He was so excited to meet his son. He thought about all the things they would do together at the Ranch. Go Catfish fishing in the creeks on the Ranch and go Deer hunting in the foot hills. He was a professional Rodeo Bull rider and it was at the Rodeo at Huston Texas that he was thrown off a bull named 'Son of Satan' and landed on his head. His neck broke and he died instantly. His best friend, Tex, was there and witnessed his fall. When Kitty got the news of Rob's death she was heartbroken as he had so many things he wanted to do with his son.

He had recently drawn up a Last Will and Testament giving the Ranch to his friend Tex with a provision that when Rob Jr. turned 21 he would be the Owner.

Tex was not pleased to hear that Rob's bastard son would be getting the Ranch that he had put so much of himself into over the years. When he went to visit Trish and Kitty he saw the baby for the first time. He was shocked to see so much of a resemblance to his friend Rob. That was it, he fell in love with little Rob and carried him around on his shoulder like he was his own son.

The Court asked Trish if they had room for a couple of other older kids. That was like asking her if she wanted a piece of apple pie.

When she met them Luke was 14 and had come from an abusive home. His mother was a drug addict and her boyfriend was a drunk who enjoyed beating Luke for no reason. He broke Luke's arm and that was the end of the family.

The Police got the boyfriend and he sat in jail for child abuse. The Mother was sent to a rehab to get sober. She decided she didn't want Luke anymore and gave him up to Children's Services.

The other was a girl named Lilly who was raped by her brother when she was 11 and he was sent to a Juvenile facility where he committed suicide by hanging. Their Dad was dead from an accident where he worked. Her Mother had mental problems and was in a long term facility.

So Lilly was alone and 12 years old. Children's Services contacted Trish and asked if there was room for Lilly. As long as she had room she would take in a broken child. It's just the way she is.

Things went smoothly until Joey's brother Newt returns from the Marines and is told that Joey went to California to beg Kitty to come back to him and that her lesbian lover shot him when he wasn't armed. He decides to inflict as much emotional damage to Kitty as possible by killing her son and then her lover, Trisha and then her.

Newt left Maine and headed for New Mexico where he heard she was.

He was also in Afghanistan and was trained as a sniper. He lost his left arm and an eye from injuries caused by an I E D (Improvised Explosive Device). It was hidden in the carcass of a dead dog. It was packed with plastic explosives and was set off by a signal from a cell phone.

He was in the Hospital when Joey died. Nearly a year passed before he even heard about it. That's when he was told the story about Joey going to get Kitty to come back to him that he loved her.

Then her lesbian lover shot him. It was bad enough that he died, but to be killed by a lesbian. This Newt could not abide at all. He and Joey hated gays and lesbians as much as they hated blacks and Mexicans. Newt had no idea that his brother was to blame for his death by attacking Kitty with a knife. He only heard the family's side of the story.

Tex was standing there when the bull was released. Like most of the time Rob rode the bull for the full 8 seconds and then during his dismount from the bull he landed on his head and his neck broke killing him instantly. Tex ran to his side but there was nothing he could do to save his friend.

At Trish and Kitty's little ranch as they called it they kept busy raising their kids and looking after Luke and Lilly. They were there by Children's Services until they turned 18. Then they could leave or stay if they wished. As far as Trish was concerned.

Kitty spent time with Lilly and she was her favorite. The Foster care money stopped coming when they are 18. This was not a problem for Trish.

Kitty finished her requirements to teach elementary school level kids. Trish taught them all how to swim in the lake by the house and they had a sail boat that she taught them all she knew about sailing. She showed them how to tack against the wind to go up wind in the boat. She had learned how when she was growing up on Lake Rumford. She was a pretty good sailor.

Newt had returned from the Naval Hospital and had a prosthetic arm and hand to replace the arm he had lost. He still had 100 % disability due to losing the eye also. He went into a severe depression when learning that his big brother had been killed by a lesbian.

This stoked the hatred and rage in Newt and he vowed to take revenge for Joey. Kitty's brother Jack told a friend of Newts that his sister was living in New Mexico. That was how he learned where she was.

He went to the Real Estate records in New Mexico to find out where Kitty and her lover were living. It was easy enough to do and when he found the property owned by both of them he started to lay out his plan.

Newt was a sniper in the marines and had 21 confirmed kills

against Taliban fighters. There were more unconfirmed kills too but he didn't want them known. One was an Afghan woman that was 700 yards away when he shot her in the head. He sometimes used civilians for target practice.

When he found the property he searched for his best snipers nest where he could watch over all their activities.

The kids loved Kitty and Trish as if they were their real parents. Robby was told at a young age that his Father was a bull rider in the rodeos. That was where she had met him.

He was told that when he was a man he would inherit his Fathers ranch in Texas. Meanwhile he could go visit "Uncle" Tex at the Ranch. Kitty didn't know how Tex felt about her Robby.

Kitty recalled in her head the night that her son was created at the Ranch in Texas. How Rob had gently held her as they made love several times that night. How he felt inside her and the smooth feeling she felt as he went in and out of her pussy. The hardness of his cock inside her. It was the only time a man had gotten her to climax. He was also the only man who ever kissed her lady parts with a gentle touch. She was also the last man that she would make love with.

Trish could see that something was working at Kitty. She seemed distracted and not her usual happy disposition. Kitty confided in Trish that she longed for the touch of a man again.

There arrangement was working fine for both of them. Yet there was something missing.

Trish asked Kitty "Do you want another baby?" Kitty replied, "Only if you will be a part of it. You know, be the one who plants the sperm from our donor."

Trish pondered thisfor a moment and then asked,

"Who shall we get for a donor?" Kitty joked," How about Luke?"

Tricia looked at Kitty and said,

"He's not old enough yet so he is out. How about Tex? You and Robby can go visit him at the ranch when the time is right and just get the seed direct. I remember that night at the ranch when he fucked me. He was very gentle and kind. A real gentleman. He knew how to make a girl feel good."

Trish thought a moment and said,

"Or, if you want me to do the deed and plant the seed, we can ask him to be our donor at a clinic and there I can finish the act of creation with the love of my life."

Kitty smiled and told Trish,

"You are magnificent love, let's ask Tex if he would sire a child who would grow up with Rob Harris's son."

Trish replied,

"I will make the call and set it up with Tex and a local clinic."

Kitty smiled at Trish and said, "Kiss me my sweet."

Trish kissed Kitty and they held each other, made love and went to sleep.

They told the children that they were going to visit Uncle Tex at the Ranch in Texas for a week of adventure riding horses and ATV's on the 5,000 acre property.

Robby had been told about the ranch all his life and now he was going to go see it. When Tex answered the phone he never could have imagined what he heard. Trish told him that Kitty and her were bringing all the kids to visit for a week.

Tex loved kids and being around them would be a treat for him. To see Trish and Kitty would be a special treat. He recalled the night after the Rodeo when they were at the Ranch and spent the night.

The time he spent with Trish was unlike any he had spent with a woman before in his life. She introduced him to some new ideas that he had not thought of in the sex department.

She was not just a pretty woman, but was very open about sex. She was apparently Bi Sexual as she was in a committed lesbian relationship with Kitty but still liked to have sex with a man. He was glad she did. He liked Kitty as well and looked forward to their visit.

When he got off the phone he went out to see the bulls that they were sending up to Huston for a Rodeo the following week.

When Trish and company arrived and got settled in Tex had the kitchen crew plan a nice Texas feast for them.

He saw Robby and was amazed at how much he looked like his friend Rob. He scooped Robby up and hugged him with a tear in his eye. He paraded around the Ranch with him on his shoulder like he was his own son.

After supper the girls laid out their idea for Tex to be a father. He listened with interest and then laughed and said, "Why not skip the clinic and just do it the old fashioned way with a 'Roll in the Hay' as we would say?"

Kitty told Tex,

"I really do like you Tex, but I want Trish to be the one who puts your sperm inside me, you do understand, right? I hope you do as we really want you to be the father of my baby."

Tex looked Kity in the eye and told her,

"O K, I will go to the clinic with you two and let Trish be the lucky one who gets to inseminate you. Can I watch? Also, I sure would like to screw Trish like we did back when you spent the night."

Trish smiled and said,

"That can be arranged, do you still have that bubble bath?" She asked Kitty,

"Would you like to watch or would you like to join in the fun?"

Kitty blushed and said,

"You told me what you and Tex did that night in the shower are you sure you want me to watch?"

Trish had introduced Tex to anal sex. He had never done that before and had not done it since.

It was a great finale to a wild day when Rob Harris had ridden "Bone Crusher" the bull that had not been ridden for five years. Rob got $10,000 for the 8 second ride. All the Sporting News interviewed Rob and his picture was in the national news as well. Trish, Kitty, and the two women from Connecticut were in some of the pictures.

That was how Joey Burke found out were Kitty had gotten to.

Kitty said,

"I sure could use a nice hot shower later this evening, I do feel a bit *dirty* from the trip. So I just might like to shower with you two."

Tex nodded toward the bedrooms and said,

"Why don't you get the kids down for the night? And I'll get a pitcher of margaritas for the big kids."

It was after midnight before the kids settled down and went to sleep. Tex and the women went back to Tex's bedroom and got undressed. Trish told Kitty,

"You can just stand and watch." She and Tex got in the shower first. Kitty watched as they lathered each other up with the bubble bath soap as promised. Tex stood behind Trish and with his arms around her he put his hands on her breasts and then fondled her wet and soapy pussy. He rubbed his hard cock up and down her ass crack. When he was well lubed with soap he put the tip in her hole. She pushed back bent over and relaxed as he slid all the way inside her.

Kitty watched in amazement as she watched her wife being ass fucked right in front of her. A brief wave of jealousy swept over her until she came back to the reality of this was to get this beautiful man to donate his sperm inside her.

She smiled at them and then walked into the shower and wrapped her arms around both of them and kissed Trish. She asked,

"Can I be next?"

The next day the children were delighted to find horses to ride. One of Tex's workers picked out some gentle ones for them.

The women took a pair of ATV's out to ride along with the kids to keep an eye on them.

Trish asked," So what did you think about last night?"

Kitty looked at her and replied,

" I didn't like it at first but when you kissed me while he was inside me I had a wonderful feeling come over me as I had a climax. It was different, but felt good." Trish asked,

"Would you do it again?" Kitty said,"

" I think I would let him as long as you are there to kiss me."

The decision to inseminate Kitty's egg with Tex's sperm was settled. They went to a Fertility Clinic in Huston where Tex made his donation and Trish kissed Kitty as she inserted the tube of sperm into her vagina and on into her uterus. Kitty laid on her belly for several hours while Trish rubbed her back.

When the Doctor came in and said, "Well ladies I am sure that the swimmers had their best chance of one of them penetrating the egg. You are free to leave and best wishes for a happy pregnancy."

Kitty looked at Trish and said,

"Do you think you knocked me up?"

Trish smiled and said, "If not we can try again, shower and all."

The next months went by and Kitty was feeling pregnant. She knew the feelings from when she carried Robby. Trish was happy and did whatever Kitty wanted.

When she started to show they told the others and they were so happy to learn they were going to have a new baby in the house.

Especially Lilly. When she was raped by her older brother she feared she would get pregnant. She had not even had a period yet, but worried none the less. Now she spent a lot of time with Kitty and asked a lot of questions about the pregnancy. She got straight answers from her.

Kitty explained how Trish and Tex helped her to get this baby. Lilly listened with great interest and asked," Doesn't it hurt when the baby comes out?"

Kitty told her,

"Yes, it does, but all you can think about is when the pain is gone you have a little baby to hold and love."

Lilly sat back and thought about it then said,

"I can't wait until Uncle Tex and Trish can give me a baby."

Kitty told Trish what Lilly said and they had a laugh at Lilly's naiveté.

Newt had driven past their home property several times. He made note of when the kids were out playing and when they were inside for classes. He scouted the hillside overlooking the house.

From his snippers nest he used a rangefinder to determine the distance to the porch and then estimated the drop of the bullet from that distance. He knew the ballistics of the 6.5 mm Creedmoor rifle he had selected for his mission.

He had set up a target at a location several miles away that was the same elevation and distance as at the house. He fired a shot at the target. He walked over to see where he had hit the target and then made a correction on the 20 power scope on the rifle. The next three shots were in the center and were nearly touching.

He said to himself,

'That should make for a quick humane kill for the kid. I don't want him to suffer, just his mom. I will get her lessy lover and then will put one in her head.'

Time passed and Kitty delivered a beautiful 6 pound 9 ounce baby girl. The kids all adored her. Trish and Kitty thought long and hard to choose a name for her. They decide on Katelyn Jo and gave her Tex's family name, Duncan. Katelyn Jo Duncan.

Luke went for a sail on the pond for a while in the morning. And fished until noon.

After lunch he and Lilly went for a hike up the hillside above the house. About halfway up they found something strange and suspicious. It appeared that someone had made a spot where they could watch the house from up there. There was a log laying across two rocks with some socks that looked like they were full of sand.

Luke said,

"This looks suspicious. Like someone has been here but I don't know why. Better tell Trish.

They went back to the house and told Trish. She went to check it out and found the spot. She looked it over carefully and decided that it was where someone had been watching them.

She had become somewhat paranoid about their privacy and was becoming more concerned about the safety of the children. She knew there were some hard feelings toward them from the Reservation people over the adoption of the three orphans. Some in the Village still thought they belonged on the reservation despite being half breeds. That the custody should have stayed in the Tribe. There was really no one who stood up to take them in. There were still a couple of hot heads that wouldn't let it go.

She decided to make herself a hiding place on the hill where she could watch for whoever was spying on her family. She told Kitty what she had found and about the socks full of sand on a log. It took only a moment for Kitty to realize what they were for.

"Trish, my brothers would have sand bags like that when they were sighting in their Deer rifles. They would lay the forearm of the rifle on the sandbag to steady it when they were shooting. Made for some accurate shots. We haven't heard anyone shooting. I wonder who was there."

Kitty and Trish did a good job on the hide they built on the hillside. They could look down on the spy's location without being seen. They couldn't believe that anyone would want to shoot at them from up here. Trish said,

"This is our place and our kids and whoever this is, they are fucking with the wrong people."

Trish recalled how in Las Vegas she saved Kitty when she was being attacked by Joey in the parking lot and how she reacted by getting her 40 caliber Glock hand gun that her father had given her when she was 18.

She and her brother, Tommy, set up a target behind the lake house. They practiced most every day and both became very proficient with it. They could draw and fire hitting the target in mid body with 4 out of 6 shots.

One time Trish unloaded 14 shots at 20 yards and hit a vital spot with 12 of the 14 rounds in 15 seconds.

Kitty had never had any experience with firearms and was glad Trish was there and was able to save her life. It did traumatize her for some time. She had a hard time getting to sleep and woke from nightmares several times a week. Trish made her visit a Physiatrist who helped her to get past the beatings and the fear that Joey had instilled in her. Then she could get a full night's sleep.

Meanwhile, Newt decided to only go to his sniper's nest three times a week. This was to minimize the chance of being found out before he could do what he came here from Maine to do. That was to kill Kitty's son to instill as much emotional pain as possible before he killed Trish. After he did that he would finish the job and kill Kitty.

He found a small town where he could hide out in the local Hotel. The people in town paid him no attention as they were used to seeing their share of ex-GI's who took to the road to try to escape the hell they had seen in war zones in Afghanistan and the Middle East.

Newt would buy a couple bottles of Jack Daniels and hole up in his room and drink himself to sleep. The next day he would head out before dawn to spend the day watching the children and Kitty and Trish. He knew their every move on a certain day. Their activities were like clockwork on the days that they held classes.

Sharply at 7 am Kitty had all the children out for morning warm up exercises. After they all ran around the yard for 5 minutes they did a series of stretches. They would then sing some of their favorite songs.

"Old MacDonald had a farm E I E I O. And on his farm he had a duck, quack, quack, quack.

"If the weather was nice they would split them up into age groups.

The younger kids would work on their spelling and math. Kitty had them all memorize the multiplication tables. She told them that it was important to know.

Luke, Lilly and Evan were in one group and Luke served as leader of them as he was the oldest. His task was to go over the previous day's work and make sure they all understood it before moving on to the that day's assignment. It worked out well and they all learned at the same rate. They were learning American History. Luke had them studying Texas and the war with Mexico.

Luke was 14 was reading and comprehending at a first year college level. Lilly and Evan were not far behind.

Kitty was really proud of what they have learned. Buddy, Patty and Robby were all reading at a higher grade level as Kitty had focused on reading skills. They were all at a 7th grade level and devoured books as fast as Kitty assigned them.

Robby really loved his little sister and enjoyed helping to care for her. He didn't like diaper detail, but did it anyway.

Katelyn was a precocious child and was crawling at 3 months and walking at 9 months. She was a happy baby and content to be with the others and enjoyed the attention she received.

Newt was getting tired of watching the happy little family and decided it was time to shred the peace and quiet. It was 5am when he left his truck parked in a grove of trees a mile away and took his rifle out of the truck. He started heading for his nest above the house where Kitty's family lived.

What he didn't know was that Trish had been watching him for a month as he came and went to his nest.

She had her own nest only 20 yards away from his. On this morning Trish arrived at her spot an hour before Newt and watched him as he made his way to his shooting location with his sniper rifle.

She had a feeling that this was to be the day when he would take his shot. She was right. Newt settled in and watched with binoculars as Kitty and the kids came out at 7 am like always.

He set up his rifle on the sand bags and looked thru the scope. At 300 yards he could see with the 20 power scope Kitty's smiling face as the kids started their exercising routine.

Newt was so fixed on watching Kitty that he never heard Trish slip silently up behind him. He activated the rifle's bolt action and slid a cartridge into the rifles firing chamber and peered thru the scope. He focused on Robby as he ran around the yard. When Robby stopped a smile crossed Newt's face and he started to squeeze the trigger. He said aloud,

"This will take that smile off your face you bitch."

The sound of the gun shot reverberated down the hillside. Kitty and the kids stopped and looked up to see Trish standing and looking at something at her feet. She walked down the hill and told Kitty,

" It's over."

After the kids went in the house to read and study, Trish and Kitty went up the hill to finish taking care of business. After checking for some identification and finding a Maine driver's license with Newts name on it.

They discovered that he was Joey's younger brother. They covered the body with rocks.

They may never find out what his plan was but they did know he was up to no good. He had stalked the family for over a month. They found a notebook with entry's that showed their daily movements. Like he had some plan that he was working on. Whatever it was didn't matter anymore as Newt was dead.

The shot they heard was Trish as she squeezed the trigger on her Glock before he could finish his shot. Blood and brains spattered the rocks and the sand bags. They covered his body with rocks along with his rifle. When they finished they walked down the hill to their home and joined the kids for lunch.

Another five years has passed...

Luke now 19, looked at Lilly, now 17, as she laid naked on a blanket sun bathing by the pond. Trish and Kitty had taken the others to town to do some shopping for clothes.

Lilly had matured into a beautiful young woman. Still petit in stature but with the curves in the right places she looked older then she was.

Luke stood and watched her as she slept. Lilly slowly opened her eyes and when she saw Luke watching her she smiled.

"Why don't you join me on the blanket?" she asked. "I would love to share it with you."

Since he knew the kids won't be back until supper time he removed his clothes and laid down beside her.

She opened her arms to welcome Luke and embrace him. She looked him in the eyes and told him,

"I have wanted this to happen for a long time, to hold you in my arms and feel you on me. Every time I look at you anymore I just want to taste you like candy."

Luke told her,

"I have wanted to hold you close and smell your sweet scent ever since you were a sweet girl of sixteen."

Lilly wrapped her arms and legs around Luke and kissed him with her lips parted and her tongue feeling for his. She could feel his cock get hard as he rubbed it up her crotch. He pushed it into her warm wetness and felt the warmth of her vagina as she opened up and let him penetrate her completely. Luke had wanted to do this for so very long.

He had only had sex with one woman before. That was one of his History Instructors at the Community College he was attending.

She was 34 and had taught him well. She showed him things that he never thought of before. She taught him how to pleasure a woman with his tongue. That her clitoris was very sensitive and he should lick and suck it. She was also very experienced in falatio.

Luke was ready to show Lilly what he had learned. As they laid naked with him beside her he asked,

"Would you like to try it another way?" She replied,

"You mean like Doggy, or Cowgirl or Standing from behind?" Luke laughed and said,

"Have you been watching porn again?" Lilly laughed and said, "I just have a wild imagination. What's your Teacher been teaching you at college?"

"How do you know about her? She is a good teacher for sure. The first time she gave me a blow job I almost came before she had her mouth closed." Lilly said,

"Like this?" as she moved down his belly and put the tip of his hard cock in her mouth. She moved her tongue back and forth along the bottom and around the head. She bobbed her head up and down as she sucked him into her. He could fell his climax coming and wanted to stop but couldn't.

Lilly wanted him to finish in her mouth and held onto his ass checks as he came. She swallowed his load and went up and kissed him.

He could taste his semen as she swallowed the last of his gift. Luke offered,

"Would you like me to pleasure you now Lilly?"

She smiled and parted her legs. Luke went down and started at her knees. He licked all the way up both legs to her crotch. When he got to her center he gently pushed his tongue into her vagina and licked his way up to her clit. He licked and sucked on it gently like he had been taught before going all the way back to her anus and then back up again.

He did this as long as she wanted him to. She had several intense orgasms and the last was a squirting one. She had never had this happen and thought she was peeing. Luke licked up her juice as fast as it past from her. She was embarrassed by this and apologized to Luke. He just smiled at her and said, "That was great, I liked it."

They laid in the sun and enjoyed the afternoon. Later Luke said,

"Would you like to fuck again?"

She looked at him and replied,

"I thought you wouldn't ask, sure, how do you want to do it this time?"

"Would you like to try anal?"

Lilly thought about it and then said,

"Only if you let me lube up first."

Luke said,

"Well, how about this sun tan lotion? That should work."

Lilly took some and worked it into her back hole. It seemed to do the job so she got on her knees and presented her beautiful ass for Luke to admire. He had another very hard cock for her and he was on his knees behind her. He had some of the sun tan lotion on his cock as he pushed gently into her. She pushed back as he started to enter. He was in about 3 inches and she started to move slowly as she experienced another wonderful orgasm. They maintained this for some time before he climaxed again in her.

The sun was going down before they went in and showered

together. They got dressed before the kids got back from shopping.

Tex and Robby were on their way to Texas and the ranch. Robby enjoyed his visits to the Ranch. He had learned to ride horses when he was seven years old. He was now ten and quite the accomplished rider.

Tex had lost his early animosity of Robby being destined to be the owner of the Ranch when he turned twenty one. He had grown to love him as if he was his own. On this trip they brought Katelyn along.

She was five now and was not about to be left behind. She had been told that Tex was her Dad and that Kitty and Trish were her Mom's. She really felt lucky to have a Dad and two Moms to love her so much. Tex was the most loving Dad and he treasured the time he had with her.

When they arrived Tex was told by his ranch Forman, Rodney, that one of their top bulls was bitten on the nose by a rattlesnake.

Tex asked,

"Did you call the Vet? What did he say?"

Rodney replied,

"Yes and he came out and gave the bull some anti-venom and is sure he will survive. Just another day at the ranch."

Snakes and Scorpions are always a threat in that part of Texas and the children were told at a young age what to do if they saw one. Leave the area and report it to one of the hands. Always empty your shoes in the morning as Scorpions like to hide inside.

Trish and Kitty were coming later in the week. Robby wanted some alone time with Tex before they arrived.

Katelyn made herself at home on the patio behind the Ranch house. She loved to read and had a collection of Dr. Seuss books that she had memorized since she was three.

Tex and Robby went out to the horse barn and picked out a pair of steeds to take on a trail ride. They rode for a while and then Robby pulled up and told Tex he needed to talk.

He had encouraged Robby to confide in him about anything at all. Robby began,

"Uncle Tex, I want you to call me Rob, just like my Dad. Robby was o k when I was little, but now I am ten, almost a teenager."

Tex smiled, he had hoped to keep him a kid for a while longer. But if he wanted to be called Rob that was O K. He thought, 'I guess that we all want to outgrow our kid names at some point.'

"O K, *Rob*, it will take some getting used to, but from now on I will call you Rob."

"Thanks Uncle Tex."

Tex offered,

"Since you are now Rob, you can call me *Tex* since I am not really your uncle."

Rob got serious and told Tex,

" I know about the will that my Dad made and I want you to know that when I turn twenty-one the second thing I'm going to do is make you my equal Partner in the Ranch."

Tex asked,

"So what is the first thing you are going to do?" Rob looked up at Tex and replied,

" Taste Whiskey."

Tex raised his eyebrows at that and asked,

"Why in the world would you want to do that?"

Young Rob looked at Tex and said,

"Cause that's what you do when you become a man."

Tex looked him in the eye and told him,

"No Rob, that's not what a real man does. A real man takes his life seriously and leaves such foolishness behind. If you want to learn about Whiskey I'll take you to an AA meeting with me sometime and you can hear the stories of how whiskey changed lives. It's not fun at all."

Rob listened as Tex told him about some of his friends who over the years had gone from being decent hard working men to drunks who couldn't hold a job or keep a relationship for long. And how one of Tex's longtime friends, Mac Davidson, had killed his girlfriend while he was driving drunk. Soon after that he shot himself.

"Yes, Rob, he yearned for his first taste of whiskey too, now he is dead."

Rob thought about what Tex said and he remembered the way that Evan, Buddy and Patty came to be in his extended family. The taste of whiskey didn't sound as exciting.

The next day Katelyn wanted to ride a horse. Tex had a Shetland pony that was just about the right size for a five year old. She was so excited and could not wait to get up on the Pony's back. When Tex and Rob were saddled up they all went out to the trail that leads to the open range.

The Ranch of five thousand acres is divided into large open range that the cattle graze in and beyond were foothills that reached to the mountains.

Katelyn was in the lead so that Tex could keep watch on her so that she didn't get in trouble. Rob rode along behind Tex. She looked back and asked,

"I am not going too fast am I, and can you keep up alright?"

They rode for several hours and when they got back to the ranch they were surprised to see that Trish and the rest of the family had arrived.

After lunch while the kids were busy outside, Tex took Trish and Kitty aside and told them what Robby said about wanting to be called Rob now instead of Robby and what he said about the Partnership in the ranch.

Kitty smiled and said,

"I knew he would do that. The boy doesn't have a selfish or greedy bone in his body."

Tex grinned and replied,

"That's for sure, he is so much like his Father. With his Native blood from his Dads side and the simple beauty and honesty of his Mother how could he be any different?"

Trish thought about it for a moment and then replied, "Being raised by two strong women didn't hurt either." Tex agreed.

Young Rob and Evan were taking care of the horses and Katelyn's Pony in the barn while the other kids went swimming.

Evan asked Rob,

"I hear that you and Tex will be equal partners when you turn twenty one. That was a dumb idea. This place is worth millions and it is all yours. Why would you just give half to him?"

Rob thought the world of Evan and looked up to him. He wondered if he spoke too soon with Tex. Rob said,

" Tex has been good to me and my sister and he and my Dad were best friends. Why would I not want to share it with him?" Evan looked at Rob and said,

"I'm just saying, you don't have to give him half. How about give him like, ten percent or so? And then share the rest with us, you know Patty, Buddy and I?"

Rob thought about it and then said,

"That is eleven years away. Let's not overthink it for now. O K?"

Evan looked at Rob and said,

" O K, but just think what that would mean to all of us. Sure we have our Moms property in New Mexico, but that is just our home, this is a going business with the cattle and the Rodeo bulls and the gas and oil wells, it makes a lot of money."

Rob thought hard about what Evan said. He knew he had to talk it over with Trish and Kitty.

The responsibility of running the ranch was all on Tex for now. In the next eleven years would he be able to run it without Tex?

He told Kitty what Evan had proposed and then they went to Trish to discuss it. Trish told Rob,

"You made a commitment to Tex and you know what that means? You are only ten, but you have been raised to be a man of your word. To go back on your word to Tex would not only be going back on your word, but would break his heart. This ranch was his best friends for three generations of his family and Tex has been working on it since he was a teen. You are a blood owner and what you decide is up to you. Evan has nothing to say about it. If you wish to give him a share it should come out of your half share, not Tex's. You have already given Tex a verbal promise. He loves you and your sister very much and he looks forward to being your Partner in the Ranch someday."

Rob held his head in his hands and thought about what Trish said and he realized she was right. She most always was.

Trish took Evan aside and explained to him what Rob and she had discussed.

That night as Kitty and Trish laid in bed they talked about what Rob and Evan were discussing. Kitty asked,

"What do you think Rob will do?" Trish replied,

"I think he will work it out with Evan and do the right thing. We raised both those boys to be responsible and to care about others feelings. I am sure he will honor his commitment to Tex."

Kitty wrapped her arms around Trish and gave her a kiss. She said,

"You always have the right answer, now let's make love." With that they embraced and held their bodies close together. Their hands felt warm as they caressed each other's soft curves and warm lady parts. Trish was the first to work her hands and mouth down Kitty's belly and gently kiss and lick her to a pleasant release. Kitty laid on her back and thought,

'I am so lucky to have met her that day in Bar Harbor Maine. She is my forever love.'

Tex took the children in to Huston to the Rodeo. Several of the bulls from the ranch were going to be in the Bull riding competition.

One of them was a son of "Bone crusher", the bull that Rob Harris had ridden for a ten thousand dollar paycheck. For a young bull he was large. He weighed as much as Bone Crusher.

Tex had offered a reward of five thousand dollars to the Cowboy who could stay on him for the eight second count.

This bulls name was Reaper.

The kids all lined up along the railing to watch the action. The bull riding was always the most exciting to see. They had watched the bull riding event every time they went to the Rodeo.

Tom Lantz was the Cowboy who drew Reaper to ride. Tom was an experienced bull rider and was a good friend of Rob Harris and Tex. He had been in Rodeos since he was a teenager. He was there when Rob died after riding a bull named 'Son of Satan'.

Tom was thinking of his friend as he lowered himself onto Reaper's back. The bull turned his head and looked at Tom, an evil look. He felt fear go thru him for the first time in all his years of ridding bulls.

The gate opened and Reaper leapt into the air while spinning around. Tom held on for six seconds before being thrown off. When he hit the ground the bull turned on him and smashed his hooves into Tom's body.

The Rodeo Clowns did their best to divert the bull's attention away from Tom. But they were too late. Reaper continued to stomp on Tom and gore him with his horns. He stood over Tom's dead body like he was claiming a prize. He pawed the ground and snorted. With a final bellow he walked away.

He looked up at the shocked audience including Tex and the kids. He stood there looking right at Tex who was horrified at the sight.

When they returned to the Ranch he told Rodney to unload the bull in a back pasture. He went in the house and got his 300 magnum and went out there and shot Reaper in the head.

A bull that Tex had raised from a calf. Tex cried for Tom and he cried for Reaper who had become a murderer. He had lost his best friend, Rob Harris to a bull and now a long time rodeo competitor and friend Tom Lantz.

After that day Tex quit raising rodeo bulls. All were castrated as calf's and sent to market. If he had not put Reaper down he feared he would kill again.

The sight of Tom being killed violently affected Katelyn the most of the kids who witnessed the horrible event. She had nightmares and would wake up screaming and peeing her pants.

Kitty took her to a child Psychiatrist to try to heal her daughter. It took a long time before she got thru the night without the terrors. The other kids were able to handle it better.

Maybe because they had seen so much violence in video games that they were immune to what happened. Trish did not approve of the games they watched and she felt it made them apathetic to the real world. She decided to get them "unplugged" from their devices and go out and be in the fresh air and sunshine.

For the first week they grumbled about it, but then they started to enjoy doing things with their hands. They built some bird houses and put them up around their home in New Mexico and at the Ranch. They repaired the boat dock at the pond.

The older kids thought they should have their games back but they knew that Trish was most often right about what was in their best interest.

The one time they recalled when Trish was wrong was when she made a birthday cake for Kitty a month ahead of her birthday. They all sang "Happy Birthday" anyway.

Back in Bar Harbor Maine, Joey's family wondered where Newton was. They had not heard from him in months. He didn't say where he was going or when he would be back.

His sister Evelyn was the only one he told where he was going. She kept it to herself because she was worried that he was going to do something bad.

Newt was really upset when he learned about Joey's death. He told her that he was going to avenge Joey's murder with some of his own. Evelyn was always afraid of her older brothers and steered clear of them especially when they were drinking.

She knew that Joey beat Kitty and had tried to chook her before she fled Maine.

When Joey found that she was in California with another woman he went nuts. Evelyn was told that Joey had gone out there to reconcile with her and beg her to come back to Maine with him. He told her that he really loved Kitty and wanted her back. She didn't know whether to believe him or not. He had always had a bad temper and it was worse when he drank. She had her doubts about him wanting to reconcile with Kitty. But she held her tongue.

He really freaked out when she left him. For nearly two months he cursed her for running away from him. When he left for California she was afraid he would do something violent.

She knew that he and Newt hated lesbians and gays even more than Black's, Mexicans and Towelheads. They thought that these people were inferior to any white man.

As teenagers they would go into Portland and find a Gay bar and wait outside for someone to leave. They would taunt the man into a fight and then they would leave the poor man severely beaten and take his wallet. They never got caught. They also like to tease Downs Syndrome people calling them "Retards". Both Joey and Newt were just plain mean people who never met their match.

Evelyn always liked kitty and was on the boat the day it hit the log and sank. She and kitty survived but the other two drowned.

Kitty was grief stricken for some time. That was when she started to see Joey. She thought it was kind of funny because she had thought of Kitty as a Lesbian.

Evelyn knew that Kitty had a thing for one of the girls that died. If Joey suspected this it may have been the reason he started to abuse her. She needed to get answers.

Was Joey murdered or was it a just killing. Also where was Newt? Evelyn started by getting the crime report from Las Vegas Police. What she had been told about Joey's death was a lie.

Joey died while he was trying to kill Kitty. Tricia Flick was named as the shooter. She was exonerated of any wrong doing and released. It was declared a matter of self-defense or the defense of another. This is not what they had been told. So if Joey was not killed in cold blood as she was told, what happened to Newt? If he was on a revenge mission? Evelyn needed to get more answers.

She learned that Kitty and Trish had settled in New Mexico.

She flew from Portland to Newark and then to Albuquerque New Mexico. She rented a small pickup truck to travel to where Kitty lived. She had their address dialed into the trucks GPS unit and she went down the road. It was a long ride thru desert, mountains and forests. She finally arrived at her destination.

She parked in the driveway and walked to the front door. Knocked and waited, shortly Luke answered the door.

"Hi, I'm a friend of Kitty's from Maine. I wanted to see her again." Evelyn explained.

Luke opened the door with a smile and said,

"I will see if I can find her, be right back, who shall I tell her you are?"

Tell her it's "Evey" from Bar Harbor.

When Luke told Kitty who was at the door she looked at Trish and said.

"She's Joey and Newts sister. What does she want?"

Trish said,

"Stay here and I will find out."

She put her Glock in the back of her pants and followed Luke to the front room. When she saw Evelyn she was surprised to see how small she was. Joey and Newt were much larger stature then she.

Kitty had only mentioned her once when she told her about the boating accident. Evelyn was operating the boat when it hit the log.

Kitty walked in the room and when she saw Evelyn she shook and started to cry. She put her arms around Evelyn and they cried together remembering their friends that they lost that day.

It was thirteen years since the accident but it all came rushing back when they saw each other. When they finally got their emotions together again Kitty asked,

"What brings you here? And how did you find us?" Evelyn replied,

"Your brother Jack told me where you were after Joey died. He told me how Joey died. I always knew he would die a violent death, it was how he lived."

Trish spoke up saying,

" It was the worst time of my life and not one I care to remember. The moment was a life or death event. He would have killed Kitty if I hadn't stopped him."

Evelyn looked at Trish and then at Kitty.

"I am so sorry for what he put you thru Kitty. He was like that when he drank. He raped me when I was twelve. I never told anyone about it. I am glad he is dead. Kitty never expected to hear this from Joey's sister.

Evelyn told them that when Joey left for California he told a friend that he was going there to kill Kitty for leaving him for another woman.

"He so hated lesbians and Gays that he just flipped out."

She looked over at Trish and said,

"I'm glad you shot him, he was just plain evil. I hated him ever since he did what he did to me when I was a little girl." Then she added,

"Newts the same way. He was told that Joey was going to try to reconcile things with you Kitty and would not believe anything else. I haven't seen him in months but I heard he was coming for you Trish. I wanted to warn you before he made trouble."

They looked at each other and then at Evelyn. Trish said, "Thank you for the warning, we will be more vigilant with what we do. Do you have a picture of Newt? Kitty never saw him as he was deployed when she was with Joey."

Evelyn reached in her wallet and produced a picture of both Joey and Newt when they were in High School. She gave it to Kitty. She recognized the man that Trish had shot on the hill side. It was Newt.

The circumstance of what happened to Newt would be a secret that only she and Kitty shared. After Evelyn left Trish and Kitty sat and pondered what had taken place.

Trish said,

"I'm glad I killed Newt. He was so close to harming you or one of the kids. "Kitty said,

"After what Evelyn shared about Joey, I'm glad he is dead too. She is such a sweet girl who I always liked. Hard to believe she had two monsters for brothers."

It was a year later that the New Mexico State police were called to investigate an abandoned pickup parked in a wooded area about twenty miles from Trish and Kitty. The owner was not able to be found in Maine or elsewhere. The truck was hauled away for scrap.

CHAPTER THREE

Deadly Seduction

W hen we left the girls they were talking about Joey's and Newton's sister, Evelyn. She came down to their home in New Mexico to warn them that her brother Newt may be coming after Tricia for killing their older brother Joey.

She has left and they were thinking about what she had said about Newt coming for Trish. They knew that threat was no more. That when he did come for her it ended badly for him.

Five years pass...

Trish returned her Glock to its safe location in their bedroom. The children were busy with their school work and they had all been doing well.

The older kids, Buddy and Robby had been instructed in the safe handling of weapons and they had developed skill in handling and firing her Glock.

Buddy said when they finished target practice on the range in the back yard,

"When I am old enough I am getting me one of these."

Robby replied,

"Tex has a full arsenal at the Ranch. When I go there we take some out to the target range he has set up. It's fun to shoot some of the big guns. Tex has a 300 Magnum that is really loud and really kicks your shoulder when you fire it."

Buddy's brother Evan joined the Army when he was seventeen and signed up for six years to be eligible for the Military Intelligence school he wanted.

The Army steered him to this based on his high test scores on entry. His training was intense. Regular Boot camp plus an accelerated course in languages. Especially Russian and Arabic. This was why he had no leave the first year.

Evan was home on leave now and was happy to see his brother and sister as well as the extended family. He was excited to see Robby and his sister Katelyn. They had grown since he saw them last.

Trish and Kitty welcomed him with hugs and kisses. They were so proud of their adopted son for the man he was developing into. He had packed on thirty pounds of muscle and grew a couple inches. His black hair was buzz cut in military style. His smile would light up the room.

Trish announced that there was going to be a wedding at their place.

"Luke and Lilly have decided to get married and they want to have the ceremony here by the pond.

"We haven't set a date yet, but I just wanted all of you to know."

Luke had finished his degree in mining engineering and had gotten a job in Texas with an oil company doing exploration for new wells.

Lilly was finishing her degree to become a Registered Nurse and had job offers from all over the country. She graduated at the top of her class.

She and Luke decided to settle near Huston since the main office of the oil company he was working for was there. So were several of the offers that she had.

Trish had offered to take another young person who needed a stable home. The Child service lady asked,

"Are you ready to take this on again?"

Trish answered,

" We are happy to help as many as you have."

"Don't say that, I have a lot of kids in need." The lady chuckled. "I do have a couple that are brother and sister who have been orphaned due to both parents overdosing on Heroine laced with who knows what. Terrible stuff out there today. They say it comes from China. But then they blame everything on China."

Trish asked,

"When can we see these kids?"

The lady replied,

"How about the beginning of the week, say Monday morning ten o'clock. In my office."

"Sounds like a plan." Trish smiled in return.

She and Kitty had great success with fostering kids and the children's service knew it. All of the kids that they had fostered had gotten a good education under the women's guidance and some had gone on to college.

Trish looked at Kitty and said,

"Sounds like we may be getting some new faces here soon."

Kitty said,

"I think we are ready to do it again."

That evening as they got ready for bed Trish looked at Kitty as she got dried off from her shower and said, "God, you are still beautiful even at 36." Kitty replied with a sly smile, "So are you for an old lady of 45."

Trish went over to Kitty and wrapped her arms around Kitty's soft body and held her close.

"I can still curl your toes for you can't I?"

She reached between Kitty's legs and squeezed her pubic mound as she had done on so many other nights.

Kitty responded by opening her legs and letting Trish run a finger in her wet crack. They kissed and pushed their tongues gently into each other's mouths.

Trish led Kitty over to the edge of the bed and gently lowered her down with her legs still over the edge. She raised Kitty's legs up and pushed them toward her head.

With them spread she could see Kitty's clit and her vaginal opening. Trish bent down and pressed her face into Kitty's crotch. She licked up her legs and back down to her center. She did this for several minutes until Kitty asked,

"When is it my turn you pretty girl?"

The next morning they got up and Started the day with the young kids, Patty, Robby and his sister Katelyn doing their class work before starting on some wood working projects.

The family had gotten a Golden Retriever puppy and they were going to build her a dog house today. They named her Ginger.

Monday morning came and Trish and Kitty went to visit the Children's Service lady at 10 am at her office.

There were two young kids sitting in her office when they arrived. A boy and girl. He was 9 and his sister was 7. His name was Adam and his sister was Penny.

When Trish and Kitty entered the office they could see that the kids were scared. They didn't know what was going to happen to them. Were these people going to take them away and do terrible things with them? Adam had heard that some foster parents make the kids do dirty jobs and beat on them for being lazy.

When Trish came in and smiled at him he relaxed some and decided to see where this was going.

The lady explained to him and his sister that these ladies were going to take care of them for a while until they could find a family to adopt them.

Adam asked,

"How long will that be? Where will we be living? Are there other kids there?"

Kitty answered him,

"We have a small Ranch out in the mountains with a pond to swim in and there are some other kids that you can play with. We home school you because there are no schools nearby. I will be your teacher. How will that be?"

His sister Penny looked at Trish and asked,

"Are you a Teacher too?"

Trish told her,

"Not exactly, I take care of all the other stuff around the place. We just got a new puppy to play with and puppies take work. Maybe you can help train her, her name is Ginger. Would you like that?"

Penny's eyes lit up and she said, "Yes that will be fun and I like puppies."

At the end of the visit they had two more kids to take care of.

On the way home Kitty said to Trish,

"This is going to be so much fun as well as work. But I'm up for it."

Trish replied,

"Yes it will be but we have had a couple of the kids move on so there is still room in my home and heart for some more."

When they arrived back at the Ranch they had a visitor. They didn't know who he was. It turned out he was from the County's land surveyor's office. He started by saying,

"You Ladies bought this land about 10 years ago, didn't you?"

Trish answered,

"Yes, what's the problem?"

He reached into a folder and brought out a sheet of paper on which was a sketch of the property lines.

He pointed to a place on the paper that was where they had built their house 10 years earlier.

"What this means is that you have been taken across. The seller of this land never had a clear title to sell it to you." Trish asked,

"So what does this mean?"

"It means that you are trespassing on land that a man named Alan Freed who lives in Albuquerque owns. The man you bought this from had made copies of the title and pawned it off as his own. "

The women looked at each other and then at the man,

"What do we do now? We have lived on this land for 10 years and built this house here."

The man said,

"I have several options for you. First I will say that you have a very beautiful home here and it is remarkable in this area. So the option one is that you can just move so that Mr. Freed can have his land back with no cost to you." Trish asked,

"What do you mean no cost? We're not moving. Go find the man we bought it from and charge him with fraud or something."

The man went on,

"He can't be found, and the second option is to purchase the land from Mr. Freed. He is a reasonable man as I know him to be. He will settle for what the bare land without the house on it is worth in today's market." Trish said,

"That's outrageous and not going to happen. I can have a battery of Lawyers here in 24 hours to protest this."

He replied,

"Go ahead, Mr. Freed likes a good legal battle, you see he is also the States Attorney."

Kitty asked Trish,

"What are we going to do now?"

"I don't know, I'll call Tommy in NY and ask him. He is closer to Dads old law firm."

Several phone calls later Trish got off the phone and told Kitty.

"Let's see what Mr. Freed has in mind for a price."

They traveled into Albuquerque and looked for Mr. Freed. They found his office and went in. The front office person, a woman who looked to be 60 asked if they had an appointment.

Trish answered,

"No we don't but it is an extreme emergency that we see Mr. Freed."

The lady said,

"I'll see if he can see you, please have a seat."

She got on the phone and asked him if he could see them. When she got off the phone she told them that he said to make an appointment.

Trish said in as calm a voice as she could muster,

"We have come a long distance to discuss a matter of importance to Mr. Freed and to us. Please ask if he can see us for 5 minutes."

The lady got on the phone again and when she hung up she said,

"He will see you for no more than 5 minutes, I will be timing it, so go in now."

Trish and Kitty got up and went into the large office of Mr. Alan

Freed.

He sat behind a large desk and motioned them to sit in chairs in front of his desk. After they were seated he asked,

"What can I do for you Ladies today?"

Trish opened by saying,

"We were notified by the Surveyors office that there is a problem with the land we purchased 10 years ago. We purchased it in good faith and have built a home on it for our kids. Now we are told the land belongs to you, that it was technically stolen from you and fraudulently sold to us. We are here to see what kind of deal we can work out with you for our property."

Freed looked at the women for a full minute and then said,

"Get out, I will see you in court."

Trish went numb as she sat up in her chair. Kitty had started to cry.

Trish replied to him by saying,

"Do you know what you are doing? We have been taking care of problem kids there for 10 years and have sent several to College."

He replied to her,

"I don't give a damn if you are fucking Mother Teresa. Get off my land or give me a million to stay."

Trish's hands ran cold as they left his office. After they got out on the street she said,

"It looks like we really got fucked by that asshole, Denver Weaver, we got the land from, and I wonder if he is really that hard to find or just hiding from the law."

Kitty said,

"We should look for him and see what we can do to get him to pay Freed. A million is a lot of money. After all he stole the land from Freed."

Trish looked at kitty and said.

"I will call Tommy back home and have him get one to the Lawyers in Dads old firm to hunt him down and to see if Freed really has a case against us."

Denver Weaver meanwhile, was living in Mexico. Near El Paso with his girlfriend Rita Gonzales.

They had concocted the scheme to steal parcels of land from the edges of large properties in New Mexico and Arizona.

They had crooked surveyors come to a property and just take a portion from the adjoining owners. The owners would not notice the loss of their land until it was already sold. Denver would take this false deed to a Realtor and offer it for sale. Most of the properties were small like Trish's.

Hers at 30 acres was one of the largest. Selling it for $600,000 cash was a great deal for them. Who would have thought that a 30 years old would have that much money?

Now ten years later Denver decide to go back to Albuquerque and see if he can do another land grab.

He wanted to see if Alan Freed had any other properties that he could steal a Deed to and sell like he did with Trish and Kitty. There was one about 30 miles east of the city that Freed had bought many years ago.

It was bought on speculation that there would be residential development going on nearby and it would be snapped up from him by a developer. That didn't happen.

Denver had his surveyor draw up a layout of the property with the borders shown with names of neighboring owners. He presented it to the county clerk to get a Deed for it. He approached his favorite Realtor and had him list it for sale. It was just about 12 acres.

Trish's brother, Tommy had contacted one of the Investigators that the law firm had on retainer and started to search for Denver Weaver. They had access to resources that can track down an Ant. It didn't take long to find him living in Mexico.

The next thing Tommy did was call a friend who worked for the FBI. He related Trish's story to him and was told,

"We have been after this Guy for years. He is pretty slippery to get as he lives in Mexico. His travels in the States are mostly done on the phone or Internet." Tommy asked,

"What's the chances that we can catch this Guy?"

"Slim to none." His friend told him.

Trish decided to negotiate with Freed so she could get him paid off. His demand for a million dollars was ridiculous and he knew it.

She hired a Lawyer from over in Phoenix Arizona to be her representative. He knew Freed and was sure he could prevail.

He called her a week later and told her,

"I sat down with Alan and we had a nice conversation. It seems that Alan had experience with the Foster care system when he was a child. I told him that the Children's service people think the world of you and what you have done with the kids that they sent to you. When I told him that you paid for their College tuition with no strings attached he relented on his demand for the million and said that if you continue to do what you are doing for the kids you can have the property for a dollar a year rent."

Trish and Kitty were absolutely giddy when they heard this. A tremendous load was lifted from their shoulders.

Now they could go about taking care of the two charges that they just acquired.

Adam was excited to see where he was going to be living. It was a lot different from where they had been before with their parents. He saw the pond and asked Kitty,

"Can we go swimming in the pond?"

She replied,

"After we get you moved into your rooms. And get some lunch."

Penny was excited to meet the Golden retriever, Ginger. She had never had a dog before and just wanted to play with her. Ginger liked the attention as well.

Trish told them,

"The other kids here are older, but they are friendly and will be happy to show you around the place. We have an indoor class room for when it is rainy or cold outside, otherwise we have class outside."

Robby, Patty and Buddy walked in as the new kids were eating their lunch. Robby was the first to speak.

"Hi guys, my name is Robby. Have you met Ginger yet? She is just a puppy but will get to be a big dog."

Adam looked at Robby and smiled. He said,

"My name is Adam and this is my little sister, Penny. She is 7 and I am 9. How old are you?"

Robb said,

"I am 15 and Patty here is 15 too. Her brother Buddy is 17. He has his driver's license so when we need to go somewhere he can drive us there. Their older brother is Evan, he's in the Army. We don't see him very often. Did you see the pond? We swim and fish in it."

Adam started to relax as he met his fellow house mates.

About that time Katelyn came bouncing into the room. She saw Penny and said,

"Hello, my name is Katelyn. I'm 10. How old are you?"

Penny smiled and said,

"My name is Penny and I am 7, when can we get in the pond?"

Katelyn looked at Kitty and then at Trish. She knew that they had to wait for one of them to watch them at the pond.

Kitty said,

"How about if we all go swimming? Bring some life jackets for the new kids as well as for yourself Katelyn."

Katelyn could swim alright but they still made her wear one.

Adam told Kitty that they had never been swimming before and were anxious to learn how.

Kitty told the kids that they were going to have swimming lessons every day after they finished with their school lessons.

Penny's eyes danced when she heard that. Adam just smiled. They were already feeling good about where they were. They both slept well that night.

A year later Robb decides that he wants to move to Texas so he can be with Tex and learn how to manage the ranch. Kitty was not happy with this. She told him,

"I just think that you should wait for a few more years before you go. You are pretty young to be heading out there. I am sure that Tex would be happy to have you around but I am just not sure I want you so far away."

Robb thought for a beat and said,

"Why don't you and Katelyn come with me?"

Kitty looked at him and asked, "Who would look after and teach classes here. Trish is not certified to teach. Only I am. These kids need me here."

Robb shrugged his shoulders and said,

"Well then I will just go by myself."

Trish and Kitty knew this day would come, but not so soon. Robb was a big boy, taking after his Dad. At seventeen he was close to six feet tall and weighed 180 pounds.

He called Tex and told him his plan. Tex replied,

"O K son, come on over to the Ranch and don't forget, you are going to get your High School diploma even if it is a GED."

Robb has started to grow a beard and kept it trimmed to about two inches long. It was as black as coal.

He announced to all the family including Adam and Penny that he was leaving for Texas the next day.

There were high fives and some tears shed. They knew that he was not leaving forever that he would be back to visit.

The older kids knew that he was destined to be a Rancher and the sooner he learned the ropes the better.

Robb left the next day, taking the Toyota Tacoma pickup truck that he bought with money Trish gave him on his sixteenth birthday. It was a long ride to the Ranch outside of Huston.

When he arrived he needed to stretch out. He liked his truck but he is a bit tall for it. Maybe a Tundra next time.

Tex met him in the driveway and told him, "Go ahead and park here to unload your stuff. You know where your room is so you can put your cloths in there awhile. We have some work to do as soon as you're ready."

Robb was excited to be working with Tex. He knew he had a lot to learn about the Ranch and how to run it.

Tex was waiting for him when he came out of the house. He said, "Get up here on this tractor and I'll show you how to drive it. We need to pick up some hay to feed the animals' they have feeders all around that we have to refill every couple days. Don't want them to get hungry"

Robb climbed up on the big John Deere and Tex showed him how to drive it and raise and lower the forks in front to pick up the hay. They drove out to where there was a long plastic bag filled with hay for the cattle.

Rob drove into the bag and took a load of hay from it. Tex then showed him the feeders that needed hay. There were seven different locations around the ranch where they were located. Robb had seen them when out pleasure riding.

He had a favorite horse that was named Rosie. She was a seven year old Buckskin mare. She liked it when Robb rode her. He had been on her since he was seven.

When he had hauled hay to all of the feeders he went back to the main barn. Tex was there talking with a young girl that Robb recognized as one of the cooks.

She was a pretty girl of eighteen with long black hair that she had in a single braid down her back. She was wearing a pair of jeans that fit her good. She was five foot five and her one hundred and thirty pounds filled her jeans just right. She has a cute little ass and a nice rack as well. Rob smiled at her and said,

"Hey, how are you Lucy? Did you know that I've moved in to learn Ranching from Tex?"

Lucy smiled back and said,

"It will be nice to see you around here without all your family. They are nice, but it's nice when they all go home."

Robb said,

"Yes, but they sure have fun here."

She replied,

"Yeah, I know and they are good eaters. Always a clean plate when they bring their plates to the dish washer. They are all good kids and I like them. I'm just saying that when they're here I don't see enough of you."

Lucy smiled at Robb and tilted her head down and flashed her dark eyes at him. Robb smirked back at her and kind of laughed under his breath.

Tex said,

"O K, we still have some chores to do at the barn"

Robb said good bye to Lucy and said,

"See you later."

She smiled and said,

"I'm making ribs for supper. I hope you're hungry."

Tex told her,

"I'm sure that when he gets his chores done he will be."

He and Tex headed to the barn. When they arrived Tex told Robb,

"OK now we are going to do a good cleanup here. I have some folks coming to look at buying some cows from me, I mean us."

He looked at Robb when he said 'us'. Robb turned and said,

"It's not 'Us' yet Tex, a couple more years."

Tex replied,

"That's true, but I already feel like partners. When we are both doing what needs done here it is an equalizer. We both have cow shit on our boots. We will both be wore out when this job is done. You can sit in on the sale proceedings tomorrow when these folks get here. You can start learning the business part of Ranching."

Robb grinned at Tex and said,

"Thanks Tex, I thought it would be a while before I came to that part. I guess it's not too soon to see you in action with the customers."

Tex worked hard getting the floors cleaned up and straightening things up a bit. Finally he looked around and said,

"That looks better. Since you are here to help out we can have this place looking like this all the time."

Robb felt like he had really done a day's work and was ready to head for those ribs that Lucy mentioned.

The Ranch had four Hands that worked on everything from fixing border fences to working with the cows during calving season.

There was always something to keep them busy on five thousand acres. Some of the land was in hay that they cut and filled the plastic ground silos in the summer and fall hay making times.

Tex and Robb headed for the house to get cleaned up for supper. As promised, Lucy had barbequed Ribs for them and the hands for supper along with mashed potatoes and green beans.

When it is just them she has one of the hired hands help her in the kitchen with meals. He is the oldest one working for Tex.

He is Harold Billingsley. He was a Rodeo Bronc rider for many years until he ended up with some bones broken along with his desire to keep 'rodeoing'. Tex knew him for years and when he needed a job and a place to live he hired him.

The meal was as good as it gets. Lucy and Harold could cook up road kill and make it taste like it came from the best restaurant in Huston.

After supper Tex went and laid down to rest and take a nap. While he was sleeping Robb went into the kitchen as Lucy was just finishing the cleanup.

He walked in and said,

"That was some supper. You really have a way with ribs. I could eat them every meal."

Lucy smiled and said,

"Thanks, I'm glad you liked them. I enjoy being able to make things that everyone likes. Harold is fun to work with too. When I saw the job offered here I was not so sure I was cut out for it. I love it on the ranch. Being able to do my job, have a place to stay and being able to go for a horseback ride when I have free time. Maybe we can ride together sometime. Would you like to do that?"

Robb answered,

"Sure, that sounds good. My horse is Rosie, which one do you like?"

Lucy said,

"I like Rosie too, but the other Buckskin is nice to ride. He is gentle enough for the kids to ride when they come to visit. Your sister Katelyn likes the pony. She's a cutie pie isn't she?"

Robb answered,

"She has always been a cutie pie. Ever since she was born she has had a lot of people to love her and spoil her rotten. Me included."

Lucy moved over on the bench and asked Rob,

Would you like to see my room?"

Robb replied,

"Sure, I'll show you mine then."

They left the kitchen and headed toward the other end of the house. Lucy's' room was the last one down the long hallway. Robbs was up the hallway next to Tex's.

She showed Robb in and said,

"Tex is the best Boss that I have ever worked for. He pays well and is kind to me. I came from a broken home and when my Father ran off and left me and my older brother alone after Mom died we ended up homeless when the bank took the house.

We lived on the street for a while and in a rescue Mission in Huston for six months. That was when I found out about the job here. I had helped in the kitchen at the Mission and learned how to cook for a group. There were about twenty to thirty men and women who stayed there. It changed most every day. My Brother Mark, and I were the longest ones there."

Robb told her,

"My Mom got pregnant by the former owner of the Ranch and she and her wife, Trish had a place in New Mexico where were lived. She and Trish took in foster kids and adopted three kids when their parents died in an accident. We are just one mixed up happy family."

Lucy said,

"It sounds like it was fun to have some other siblings or whatever like that. My brother Mark was my only family and then he joined the Marines to get into something solid. He craved the discipline that they gave him and he advanced in the ranks to lance Corporal in two years. He thinks he will make it a career I hope he does since he likes it."

"One of my "Brothers", Evan is in the Army. They have him in training for some kind of Intelligence job that he can't talk about, probably spy stuff." Rob shared.

Lucy said,

"That sounds interesting. You mentioned your Moms wife, is she a lesbian or what?"

Robb told her,

"I guess that's the label that people put on same sex couples. I just think that I am lucky to have two people who are in love and care for each other to love me."

Lucy said.

"I didn't mean anything bad about it. I have friends who are lesbians and some who are bi. That's just who they are. Their normal people who just happen to be attracted to someone of the same sex. If I found a really pretty girl I might be attracted as well. You know what I'm saying?"

Robb looked at Lucy and then said,

" I understand. I am attracted to a pretty girl and she is right here now. What do you think of that?"

Lucy smiled at Robb and said,

"I am attracted to some handsome young man who is right here now and I really want to kiss him on his sweet mouth."

With that she reached over and took Robb in her arms and pressed her lips to his. She parted hers and he let the tip of his tongue slip into her mouth. He tasted the sweetness of her tongue as it moved over his.

He could also feel his cock getting hard. This was the first time he had a girl kiss him and he liked it.

Lucy had several men friends who taught her how to pleasure a man.

She reached down and touched his hardness thru his pants. Robb had a breath of air sucked into his lungs. He had never felt what he was feeling now. He knew that this was going to be a defining moment in his life. Should he let it happen? Lucy made the decision for him.

Before he knew what was happening she had unzipped his pants and slipped his cock out where it had more room. She gently stroked it in her hand. He reached for her crotch and she parted her legs so that he could feel her warmth. Robb asked Lucy,

"Can I take your pants off? I want to take mine off."

Lucy took her pants off and he could see her lacy panties and her sweet crotch. He slipped his off and his cock liked the freedom. It stood out straight. Lucy stroked it gently and then slipped it into her mouth.

Rob had never felt anything like it before. He ran his hand down into her panties and felt the warmth of her pussy. Lucy stopped what she was doing and asked Rob,

"Would you like to lick me down there?"

Robb replied,

"I've never done it before, can you tell me what to do?"

Lucy moved to where Rob could see her warm pussy. She said,

"Just lick me between my legs. I'll tell you when you are doing it right."

Robb started to lick Lucy's clit, he moved down to her wet vagina. He liked what he was doing and she seemed to be enjoying it. Lucy groaned and said,

"Oh yes, right there. I love what you are doing. Suck that little bud right there. You can lick my pussy all day. You are doing it right. Do you want to fuck me now or would you like me to suck you off?"

Robb said.

"Yes I want to feel it all, I want to feel you sucking me but I want to feel me inside you too, OK?"

Lucy replied,

"'OK, we can do that."

She let him lay down on her bed and she took his cock into her mouth again. She turned around into the sixty nine position with her pussy at his mouth.

They pleasured one another for a while and then switched to her on top in cowgirl position and fucked slowly to completion.

Robb had never had such an explosive ejaculation like that before in his life. He wondered if she would get pregnant.

He asked her as they laid in her bed.

"Lucy, do you think you may get pregnant?"

Lucy smiled at Robb and replied,

"No, Robb not this week. More likely next week. I don't want to get pregnant, I just wanted to fuck you Robb. Is that alright?"

Robb smiled and replied,

"Good to know, I might want to do it again. I think I'm going to like living here."

Patty liked having Ginger for the family pet. A Golden needs a lot of care to keep them looking good.

She enjoyed brushing her and trimming her hair and her toenails. She gave her a bath every other week to get the dust and smell from swimming in the pond off of her.

Trish told her that she should open a Dog Grooming shop when she was older.

Patty liked the idea and carried that thought thru until she was eighteen. She started small and advertised her services to the few local neighbors. There were a few that had some small dogs that were brought to the house where Patty set up a "Grooming Parlor" in the house with Kitty and Trisha's blessing.

With the owners permition she would let their pets play in the pond before she did there grooming.

Her little business was growing slowly. She made enough money from it that she purchased a Chevy Van and installed a washing area and a blow dryer to finish the cleaning job.

This allowed her to reach out to customers who lived farther away from her home. When she could get closer to towns where there were more small pets she started to see the potential for the business.

Kitty encouraged Patty to take an online business course on how to run a small business.

She did and finished the course in only a year. She talked it over with her 'mothers' and they decide to let her leave home for the big city.

Patty looked at Albuquerque area as a potential location for her shop. She scouted several areas and decide to locate in the suburb of Nob Hill on the east side of the city.

It grew up along the old Route 66 that was by-passed by the Interstate route I-40. The residential population looked "Doggy" to her. She found a mall that had a vacant store that she was able to rent for a reasonable price.

Patty moved in and proceeded to set up her grooming business. She had no sooner had her sign put up when she had her first customer.

The man walked in with his Apricot Poodle on his arm. He smiled and told Patty,

"My name is Donald Nelson, This is Molly, she is my baby and I hope you can do a good job with her, she is a sweetheart and I needed to find a new groomer for her. The last one died in a car wreck."

Patty replied,

"That is tragic to hear. How long ago did that happen?"

He told her, "Fiona died six months ago and I have not found a Groomer that I can trust. You see Molly is sweet but she can be a bit of a biter when it comes to strangers. Would you hold her for a moment so I can see her reaction to you?"

Patty reached for Molly and at first she growled for a moment then licked her hand. Mr. Nelson smiled and said,

"Wonderful Molly, you have found your new groomer."

The shop did well and after six months she hired a young girl to help her as the shop had expanded into handling some dog related supplies. Like collars and toys. Along with some treats.

The girl's name was Tina Frost. She was 19 years old and was attending Community College on a part time basis so that she could work to pay for it.

She had long black hair that hung nearly to her waist. She was 5' 6" tall with brown eyes with just a touch of blue green. Tina was slim and weighed about 105 pounds. She appeared to be of mixed race like Patty.

After working with her, Patty developed more than a working relationship with Tina. Tina liked the affection that Patty showed her.

One day when the shop was done for the day and the last customer had left with their canine companion, Patty reached over and took Tina's hand. She gave it a gentle squeeze and Tina turned and smiled at Patty.

Patty pulled her into her arms and gave her a light kiss on the lips. Tina responded by pressing hers to Patty's and opened her mouth just a little to let her tongue slip out and touch Patty's lips. She pulled her up against her body and placed her hands on Patty's butt cheeks and squeezed them slowly as she poked the tip of her tongue into Patty's waiting mouth.

They shared a long lingering kiss as they each fondled the others pussy's and when Tina opened her shirt and pulled her bra up Patty went down on her perky titty's. Her nipples were getting hard as Patty sucked on them.

Tina sighed and told Patty,

"It has been a long time since anyone has touched me like you are doing, I like it.

Patty looked up at Tina and said,

"I wanted to do this ever since you walked in. Let's go over to my apartment and have some real privacy.

They locked up the shop for the night and headed over to Patty's place. When they arrived they went into her first floor apartment and closed the door.

Back at the Ranch Tex was going over with Robb his ideas for making the place into a working Dude Ranch operation.

They would build a bunk house to put up their guests and expand the kitchen so they could feed them as well as the Ranches' regular help.

Robb liked the idea of having a turnover of new people every two weeks. It would be long enough to have them be half competent to do the chores around the place and chase some cattle. It sounded like it could be fun. Especially if there were some Cowgirls coming in.

After having sex with Lucy several times a week he really had learned how to pleasure a woman. He was ready to try some other pussy's to see how they felt. He wondered if fat girls felt different. He just might get the chance if one showed up for horseback riding lessons.

Tex had plans drawn up for the bunk house and the kitchen addition so that his contractor from near Huston could get started. He was told it would only take a few weeks to finish after the concrete base was cured.

The bunk house would have six private bedrooms and two shared bathrooms.

Robb and Tex decide to get more horses to accommodate their guests. They went to an auction outside of Huston one Saturday and were able to pick up six nice looking young steeds to bring back to the Ranch.

The next thing they had to do was to train the new animals so that they could be ridden safely by different people. Sometimes a horse can get an attitude about someone and toss them off their back or kick when they are attempting to mount.

It took Robb and a couple of the Hand's just a few weeks to get all six into gentle riding condition. They were not really that bad to work with. They could not have gotten any better horses then these.

Back at Trish's and Kitty's home the new kids were blending in well. Penny and Adam were the only ones that were being home schooled by Kitty at this time so they learned at a rapid pace and Kitty was happy with how they were doing.

Penny had an artistic streak and loved to draw pictures of Dogs and Cats. She did quite well and Kitty had some of them framed and hung on the wall in the front room.

The Case worker from Children's Service's was pleased as well.

She watched how the kids interacted with their Foster parents.

She reported back to her office that everything was in order as always. The kids were safe and their schooling was ahead of their peers. She wished that all the foster situations were as good as this has always been.

She asked Trish and Kitty if they had any thoughts about adopting Adam and his sister. Trish answered,

"We have been waiting to see if your agency had anyone in mind first before we said anything about it. Yes we would take them in a heartbeat. They are the sweetest well behaved kids we've had."

It was a week later the call came for them to appear in Family court for the adoption. They were now Adam and Penny's legal parents.

When they got back to their "forever home" they had a celebration by the pond and everyone went swimming.

Penny showed them how she had learned to do the back stroke. Ginger went swimming too.

Patty closed the door after Tina had entered. She took Tina's coat and hung it in the closet. Tina stood in front of Patty and extended her arms. Patty went to her and they kissed.

Tina started to undress Patty as Patty was working on Tina's shirt and Jeans. When both girls were down to their panties they went to Patty's bedroom and laid down on her bed.

While Tina was on her back, Patty went down to her feet and slipped her pink panties down her legs. She removed them and then she took hers off too. She worked her way up between Tina's legs. Stopping to lick and kiss her legs from her ankles to her knees and then up her thighs. She did this to both of Tina's legs before she reached her crotch.

When she got close she breathed her warm breath on Tina's pussy.

Tina gasped and spread her legs apart so that Patty could get up close to her clitoris. Patty licked her clit and gently sucked it until it got hard and poked out from its hood. Patty put a finger into Tina. It was wet and warm as she moved it in and out.

She put her tongue in Tina's vagina and licked up her juices while her finger kept working. Patty worked another finger in and then another. When she had all three in Tina let out a gasp as she had her first orgasm. She smiled at Patty and then said,

It's my turn now.

Robb looked over at Lucy and said,

"You know what? I don't know what feels better to have my cock in your pussy or in your mouth."

Lucy smiled at him and said,

"You can have it both ways if you like. I 'm not sure if I like your tongue in me more or your cute little cocky."

Robb told her,

"It works for me too. So are we going to do it or just talk about it?"

Lucy cooed and said,

"I like to talk dirty to you. Do you like it when I talk dirty to you? I see your pants have a lump in them. Mine are just getting wet. Want to feel my wet panties?"

Robb slipped his jeans down to his knees and said,

"You go girl. You know what to do."

With that Lucy slipped over and bent down so that she could put the tip of Robb's cock in her mouth. After she sucked for a few minutes she asked,

"Are you ready for some wet panties yet?"

Robb told her to finish him off and then he would do her too. She went back down and gave him as good a complete blow job as she could and swallowed every bit of his seed.

Tina told Patty,

"Get up on your knees so I can see your pretty ass."

Patty did as she asked. Tina got behind her and started by licking all around her cheeks. She followed the top of her crack down to her anus.

She ran her tongue over the entire area and pressed it down hard. She wiggled it back and forth over her opening and then put the tip inside.

Patty moaned as Tina worked her way down to her opening. Tina licked both of Patty's holes until she could feel and taste her flowing juices. Patty had a series of intense orgasms as Tina kept licking and sucking all of Patty's lower parts. After they were both sated they sat on the bed and talked.

Patty looked at Tina and said to her,

"I think I love you, maybe it's just that what we did was so sweet and loving that I can't imagine anyone else doing what we did to pleasure each other the way we did."

Tina smiled at Patty and replied,

"I have done it before when I was in High School with one of my Teachers. She kept me after school one time and showed me how to do stuff. She did it to me and it felt so good I wanted to keep doing it. So we did every Tuesday. I would do her and she would do me. She would give me a ride home afterward.

"She got caught giving a boy a blow job one day and she got fired."

Patty said,

"That was back then, this is now. Can we keep our business relationship and our personal separate? I hope so as I want to be near you all the time."

Tina thought about it and then told Patty,

"I think we can work it out all right. We just have to be cool when we are in the shop, O K?"

Tina looked at Patty and said,

"We can keep busy at the shop and then when the lights go out we can let our passions blossom. Sound good?"

Patty agreed and they embraced and kissed before heading for sleep.

Tex was settling up with the building contractor that he hired to put up the bunkhouse and the enlarged kitchen.

He was getting closer to opening up his Dude ranch. Robb had found a good deal on some gently used saddles and other tack for the horses.

Robb had designed a web site to attract business. They also advertised in the Dallas Fort Worth area along with Huston. He figured there would be some people in those places that would like a Ranch vacation and had the money to pay for it.

Harold purchased additional kitchen ware and dishes for the new kitchen. He and Lucy worked on getting that ready for when they would be feeding a crowd.

Lucy suggested to Tex that he consider having a wedding venue as long as they were changing the business model for the Ranch. They could offer weddings on horseback. Or other Cowboy themed events. Tex said he would think about it.

Back in New Mexico at their little ranch Trish and Kitty were kept busy raising their newly adopted kids.

Adam and Penny were as happy as could be and they loved being with Trish and Kitty.

Life was fairly simple and Kitty had the kids' reading at a Middle School level. Their spelling and math were also at a higher level considering they were only 10 and 8 years old.

Penny really like to draw pictures of dogs and cats. She was now doing some landscapes using the view out across the pond and into the forest as subjects.

They bought her an easel that she could use to put her paints and canvases on when she was working on a project.

The nearest town was Magdalena and it was 15 miles from their home. In the town there was a place that local Artists could show their work and offer it for sale. Kitty took some of Penny's pictures in and set them up.

The owner called her two days later and asked if she had more pictures that the first ones she brought in were sold.

Penny was so happy that she jumped up and down for 5 minutes and then went out to do some more pictures for the store. She was so proud of herself to have people actually pay for her work.

Adam had a Guitar that he liked to play. He was self-taught as there were no music teachers in Magdalena except for an older lady who taught piano lessons.

Kitty recalled that her Dad played the mandolin when she was young.

She missed the old days in Maine. She and her sisters Betty Jo, Darla and their two brothers, Jack and Willy would all gather around as her Dad played and her Mom and all the siblings would sing along to whatever song Dad chose to play. There were a lot of fun filled times back then when in the winter the wind blew and the snow flew. Kitty didn't miss that weather. Here in New Mexico it got cold at the altitude they were at but it didn't get much snow.

Evey had left Trish and Kitty and flew back to Maine.

She decided to get Joeys lobster boat back on the water after she had it completely refitted and re-painted.

She chose to rename it the Kitty Kat.

She had been fishing for lobsters out on Penobscot Bay ever since she was 12 years old.

That was also the year that Joey raped her. It traumatized her for a long time. It was not the way a young girl should be initiated into having sex.

He held her down on her stomach and forced his hard cock between her legs. He finally managed to get it in her vagina. She was a virgin and it was the most painful experience she ever had.

He shot his load inside her and she feared she would get pregnant. Having her brother's baby she feared could be deformed or any number of things can go wrong from incest. She had not even had her first period.

Here she was on the same boat that he had raped her on all those years ago. She had gotten over it for the most part. But she never had a sexual relationship with a man ever since.

Evelyn liked the water and being out on the boat was a wonderful way to make a living. She had lobster pots spread out over several locations there in the bay. There were very few women who did this as it is hard work and long days on the water.

She is very selective with her catch. She measures everyone to be sure they are mature and she puts all the females back in the water. Her buyer on the dock knows what he gets from her are all premium lobsters.

One day as she was getting ready to push off from the dock Kitty's older brother Jack stopped by and struck up a conversation.

"I see you have Joey's old boat looking good there on the water. It's been, what two years since the incident out west?"

She replied,

"I'd rather not talk about it. I put Joey out of my head. And that's where I want him to stay. You see the new name on her? The Kitty Kat. That's to honor your little sister for dealing with that ass hole. He nearly killed her out there. I'm glad Trish did what she had to do. I have no sadness that he is dead." Evelyn went on, "I went to New Mexico and visited with Kitty and Trish for a day. I told them that I hold no grudge against them."

Jack commented,

"I'm glad you did that. Sometimes you just have to face up to the reality of what happened. By the way that's a lot of boat for a small woman like yourself. Can you use a deck hand to help with the pots? I know it's a lot of work. I got laid off at the paper mill and could use a job. I helped my dad when he went out for 'lobsta' so I know what to do."

Evelyn looked at Jack and then at her boat. She told him,

"I could use a deck hand. Over the summer I had Dave the College boy but he's back to school. I don't pay a lot of money because I don't have a lot to give."

Jack waved his hand and said, "Just stop right there. I never asked for what the wages would be, did I?"

She said,

"I guess we can decide on that later. Come aboard and let's go get some 'lobsta' as we say down east."

Jack was in fine physical shape for a man of 40. He worked out with free weights and ran a mile every day in the morning and again in the evening. Working on her boat was going to be no problem.

They got along good and they really hauled in the lobsters. Jack fished for bait fish to put in the pots. Evelyn was glad Jack stopped by that day.

One evening when they got back and unloaded their catch she

said,

"Let's go grab a cold one. We earned it today." Jack agreed. It was the best days catch they had all week.

They went to a dockside Tavern and ordered a couple of Bud's. They sat at a table along the wall. The waitress came and gave them each a menu. Jack said,

"I'll have that Turkey special that's on the menu. Mashed potatoes and filling. Does it get any better than that?"

Evelyn scanned own over the menu and decides to have a French dip with au jue.

When they finished their dinner it was past 10 o'clock

Evelyn said,

"Since it is getting late why don't you just stay at my place tonight rather than driving the ten miles to your house and then back in the morning. I have a guest room you can use."

Jack replied,

"That sounds like a plan, let's go"

From the dock where they were it was only a mile off Route 1 to her house.

When they arrived she parked her truck in the driveway and they went in the house.

Evelyn showed Jack where he could sleep in the spare room. The bed looked like he was not going to be awake long. He wasn't.

Evelyn went to her bedroom and pulled down the sheets and blanket. She stripped off her pants and shirt and headed for her shower.

As she was washing herself she thought about Jack. About his trim body and his six pack abs that showed when they were working on the boat. It had not come to her mind for a very long time that her body yearned for the gentle touch of another person. The touch that only a man can do.

She got into her bed and laid there awake for a long time. When she was sure that Jack was asleep she went to his room and watched him as he slept.

She put her hand down in her panties and stroked her pussy as she watched him sleep. As she ran her finger tips across her clit he rolled over in his sleep and she saw that he was naked. His penis was there on the bed. It looked like it was at least eight inches long and it was looking hard. She wanted to reach out and feel it as he slept. Should she? Could she? Would she?

There was only one way to find out. She crept silently over to the side of the bed and gently laid her hand on his member. She marveled at how it looked. He had been circumcised as a baby and the glans was a dark shade of pink. Like the inside of her pussy.

She lowered her head so that she could smell it and then she touched it with her tongue. She felt it twitch a little and it seemed to get harder. She ran her tongue over the pink tip. She wanted so to just take it into her mouth and run her tongue all over it. To know that if she did suck it there would be a finish when his fluids would pour out the small hole on the tip. She wondered what that would taste like.

She had not ever had a man. She had never had a boyfriend all thru school so she never had any physical contact, meaning sex. Her pussy longed for it to slide in and out and then make it even wetter then it was right now. She took her fingers from her wet pussy and put them in her mouth. She liked the taste. She thought, maybe I should be a lesbian if all girls taste as good as me. She smiled as she remembered Kitty. Wet Kitty. If I had known then what I do now I would have licked her pussy until it spilled over.

She looked down at Jack as he slept and decided to go ahead and suck him off. She lifted his cock up and slid her mouth down over it. Being careful not to wake him up. She closed her mouth and started to suck. It felt strange, like some kind of intruder. She continued to suck as it got bigger and harder.

After about five minute she suddenly felt something slick in her mouth. It tasted a bit salty and had the texture of egg whites. She swallowed it and kept sucking to get some more. She thought '*So that's what gissim tastes like.*' She got up and went back to her bed.

She didn't know it but Jack was a light sleeper and he felt it when Evelyn first touched him.

He laid with his eyes closed while she gently licked the head of his cock. He felt his sphincter tighten as his cock got harder. He was tempted to wake up and maybe fuck her.

Instead he opted to pretend to be asleep and see what would happen. As she sucked his cock he felt how gently she did it. He never felt her teeth on it and when he finally released his load in her mouth she must have swallowed it because he never found any on the sheets after she left.

He thought as he laid there awake.

'*This could be the best job I will ever have.*'

Buddy got a full scholarship to University of New Mexico in Albuquerque. He wanted to study Bio Engineering.

The study of and manufacturing of medical Devices. He got along with his professors and carried a 4.0 Class ranking all the way thru College.

He went on to grad school and got his master's degree in Medical devise engineering at M I T.

The first year he was working in the Industry he came up with a new design for a heart valve. It was a success and has saved many lives.

Evan went up thru the ranks quickly to the rank of Major. One day a man approached him on the base and said,

"Hello Major Flick, my name in not important. I would like to talk to you about a career change. I know you have been in the Army now for what, six years?"

Evan looked the man over and replied,

"Yes, that is correct, six years this past month. Who do you represent?"

He replied,

"A little organization based down in Langley Virginia called the Central Intelligence Agency. Or CIA for short. The name most folks know us by."

Evan asked,

"How am I being picked for the job?"

The man replied,

"We have been watching you now for several years and we like what we see. I am extending an invitation for you to come to Headquarters in Virginia to begin training as soon as you can wrap up what you are working on here.

I have already spoken to your Commanding Officer about this opportunity. He said he would hate to lose you but he agrees this is what you have been trained for the past six years."

Evan looked the man in the eye and said,

"I'll get things in order and see you in Langley."

After six months of additional weapons training and language and dialect understanding he was sent on a team mission to Eastern Europe.

There is a Cyber hacker somewhere in that region that has been running a ransom scam on middle to large size businesses in the U.S. and several European countries and they have extorted nearly a billion dollars' worth of Bit Coin ransom to release the affected computers upon receipt of the ransom.

Evan and the team are now located in an abandoned warehouse in eastern Ukraine. It is suspected the Hacker is operating from somewhere in this area.

The team has local undercover operatives that have infiltrated the hackers own system after following the electronic pathway back from the ransom victim.

They are very close to having the exact location. Evans senior agent explains that when they get the go ahead to hit the hackers' base of operations they will meet resistance.

"So everyone needs to be on high alert when we go in. The place may be booby trapped. Our operatives say they are well armed with full automatic rifles and handguns."

Evan checked his weapon and felt comfortable with it. The clip was full and he had two extra clips. He had qualified as Marksman at every qualification. He had been handling firearms ever since he was a teen back on the Ranch.

Trish had felt it was important that all the kids as soon as they were 16 learn to safely handle weapons. She trained them with her 40 cal. Glock.

The word came from their operatives that the exact location had been found and the team readied for the attack on the hackers.

When they arrived they split up with Evan taking his men to the rear of the building to prevent an escape by the back door.

The leader and his men went to the front and on command they forced the front steel door open with a shape charge at the hinges.

The men inside were taken by surprise and raised their hands in the air. There were three who went out the back door in an attempt to escape.

The first two were dropped like flies as they pointed their automatic weapons at Evans team.

The third got off a burst in Evans direction and one of the bullets hit him in the neck. Blood squirted out and it was shurly a mortal wound.

His team mates tried to staunch the bleeding but it was to no avail. He died at the scene.

His body was sent back to the states and Tricia and Kitty asked that he be buried on their property. This was OK'ed by the Agency and an Honor guard was dispatched from Langley Headquarters for the services .His Commanding officer from the Army was in attendance.

He told Buddy and Patty that Evan served with honor and was one of the bravest men he ever knew. It was a privilege to serve with him.

The Director of the CIA also spoke of Evan as a brave and loyal agent who will be missed by his team as well as all those who knew him.

His mother's and siblings made a memorial garden behind the house and his ashes were interred there.

After the service Luke and Lilly returned to Huston where they lived. Luke went back into the field in search of new land to drill for oil.

He had gotten a promotion to "Head of exploration" with his own office in the corporate headquarters. He still enjoyed going out with the men who did the preliminary findings.

He was the one who along with the company's legal team acquired the land from the owners or negotiated a deal with them to keep the land and allow an easement for the company to drill exploratory wells to determine how much oil was present.

If it was what his company was after they would setup a royalty program with the owners.

Tex had dealt with the company that Luke worked for and they were good to their word.

Robb Harris Sr.'s Father had them come in and drill a number of test holes and they found an abundance of likely spots on the Ranch that had oil.

He set up a deal where he would keep the land and lease the wells to the company.

He could keep running cattle on the land and have the oil as a bonus. Best of both worlds.

Luke and Lilly came out to the Ranch to visit often and enjoyed spending time with Robb when they were there.

Lilly liked her job as a surgical nurse in one of Huston's Hospitals. She was very busy and often worked weekends.

Luke would go to the Ranch those times to ride

Horseback into the hills.

Robb and Tex were very busy with the Dude Ranch business and they had a full house most of the time.

He liked to eat at the "Chuck Wagon" that was build alongside the kitchen when he was there. It served as a dining hall for the guests and the Ranch crews.

He would strike up a conversation with Lucy some days. He listened as she spoke of being homeless for a while until she found a job and place to live here. There was something about her that was appealing to Luke.

One day when he was done eating and had helped her and Harold to clean up after lunch he suggested they take a ride out on some of the foot hill trails. Lucy liked the idea and said,

"That sounds like fun. Wait here while I get dressed for a ride.

Just have to be back to help with dinner about six. We serve at eight when all the Dudes are back."

They left and went out one of the trails that was less used by guests. They had ridden for about four miles when Lucy said,

"Let's take a break and rest for a bit."

She got off her horse and took a blanket down off him and laid it on the ground. She motioned to Luke to join her on the blanket.

They laid down and looked up at the sky. There was not a cloud to be seen.

She looked over at Luke and smiled. A smile that only meant one thing.

Luke turned toward Lucy and she reached for and touched him on his cheek. He looked at her and smiled back. It wasn't long before she had kissed him and put her arms around him. Luke had never been with any woman other than Lilly and was curious how it would feel to be inside her. He returned her kiss and then asked,

"Would you like to get more comfortable? Like take off your pants?"

Lucy giggled and asked,

"Would you like to take yours off too?"

Nothing more was said and they removed their pants. Luke was already sporting a nice hard on and Lucy looked at it and took it in her hand. She stroked it for a while and then subsequently put her lips on the tip. She licked it around the end and sucked it slowly into her warm, wet opening.

Luke laid back and let her pleasure him. He had a release and she allowed it to go down her throat.

Luke turned over and placed his own head between Lucy's legs. She put her fingers on her pubes and parted them so Luke could plant his tongue inside her wet vagina.

He licked and licked her wetness until she experienced an orgasmic ejaculation. Some call it a squirting orgasm.

Lucy looked at Luke and said,

"Was that o k? I couldn't stop it."

Luke grinned at Lucy and replied,

"It's ok with me. I like your sweet juice. How was mine?"

A while later he fucked her before they headed back to the ranch house.

Robb always liked it when Luke and Lilly came to visit. He especially liked to see Lilly. She was a beautiful woman and he remembered catching Luke and Lilly back in New Mexico making love. All the other kids went shopping for new clothes but he stayed home.

He had been watching Lilly from up at the house while she laid on a blanket naked. Luke showed up and they talked for a minute before he stripped down and laid on the blanket with her.

Robby watched as they gave each other oral and then they fucked. It was too much for him to watch without stroking his own cock. He felt it coming about the same time he could hear and knew that Luke was shooting his load into Lilly. He never forgot that day.

The next day Robby asked Patty if she would let him do something that he saw Luke doing with Lilly.

He said,

"I think you'd like it. Lilly did."

They went into her bedroom and he told her,

"Take off your panties and lay on the bed and let me see your crack."

Patty did as he asked and spread her legs apart so Robby could see her girl parts. When he did he could feel his cock getting hard.

Just then Kitty walked in and said,

"I see something going on that shouldn't be. Get your pants back on young lady and go outside. I will have a talk with Robby."

His face was so hot he thought it was going to melt. Kitty sat him down on the bed and said,

"I know that you are coming to an age where you are curious about things. Experimenting with Patty is only going to make it worse. There are things that kids do and things that adults do. Kids must wait until they are adults to do adult things. You will be able to do these adult things soon enough. Do you understand what I am saying?"

Robby answered,

"Yes mom, I just saw Lilly and Luke doing stuff and wanted to try it. They looked like they were having fun."

Kitty thought about it and knew what she needed to do.

The next time she was in town she went to the Drug store and bought a box of condoms.

Lilly stayed at the Ranch house while Luke went out with his Geologist to look at a section of the ranch that he thought would be a good location for a new Natural gas well.

With modern fracking techniques they can extract far more gas then they could in the past.

Robb sat with Lilly at a picnic table on the patio where they held parties. He enjoyed spending time with her.

She was always his favorite of all the foster kids back in New Mexico. He told her,

"I remember watching you and Luke on a blanket one time by the pond. Do you remember that?"

Lilly looked at him and asked,

"Just what did you see that day for a ten year old? Refresh my memory?"

He smirked at Lilly and in a low voice,

"I saw the two of you pleasuring each other. Looked like fun, was it?"

Lilly's face started to get warm.

"What do you mean pleasuring?"

"You know doing things with your mouths. It looked like something I would like to try."

Lilly looked around and saw no one close by so she replied,

"I'll bet you have done it with Lucy, haven't you?"

Robb snickered and said,

"How did you know?"

"She told me you two did it. She is a really hot girl isn't she?"

Robb struggled to keep from touching the hard on that he had just sitting here talking almost dirty with her.

Finally he asked,

"Would you like to go inside and play?"

"What would we play with?" She asked as she saw the swelling in his pants.

He replied while looking down himself at his boner,

"Anything at all that you would like to play with."

She reached over and laid her hand on him and gently squeezed it.

"I'm ready to go get a cold drink Robb, how about you?

They got up from the table and walked into the kitchen where Lucy was cutting up some lettuce for salads. She looked at Lilly and asked,

"So what are you two up to? No good I hope." Lilly replied,

"Why don't you put down that knife and join us?" Lucy looked at Robb and asked,

"Are you up for a three some?"

Robb kept walking across the kitchen to the hallway back to his room. Lilly and Lucy followed him.

The women took turns licking Robbs stiff member.

Lucy liked to put the tip in her mouth and gently bite it.

This sent what felt like an electric shock thru to his prostate. He started to leak a little bit of semen that ran down onto Lucy' tongue. She tasted it and pulled away and told Lilly,

"Do you want to do this while he is leaking some precum. The main event is yet to happen."

Lilly licked the semen from the tip on Robbs cock and then took it into her mouth all the way to her throat. She moved in and out several times while deep throating him. It was almost enough to make him release his load.

He managed to avoid it by thinking of something else. He would think about saddling his horse and taking a ride out in the green pasture. He learned this way to control his ejaculation. Sometimes he could go ten minutes longer by doing this.

He pushed her head away and said,

"Let's see some girl on girl stuff before I give you my present. O K?"

The women looked at each other and then they kissed. Lucy was the first to explore Lilly's body. It was not long before Lilly reciprocated and went down on Lucy. Her mouth dropped open and she let out a gasp. She thought.

'I've had my puss licked a lot of different times, but this is the best. I guess what they say is true. Only a woman can really get another woman off the way she should' Lucy experienced a series of orgasms like never before.

Lilly had only ever licked one pussy. That was when she was in college. She and her roommate would pleasure each other on a regular basis, but she still liked a hard cock. And now she could feel Robb coming up to ride her doggy while she was licking on Lucy's pussy.

It was a little while later Lucy said,

"Let's trade places."

Lilly backed off and Robb pulled his still hard cock out of Lilly.

Lucy went down on Lilly while Robb kneeled behind and entered Lucy and rode her to a sweet ejaculation. He kept his cock in her for as long as it would not slip out. Finally it did. He smiled at the two women and said,

"Now wasn't that a fine way to spend an afternoon?"

They smiled back and told Robb.

"Maybe next time it will just be the girls."

Luke got back in time for supper and they all sat around the table with Tex, Robb, Harold, and three of the Hands.

Luke's Geologist had to return to Huston to review his findings with the Drilling Team.

The list of Guest's that were staying in the bunk house was growing. Most of the rooms were rented. Some were staying for one week and others signed up for two.

Brad Weeks was one of the two week Cowboys. He was 34. Six feet tall and with blond hair that he wore in a Mullet style he was drop dead handsome. Or so he thought.

He had been born on a Ranch in Oklahoma but left it when he went into the Marines and his parents sold their ranch because his dad fell and broke his back. He was partially paralyzed from the hips down. He couldn't work anymore so they sold out.

Brad wanted to feel the ranch life again so when he saw this opportunity he signed up. He works in Dallas for an oil field development company. He is trapped in an office at a computer for fifty weeks a year. This was his vacation. He thought,

'*Sunshine, fresh air, good food and looky there. A sweet girl in the kitchen. I'd like to fuck her sometime in the next two weeks.*'

He had a single room to himself. He thought that would work out fine.

'*Now how to get some free time to talk to her. She seems to have a thing going with the one Boss, Robb. I know he's banging her. Maybe there is room for one more. She sure has those 'Bedroom eyes.'*'

The guests were fed well. From rib eye stakes and barbequed ribs a couple times a week.

Breakfast was a choice of Sausage gravy on Busquets, or your choice of things to be put in a three egg omelet. Hot coffee in large mugs. A real Texas experience. Yes, there was hot Sause on the tables.

Several of the other guests were married couples who wanted to get away for a time from the city life. One couple was Ira and Sue Ranck.

They were from over in Louisiana. Sue came from a family who owned some oil property on the Gulf Coast. They were in their 60's and had more money than anyone should have. Her oil just kept coming out of the ground and the money kept piling up in the Bank.

Another couple were from Ohio and had made enough in the Real Estate business to retire at fifty five. They came to the ranch just to get out of Ohio for the first time in their lives. He is Randy Freberg and she is Mrs. Rosy Freberg. They never set foot on a farm or ranch other than to sell it. This was going to be a whole new experience.

There is an apparent Gay couple who are from Albuquerque New Mexico.

They are both Lawyers there. The younger of the two is named Sam Nestle who is a prosecutor and his partner is Alan Freed, who is the States Attorney.

They try to get away a few times a year where no one knows who they are. They have had a down low relationship for 20 years.

At this time there are two empty rooms in the bunk house.

Tex and Robb decide to charge each person $1,500.00 a week. This was all inclusive with meals and the room.

Tex said,

"If I knew people would pay me to work here I would have started it a long time ago."

Robb agreed. He was still a few years away from inheriting the Ranch but he too could see that they made the right decision in getting away from the rodeo bulls.

He had made a verbal promise to share the Ranch with Tex after he got full title to the land. But his half-brother Evan had suggested that he share the Ranch with him and his siblings.

Evan was in the CIA and died while on a mission in Eastern Europe. His remains are on his mom's property in New Mexico. His two remaining siblings are Buddy and Patty.

Buddy was an engineer for a big company in Kansas City. He moved there after his heart valve device won federal approval. He found a company who wanted to manufacture them for him and give Buddy a handsome royalty.

He and his wife Brenda were happy living in a suburb of K C named Olathe. It is a nice quiet community that is close by to the city. Buddy can get to his office in 20 minutes.

Once a month they fly out to Albuquerque and rent a car to go out to the small ranch where he and his sister and brother grew up. They always brought flowers to place on Evans grave.

On this trip they had some happy news to share with his mom's. Brenda was expecting. The baby was due in February. It is a boy.

Trish was excited to hear the news. She couldn't wait to tell Kitty who had gone up to visit Patty in Nob Hill where she and her partner ran a Dog grooming Salon. It had become the place where the upper class brought their dogs for grooming.

Patty and Tina had expanded the shop to the space next door to them in the Mall to accommodate their growing business.

When Kitty arrived the shop was buzzing with excitement. Patty had hired three more Groomers to take care of the customers who were coming in with their Pets.

Kitty's phone rang just as she walked in the door. It was Trish.

"Guess what Kitten? We are going to be Grandparents."

Kitty's mouth dropped and she asked,

"Who are the Parents?"

Trish replied,

"Brenda and Buddy came in this morning and told me. I am so happy for them. He has been so successful with his business and they have a nice home. Now they can fill it with kids."

Kitty grinned and said,

"I'm so glad for them too Bren is such a sweet girl. I know she will be a great mom." Just then Patty came up and gave Kitty a kiss on the cheek. She asked,

"Who was that on the phone?" Kitty replied,

"Guess who is going to be an Aunt? And guess who will be a Grandma in February?"

Patty beamed and asked,

"Who?"

"Bren and Buddy are expecting a little boy. Isn't that exciting?"

Back on the Ranch, Robb took Brad Weeks out to a section of fence that had been in need of repairs for a while. He decided to have him help with the repairs.

It had been a while since Brad did any manual work so it took him a time to get in the swing of it. By then he was able to keep up with Robb until the fence repairs were done.

Robb made note of Brad's happy manner and cheerful disposition. It made the day go well.

Brad told Robb,

"You know what? I like working with you. What say we hang out in the evening? You can bring Lucy along and we can have some fun together. Sound like a plan?"

Robb could see thru Brad's motive and decided to go along with it for fun. He said,

"O K, I'll ask Lucy if she would like to hang out with us. She is a lot of fun to be with."

Brad thought that if he had Robb along she would be more comfortable with him and then he could get closer to her later. He surmised they were having sex and now it was his turn.

Lucy said that it sounded like a nice way to spend the evening. And maybe she could get this hunk of man to herself for a while.

That evening the three of them went for a short trail ride under the moonlit sky. They got back to the Ranch about 10 o'clock.

Robb said,

"I think I'll turn in for tonight. Get a good night's sleep Brad. I'm going to work your ass off tomorrow."

Brad laughed and told Robb,

"Bring it on Boss man, bring it on." He looked at Lucy and asked,

"You don't have to go in yet do you?" She looked at Brad and then asked,

"Can I see your room in the bunk house? I haven't had a chance to see how they are fixed up." Brad said with a grin,

"I'd be happy to show you my room. It's pretty nice for a bunk house."

She grinned back at him and watched as Robb went in the house for the night. She knew what brad had in mind because that was on hers' too.

They went in the Bunk house and entered his room. He closed the door behind them. Lucy looked up at brad and then told him,

"You want to get in my pants, don't you?"

Such a direct approach was O K with him and he replied,

"I like that in you Lucy and you are right. I 've had my eye on your cute little ass for the past week and hoped we could get it on some time."

Lucy stepped up to him and reached up to kiss him. Brad leaned down and their lips met. He held her close as their tongues encountered each other. He reached around her and put his hand on her ass and squeezed it gently. She moaned a happy moan and returned his squeeze. Not on his ass but on his growing manhood in her hand.

Brad removed her blouse and bra and then undid her jeans. She kicked off her shoes and pulled his tee shirt off.

He unbuckled his belt and let his pants drop to the floor. Lucy fell to her knees on the floor and pulled his shorts down to expose his large cock. When she saw it her eyes opened wide. It was the biggest one she had ever seen.

She put the tip in her mouth and started to lick it and then she sucked it in and stroked it at the same time.

Brad liked the way she took control. He picked her up and with her legs wrapped around his hips he tried to enter her wet pussy.

It would not slid in like he wanted it to so he laid her on the bed. He went down on her and thought that if he could get her hot enough he could enter her more easily.

This didn't seem to help as much as he hoped. He went back down and continued to eat her out until she came again and again.

Her body shook and her toes curled with delight. He liked that he was able to get her to have multiple orgasms, but he wanted his too.

He pushed her head back down onto his big cock and forced himself inside her mouth as far as he could.

He moved in and out until he came in her mouth. He could feel her throat as she tried to swallow his large load of cum. She was gagging and pushing him away but he kept pushing into her and cumming until he could cum no more.

When he was done he got up and said,

"How was that my little slut? Did you get enough? Huh?"

Lucy didn't move. He looked at her and saw she wasn't breathing. '*It can't be. Is lucy dead?*'

Brad was in a panic. He had not expected to have her die on him. What was he going to do now?

Sometime in the middle of the night he got a horse saddled up and put her on in front of him as he sat on the saddle. He rode quietly out under the moon lite for several miles. He went out to where there were a lot of rocks and he laid her body on the ground and covered her with more rocks until she was completely covered.

He went back to the ranch and went to bed.

The next morning found Harold cursing about Lucy not showing up for breakfast. He was working hard to get the morning meal ready for the guests and the hands.

Robb was up and wondered where she was too. The last he saw her was when he left her with Brad. When he saw Brad he asked him,

"When did Lucy come back to the house last night? I don't care what you two did, it's just not like her not to be up for breakfast."

Brad shook his head and said,

"She left at about one. As far as I know she went back to her place. I didn't see her after that."

Robb was not sure he was telling the truth. But how could he get to the truth about what happened to Lucy.

CHAPTER FOUR

The Story So Far

When we left the last story Lucy had disappeared and no one seemed to know where she may have gone. The last one to see her was Brad Weeks, a Dude ranch client.

He, Lucy, and Rob had been hanging out that evening talking and drinking some beer until Rob went in the house to go to sleep.

Brad and Lucy went into Brad's room in the bunk house where the Dude ranch clients all stayed.

They had oral sex and Lucy chocked to death when she had Brads huge cock in her mouth. When Brad realizes that she is dead he panicked.

He took her body out to the back part of the Ranch where he found a pile of rocks that he was able to bury her body with.

Brad went back to the bunk house and went to bed.

The next morning Lucy was missed right away by Harold, the other cook at the Ranch.

When Rob showed up Harold asked him,

"What did you do with Lucy? She didn't show up for breakfast and there are a lot of things to be done for the guests. You didn't get her drunk last night did you?"

Rob replied,

"The last I saw her was at 10 o'clock when I went to bed. She was still hanging out with Brad. I'll go over to his place and get him up for work anyway. Maybe he knows where she is. Maybe she spent the night with him. I'm not her keeper." He shrugged and walked away.

Rob went to Brad's room and knocked on the door. No one answered at first. Then a sleepy Brad opened the door and asked,

"What time is it and what the fuck do you want?"

Rob looked in the room for Lucy and when he didn't see her he asked,

"Where's Lucy? I know you were with her after I left and if I know her she probably said something like 'Wanna fuck', now where is she?"

Brad wiped his eyes and said,

"I don't know. She left at 1 o'clock and I went to sleep until you came hammering on the door."

Rob said,

"Well she is missing and it's not like her to miss breakfast time. She has worked here for nearly a year and has never missed a morning."

When Tex found out that Lucy was missing he couldn't believe she left. She had an old Honda that was parked out by the barn under a lean to of a garage. He looked there first. When he saw it was still there he told Rob,

"I suspect foul play here. You say Brad was with her the last you saw her?"

Rob replied,

"Yeah, at about 10, I went in and went to bed. She and Brad were still hanging out at a picnic table by the bunk house. I figured he took her inside later and probably had sex with her."

Tex looked at Rob and asked,

"Why do you think that? Have you been doing her too?"

Rob's face got red and he answered,

"I have to answer, yes, because you probably already know the answer."

Tex half smiled and he replied,

"Your right, I know just about everything that goes on around here it's my job to know things. That's what it takes to manage this operation. The sooner you realize that it is part of running this place the better. Now let's go and question Brad. See what he really knows. Then we will call the Texas Rangers and let them handle it."

✳ ✳ ✳

Alan Freed rolled over in the bed and kissed Sam on the cheek.

"Wake up sleeping beauty, it's time to go shovel some cow shit before breakfast."

He then went under the covers and stroked Sam's soft cock. It wasn't long before it raised its head and entered Alans waiting mouth. He sucked slowly on it as Sam put his hand on Alan's head. He let him suck on him for a while and then when it was good and hard he asked Alan,

"Would you like me to fuck you now?"

In reply Alan rolled over and got up on his knees. Sam proceeded to put on a condom and lubed Alan's asshole.

He slid it in as he had so many times when they went on these private vacations. There was just something about how Alan liked to be fucked in the ass and how he allowed Sam to reach around and stroke his cock until he ejaculated.

The pressure on his prostate from Sam's cock made for the best of morning delights.

When Sam had come in Alan's ass he pulled out and laid back on the bed. Alan went down and licked the come from Sam's cock.

This is how they spent part of their day before going to do their assigned chores on the Ranch.

✳ ✳ ✳

Ira and Sue went to bed around 10 o'clock that evening and after a quick fuck they were asleep in no time.

Around three in the morning Ira was awakened by a strange sound. It didn't last long, but it raised the hair on his neck. It sounded like someone mumbling,

"HELP ME."

It stopped and he went back to licking Sue's pussy. He liked it when she let him do it when she was sleeping.

When she would wake up with his mouth on her she would pretend it was someone else, anyone else.

Because as much as she enjoyed this she knew he would want her to suck him off when he was done. The good part was he liked to lick her pussy all the way back to her ass hole. This would really fire her up and sometimes she would have a squirting orgasm.

On those nights she would suck him off but pull off before he came. She didn't like his come. She knew that some other men tasted better. This came from experience. When Sue was a young woman of 18 or 20 something she had a reputation around Baton Rouge for being a Cock sucker of renown.

She had even worked a "Glory hole" establishment where she picked up an extra $20.00 for every man she made come while she was in a room with holes in the wall that they stuck their cocks thru and someone would suck them off. They had to guess if it was a man or a woman who pleasured them. If they guessed wrong it would cost them another $10.00.

It was a sleazy way to make a living but she had no other skills.

Then she received a letter from an Attorney's office. She opened it and it read.

Dear Ms. Sue Brooks

We are privileged to advise you that your Mother's late Grandfather had left her a property on the Gulf Coast where there are a number of active oil wells. Since your mother has past, the Estate goes to you. You are the last living descendent. Contact our office for details. Congratulations Ms. Brooks.

Sue had been estranged from her mother for years and she had no idea of what this could be but it sounded like she was done sucking cocks.

✳ ✳ ✳

Randy and Rosy were a bit different from most couples they just liked to watch others having sex and then masturbating. Sometimes they would just watch porn and watch each other doing it.

Randy liked to watch old lesbians licking each other or young girls getting it on. They each had their own TV's so they could have their own favorite channel.

Rosy liked to watch the gay channel where the muscular studs would be ass fucking some skinny kid. The Kid seemed to like it. When the guy was ready to come he would hold the kids head and shoot it in his mouth. This would really get her to cum.

On the rare times that they have actual sex together they have mirrors on the celling of their bed room so they can watch themselves. There are mirrors on the side walls as well. That way they can think of themselves as the porn stars.

✳ ✳ ✳

It was a rainy, gloomy day in Bar Harbor. Evelyn debated with herself about even going out today. She knew that Jack would be on his way to the boat so she decided to go ahead and meet him there.

Around 8 o'clock he arrived at the dock. She was waiting for him. He asked,

"What do you think? We going out today?" She replied,

"Well there is no wind just rain so I think it will be safe. Maybe not a great Lobster day. They seem to like the sunny days to crawl around down there."

"That's what my dad use to say. He would just stay at home on rainy days. So what do you want to do?"

"Were here now and I have some bait for the traps so we might as well give it a try. Worst come to worst we head back in and call it a day."

They pushed off from the dock and headed out in the Bay. They removed the lobsters that were in the traps and rebaited them. They had serviced about 35 traps when the rain started to come down in serious fashion.

Evelyn asked jack,

"What do you think? Looks like it's not going to give us a break today."

Jack answered,

"I think you're right. Let's call it and head back in."

They turned around and went back to the dock. She dropped off the lobsters that they had picked up and then headed back to her house.

Evelyn turned into her driveway and parked her truck. She opened the door and Jack followed her inside.

She said,

"Let's get these wet clothes off and into the dryer and then get some food in our bellies."

Jack was all for that and he made a ham and cheese sandwich while she went into her bedroom to get out of her wet clothes. She left the door partly open while she disrobed.

She told him,

"Come in here I want to show you something you might like to see."

Jack finished his sandwich and walked into her room. His eyes went wide and he smiled and said,

"I sure do like what I am seeing."

She was laying on the bed naked. He finished taking his clothes off and climbed in beside her. She asked,

"So what would you like to do jack?"

"I'll just show you if that's OK with you."

He could feel his cock getting hard just looking at her nude body. His eyes went from her toes to her warm lips and back down to her hips. He moved in between her legs and went down to lick her center. She gave a low moan of pleasure as he licked her clit and moved down to her pink vagina. Jack wiggled his tongue from her clit to her pussy hole and back again. Evelyn had never had a man or a woman for that matter to serve her needs so completely. She ran her fingers thru his long hair and raised her hips up so that he could push his warm and wet tongue into her hole. At last he pulled himself up and pushed the tip of his cock into her wet vagina. She was tight but wet enough that he could slide in until nearly all of his eight inches were inside of her. She looked into his eyes and he into hers. They kissed and let their tongues dance into each other's mouths. When he felt his climax coming soon he stepped up the pace and she responded by putting her legs around him and holding him inside as he released his warm seed. She felt the warmth of it and smiled as she felt him growing soft. At last he slipped from her and knew that he had made her happy and satisfied.

They stayed in bed the rest of the afternoon and listened to the rain as it hit on the steel roof of her house. They fell asleep in each other's arms.

Back in Nob Hill Patty and Tina arrived at their shop to find the front door had been smashed in. Walking inside they saw where supplies and equipment had been tossed about the floor and graffiti was sprayed on the walls.It read.

LESBIANS GET OUT
YOU'RE NOT WELCOME

It wasn't long before the Police arrived and in surveying the damage and the writing on the wall the one officer remarked.

"Looks like vandalism and a HATE crime. We see some of this more and more. Do you have any enemies that you know of?"

Patty told him,

"Not that I know of. But that doesn't mean we don't have at least one, obviously."

"Notify your Landlord about the damage to the door and the lost materials. We will inform our Captain with regards to the graffiti and attach a hate crime to the charges when we catch these people or person responsible. It is a serious offence on top of the vandalism."

Patty called Trish and reported what had happened.

Trish was incensed when she heard about it.

She asked Patty,

"Did the Police make a note of it when they were there?"

"Yes Mom, they did and they told me that it was an extra felony charge when they get whoever did this."

Trish replied,

"I would hope so. The Gay panic defense doesn't hold up in a murder case. Why would it be for this case?"

Patty asked,

"What is a Gay panic defense?"

Trish explained,

"It was something that Lawyers have tried to get their client off for doing something to a gay or lesbian person because their client was panicked to do it because the victim was gay. This was a cop out and they knew it. That is why it is not allowed in most States anymore."

The Police returned to the salon and told Patty,

"The surveillance camera on the building got a real nice shot of the license plate on the pickup that was here and dropped the bad guy off to do his handiwork. It was reported stolen by the owner. He thinks it was a relative who stole it. We are going to pick him up now."

The landlord was not happy about what had happened to the girls shop. Let along the damage to his door. He told patty and Tina that,

"If you are going to be a distraction here for the other businesses and customers then I will have to ask you to leave. I don't like it but that is just the way it is."

When the word got out that they were going to be evicted a group of other businesses and Gay rights advocates stepped in and told the Landlord that if they were out then the other shop renters there were going to leave too and leave him with empty Real Estate. (Money talks, bull shit walks.) They got to stay. The notoriety that came from it only increased their grooming business. When it became available they rented the store next door and hired three more groomers.

✳✳✳

Back in Texas the 'Dude' ranch business was taking off and Tex was happy to find people who wanted to pay him to work there. He and Robb were getting ready to roundup some cattle to sell off before winter so they wouldn't have to feed more than they had hay for. Of the current crop of Dudes they felt there were some who would be able to help with the roundup.

The first was Krissy Karr from Washington DC who had a good

riding background. She worked on a Horse farm outside of the city when she was a teenager and had done some Barrel racing at a Teen Rodeo for several years. She is working at the Pentagon as a computer programmer.She is thirty and single. Long brown hair and brown eyes. 5' 8" tall and a smile that could light up a dark room when she walked in. Robb knew right away that she was special.

Tex chose two of the others to help with the roundup. One was proficient with ATV's and would take one of the side by sides so that he could take a passenger along with him.

When the day came to move the herd of fifty head of cows and steers to the loading corral a half mile west of the main barn Robb took Krissy and a couple of the regular hands out to the north pasture to start moving the animals to the loading area. It was about five miles from the pasture to the corral. When they arrived at the pasture Robb had the hands work around the back of the pasture and start to move the cattle along the fence to the gate leaving it open for the rest to follow. As they moved their charges toward the loading area the others moved alongside to keep the cows going in the right direction. By noon they had the first fifty ready to put on the Cattle haulers truck. Each day they would move another fifty to the trucks.

Krissy signed up for two weeks and at the end of the first week she and Robb had become more than friends.

They took a picnic basket along with them and headed out to the western pasture where they found a small grove of cottonwood trees and Robb put a small table down on the ground and a couple of picnic chairs to sit on. They had their lunch and then laid down on a blanket to look up at the sky with its puffy clouds rolling by. He reached over and took her hand in his. She grinned at him and said,

"Now what cowboy? What do you want to do for dessert?"

Robb smiled at her and asked,

"May I kiss your sweet lips?"

Krissy winked at him and said,

"Not if I kiss you first. Then it will be your turn. OK?"

With that Robb puckered up and closed his eyes. Krissy moved over on the blanket and planted one on him. He pulled her close to him and returned the kiss to her with his lips parted and with his tongue tip touching her teeth. She opened her mouth and sucked his tongue into her sweet mouth.He reached over and squeezed her ass cheeks. She made a little moaning sound and then she moved over on top of him. She pressed her pussy up tight to his hardening erection. He pushed himself up against her and then she got up and removed her jeans and boots. She took Robb's boots and pants off too as he laid there on the blanket. When she had them both naked from the waist down she straddled him and pressed his cock into her pussy. As he slid into her she watched his eyes as he went in deeper and deeper. She stopped moving and then she clamped her vaginal muscles on him and released and squeezed again and again. He had sex with several different women and none had ever done this before. He liked it. She alternated between squeezing and moving her hips up and down on him until she felt his hot release inside her as she had her own orgasm. She continued to move up and down and front to back on him until at last he slipped from her wetness. She slid up his belly and put her shaved mound on his mouth. Robb licked and licked her until he felt another erection starting. He slid her back down and rolled her over so that he could fuck her from behind. They laid on their sides and continued to copulate for over an hour. When he finally had another ejaculation. This time Krissy went down on him and licked their combined juices from him.

When she was done she asked him if he was OK with what she did.

"You know, making you eat me after we fucked. Then me licking you clean the next time. I know I liked it. Sometimes a guy gets funny about doing me like that."

Robb just smiled and said,

"I liked it both ways. When you did that it just showed me that you really do like me enough to do what you did." She smiled at Robb and said,

"You don't know how much I wanted to do that. I did that with a boyfriend one time and he got up and slapped me across the face and said, don't ever do that again. So I never did as that was the last time we did anything. I just think it is a natural thing to do if you like someone and it doesn't hurt anyone, then do it." Robb thought about what she said and then replied,

"You know what Krissy? I liked the taste of you on my tongue and if you liked my taste then it's O K with me to do it some more."

After that day whenever they had the privacy to indulge they did.

Krissy went back to Washington and gave her notice. She then packed up her things and moved to the ranch to be with Robb.

✳ ✳ ✳

Kitty and Adam took the sailboat out on the pond one day to just practice their tacking skills with the little boat.

When they got to a certain place on the pond and the wind was right they could smell something dead nearby. They were curious to find out what it was so they moved the boat back and forth until they found the source of the smell. It was the body of a young girl.

They went back to the house and called the Police. They called the county Coroner to come out and supervise the removal.

They checked on missing persons to try to find out who she was. It wasn't long before they found that she was a missing person from Magdalena who had disappeared a week ago. That seemed right with the amount of decomposition that had occurred to the body.

They interviewed some of her friends from school and found one girl who knew a lot about her friend. She told the Police that she was involved with a man she called Franky. No last name. She told them that he was a Photographer who took pictures of her and then paid her to have sex with him.

The Detectives had no problem finding the right man. He was Frank Banks. A professional Advertising photographer who did magazine and Newspaper ads and used some young people as models.

The Coroner found the cause of death to be strangulation. Manner of death was homicide. She was also four months pregnant.

They picked up Frank Banks and after they interviewed him for several hours he confessed to killing her and then burying her out in the country. They asked him to show them where he buried her body.

He took them out to where he said he had done it and when they arrived they were surprised to find the empty grave with drag marks leading down to the pond where Kitty and Adam found her. Crime scene tapes were still there.

The Coroner made no mention of animal activity where a Bear or Coyote had bitten her and drug her away from the burial site to the water. That was another mystery.

✳ ✳ ✳

Mike Brown was a poacher who had been hiding up in a tree a hundred yards from where he saw a man carrying a body over his shoulder. He saw him lay the body on the ground and cover it with dirt and rocks.

Mike was waiting for a Deer to come by so that he could shoot it with his cross bow. He was known to be a market hunter who would kill a number of Deer and Elk to sell to anyone who would pay his price for a trophy head or for the meat.

After he saw the man leave and heard his car move from the area Mike went to see what he had buried. When he arrived there he started to poke around in the rocks and dirt and soon found the arm of a young girl. He dug some more and uncovered her face and upper body. He pulled her from the shallow grave and looked at her for a while. He thought,

'She sure was a pretty girl. Who would do something like this? She looks like she was pregnant too. What a shame. Wonder what it feels like to fuck a dead prego.'

When he was done having sex with her corpse he drug the body down the hill to the water and dumped her in.

It was several months later when Penny had gone up on the hill side to be able to see across the pond to where the trees went up the mountain. It was an appealing place that she had always wanted to do some drawings and some oil paintings of the scenery there.

She had hiked up there on that clear blue sky day when the Aspen trees had their full yellow fall colors and the Cedar and Loblolly pines dark green and the blue reflection of the sky on the ponds water were everything she wanted to show in her paintings.

She had become a successful artist in her own right for her age and was selling all that she could paint. She had been showing at Taos and in Magdalena and her work was selling at advancing prices. She had set up her easel and was just getting started on a canvas when she heard something in the trees to her right. She looked that way but couldn't see what had made the sound. She had been taught from the time she was a small child that when you think you hear or see something you should just keep still and continue to listen. You never know what you may see or hear.

Penny sat still and looked over in the direction that she thought she heard a sound. Then she saw it. It was a man up in a tree with some kind of a bow and arrow. She knew that it was not hunting season yet in that area so she just sat quiet and watched.

As she did she saw an adult Mule Deer move from the trees down the hill to where she saw the man in the tree stand. He had not seen her and was now fixed on the Deer at hand. It was a magnificent Buck with massive size antlers. It looked like it had at least ten or twelve points. She saw the man in the tree draw a bead on the Deer with his bow. She heard the theek of the arrow as it left the bow and heard the kathunk as it hit the bucks' chest cavity. It jumped a few steps and then dropped down on its side. It stopped moving shortly after it hit the ground.

Penny knew it was dead and that the man who shot it was not a legal hunter. Her family doesn't allow any hunting on their 30 acres except by family members.

She slowly turned and packed up her art equipment and headed down the hill toward the house. She turned in time to see the man coming toward her at a run. She dropped her stuff and started to run herself. She couldn't outrun him as he was faster then she was. What he didn't know was that she carried her mom's 40 Glock with her when she went out into the mountains to paint. There could be a pack of Coyotes or even a Mountain Lion that could take her for an easy prey. Penny didn't like the looks of him gaining on her so she stopped and pulled the handgun from its holster and pointed it at him.

When he saw it he slowed to a stop and looked at it in disbelieve. Who did this little girl think she was to be pointing a gun at him? He didn't even believe it was real until she put a shot right in front of him and sprayed dirt and rocks up at his face.

That was when she pointed it directly at his face and he froze in place and raised his hands. He said,

"What are you doing little girl? Don't you know it's not nice to point guns at people? I'm not going to hurt you now put it down. O K?"

Penny didn't say a word she just kept it pointed at his face. She remembered then that Kitty had warned her that there are more dangerous things in the mountains then lions. She believed that this was one of them.

Back at the house Trish and Kitty were just finishing up the laundry and hanging it out to dry when they heard a gunshot back on the mountain. Then another shot rang out and then another. Kitty said.

"I think we should investigate that shot. Penny may have shot a predator and we need to be sure she is O K."

They hurried up the hills as fast as they could and then they saw Penny holding the Glock with both hands and a man they recognized as Mike Brown. The poacher with his hands up. Penny said to Trish,

"He shot a Mule Deer over there at the edge of the woods. He was coming after me because I saw him do it."

Trish took the gun from Penny and told her to go back to the house and call 911 and report a Game violation here at the ranch.

"We need a Sherriff or a Game Warden as soon as possible so the meat doesn't spoil."

Penny did what she was told and was able to get a Game Warden right away. She was only five miles away and told her that she would be there in about ten minutes.

Mike didn't like the idea of being taken down by a twelve year old girl even one armed with a handgun. He watched Trish and decided that she was not going to shoot him if he tried to escape. He turned his back to her and took off running for his ATV that he had stashed in the trees.

He didn't get far when he heard the shot and felt the bullet hit his leg. He had no idea that she was as good a shot as she was. If she wanted to kill him she would have. She just wanted him to be there when the Law arrived.

Warden Dolly Matson was a ten year veteran of the game Commission and had heard of Mike Browns reputation as a poacher and had hoped to nail him someday. Today was the day.

Trish told him to tie his belt around his leg to slow the bleeding. She kept her distance from him as she was sure he would try something else to disarm her.

Warden Matson handcuffed him and called for an EMT to come to assist in getting him back to the road so she could transport him to jail. She was able to salvage the Deer meat and it was taken to the County food bank.

✳ ✳ ✳

Back at Patty's shop her first customer had sent a letter to the local Newspaper expounding the skill and care that she had used in grooming his Poddle, Molly.

The letter led to more new customers seeking grooming for their dogs. One of them was a wealthy show dog owner, Lois Lawrence who has a Portuguese Water dog like the one that the first family in the White house had. His name was Sparky and was a best in show winner at many shows.

She brought him in for grooming ahead of a coming show in Denver CO the following week. Sparky was not just a top show dog but was in demand for stud service. Some of his pups were destined to be show dogs themselves.

After they had finished grooming him Lois asked,

"Would one of you be able to come with us to Denver to take care of his final touchups before the show? I am willing to pay you well for your trouble including all expenses."

Patty looked at Tina and asked,

"Would you like to go to Denver? I can hold down the fort here with the other groomers. It may be an opportunity to meet up with some other owners too."

Tina's eyes lit up and she replied,

"Sure, I'll go. Never been to Denver before."

Lois told her,

"O K, I'll pick you up on Friday morning and we will fly from Albuquerque to Denver. We will get a room at the Hotel where the show is being held."

Tina was excited to be going to her first Dog Show and be grooming one of the top dogs in the show.

They arrived in the afternoon and got checked into their room. There was a crate for Sparky in the room as well.

After they got settled in Lois suggested they head down to the Hotel's restaurant for supper. Tina looked over the menu and asked Lois,

"I see they have Surf and Turf. What's that?"

Lois told her,

"That is a Lobster tail and a steak. Would you like that?"

Tina looked at her and asked.

"May I?"

Lois replied,

"You certainly may. Whatever you would like to have. You are my guest this weekend."

When they finished their meal they went back to their room. Lois went into the bathroom and took a hot shower. When she was finished she told Tina,

"Your turn now. I left plenty of hot water for you. I will wash your back if you would like me to." Tina smiled and replied,

"That sounds nice. Patty and I wash each other's backs when we shower together. We even wash our fronts."

Lois smiled and said,

"I would like to wash your front too. Would you like to wash mine?" Tina smiled back and told her,

"Anything you want to do is fine with me."

Tina got in the shower and got lathered up. The next thing she knew Lois was back in with her and had a wash cloth full of soap and was washing Tina's back. She turned around to face Lois and she washed Tina's breasts while looking into her eyes. Tina put her arms around Lois and pulled her to her. She experienced a tingle that started in her butt and went around to her pussy. Lois rubbed her washcloth over her pussy while Tina went down and kissed Lois's tits. They got rinsed and dried off.

They went to bed naked and kissed each other's lips. Lois snaked her tongue into Tina's mouth and enjoyed the taste and feel of their tongues as they twirled around in their mouths. First Lois in Tina's and the Tina in Lois's.Lois put her hand on Tina's pussy and stroked it gently while running a finger inside her. Tina returned the gesture and then Tina turned to the sixty nine position with Lois on the bottom. She held Tina's ass cheeks while she licked her clit and wet vagina. She slipped a finger inside Tina's asshole and wiggled it in circles. Tina moaned and put her whole tongue in Lois's wet pussy. They worked each other's girl parts until they were both on the edge of a wonderful, tingly orgasm. Tina rolled off Lois and took the bottom position for another round of licking and sucking to another wonderful finish.

For a woman of sixty she had perky tits and she had her pubic hair neatly trimmed. Tina shaves hers off smooth so she looks like a twelve year old girl. Her clit pokes out of its hood like a miniature penis. Lois liked the feel and taste of Tina. She pulls her legs up and ran her tongue over Tina's sweet clean anus. Tina gasped and wallowed her tongue over Lois's wet pussy.She would never have thought that having sex with an older woman could be so much fun.

The next day they woke up and had another round of oral sex with each other with some good finger fucking to go with it.

The Show started at one in the afternoon and ran until six. When the Best in Show was picked by the Judges. Sparky took home the trophy again.

On the flight back Lois suggested the next show Patty could go with her and then alternate with Tina at the future shows. Tina liked the idea and took Lois's hand in hers and said,

"I know Patty would love to go with you next time and then we can both go to the next show together." Lois smiled at Tina and said,

"You are a special girl and I can see why Patty loves you so much. You do like to share don't you?"

Tina smiled and said,

"We have been partners for some time now and we have no secrets from each other. We do enjoy making love together and I know you and Patty will have as good a time as we had last night. God, you are amazing and so sweet in bed."

Lois looked at Tina and remarked,

"If I didn't know better I would have sworn you were just a tender young thing who likes to pleasure your partner no matter how young or old they are. I know you made this old woman's heart do flip flops last night and again this morning. I'll bet you and Patty can go all night can't you?"

Tina snickered and confided,

"You're not bad yourself. Can I ask you a personal question?"

"Sure just name it."

"Do you ever have sex with a man? Just curious."

Lois didn't miss a beat and replied,

"Sure I like a hard cock sometimes. Do you?"

Tina looked up at the ceiling and replied,

"Well yes, I don't make a practice of it, but yes, I like to suck one off and get his load. Then I kiss him and see if he likes it when I share his load with him. Do you ever do that?"

Lois thought about it and then replied,

"You know what? I have learned something from you this weekend. I'll have to try that next time."

✳ ✳ ✳

One of Tex's cowboys came in one day and told him,

"I was out on the north pasture today and saw a couple coyotes eating on something. I took a shot at 'em and hit the one and the other ran off. I went over to see what they were working on. I think I found Lucy."

The Rangers went to Brad's work place and placed him under arrest for her murder.

Robb was shocked when he heard that she had been found. He blamed himself for letting her be with Brad that night. He just had to move on.

The Dude ranch was really taking off and they had most of the summer and fall booked full. One day Robb saw a young woman show up from Duluth Minnesota. She was the answer to his fantasy. He always wondered what it would be like to fuck a fat girl.

Jill Ayers was just that. She was 5' 7" and weighed 240 pounds. She was excited to be there and couldn't wait to get on a horse and learn how to ride. When she saw Robb she wanted to ride him too.

When all the guests had arrived and they had their supper Robb took Jill for a walk out to the horse barn where he showed her the horses that they would be riding that week. The full moon was as bright as daytime and they walked back up to the Bunk House where her room was located. Before they got back he stopped and took her hands and put them on top of his shoulders and then put his hands on her hips. Before he could say anything she kissed him on the mouth. Robb parted his lips and invited her tongue to visit his. They French kissed for a few minutes and then she asked,

"Would you like to see my room?" Robb replied,

"Which one is yours? Oh, I know you're in number six, right?" She replied,

"How did you know that? Oh I know. You probably assigned them. Didn't you?"

Robb smiled at her and said,

"You got me. Yes, I did that because I wanted you to have some privacy and that room is the best."

Jill replied,

"Thank you Robb. Come on in I'll show it to you. And anything else you want to see is fine with me."

As they walked he held her hand in his. She looked up at him and smiled. She just knew she was going to get fucked the first night here.

The next day when the rest of the guests were at the horse barn getting saddled up for the days instructions she noticed a very pretty black girl with her white husband. Jill saw the way she looked at her and winked and smiled at Jill. She thought,

'I wonder if she would like to visit with me some evening. Maybe Robb can fuck both of us. Or am I dreaming. She sure is pretty and her teeth are as perfect as can be. Must have had braces when she was a kid. I just want to kiss her and maybe get to lick her puss. Now I am dreaming.'

Lisa and Jeff Prentiss from Mississippi went to College at "Ole Miss". Jeff was from West Virginia and was as white as he could be.

Lisa was a beautiful Black girl right out of high school and the first time away from home in Alabama. She was the first in her family to go to college. They met at a frat party the first week of classes. She wanted to fit in and so she drank some beer and when Jeff asked her to slow dance she looked at him and thought,

'I wonder if he knows I'm Black. Sure he does. He just wants to see if he can get in my pants. I sure do want in his.'

As the evening went by he asked her if she would like to go upstairs and make out. Lisa replied,

"I don't mind if I do. What's yo'all name? I'm Lisa."

Jeff smiled and said,

"That's a sho 'nuf purtty name fo a purtty gal."

He took her hand and led them to a bedroom. They continued

to slow dance and rubbed their bellies together. It didn't take long before she could feel his cock get hard. She rubbed against it and put her arms around him and held him close. He felt her soft ass and pressed against her warm pussy.

They got naked and he pushed into her wetness. She responded by putting her hands on his ass cheeks and squeezing them with her warm hands. It was not long before she felt his hot load flow into her.

They got married in the spring before their daughter was born. He got a job as a car salesman in Biloxi and she stayed home and was a good mom who just liked to fuck Jeff every chance she got. In three years they had three kid's two girls and a boy.

While they were riding the next day Jill invited Lisa to join her and Robb that evening. Lisa said,

"That sounds like fun. Jeff is going to go play cards with some of the other men."

Jill told her,

"That's cool. I'll invite Robb to come visit with us while Jeff goes play cards. We will find our own games to play. Sound good?"

That evening after supper the men started playing poker and drinking whiskey. Lisa, Jill and Robb played with each other. Lisa was sucking Robb's cock while Jill was eating Lisa's wet pussy. She had never done a Black girl before and liked seeing how pink the inside looked. She always thought it was just Black like her skin. Jill knew her pussy was pink inside but didn't know that some black girls have pink and some are Black. It didn't matter to her as she just liked to lick it until it got really wet. She rubbed her face in Lisa's juice.Lisa could feel Robbs load coming at the same time Jill was making her come too. Lisa wondered if she was going to get pregnant again. Not that it mattered since Jeff had a vasectomy and was done shooting live rounds. Lisa did want another baby. When they were done Lisa said,

"Well that was fun. Let's do it again before the week is over."

Jill wanted to keep doing it all night with Robb now and was happy that he still wanted to fuck her after Lisa had drained his pipes.

Robb decided to let Jill down easy and so he told her,

"I think we should just cool it for now. I have a lot of things that I need to do around here and as much as I enjoy the distraction, I really have to take care of the business at hand before I get involved with anyone. You understand?"

Jill was hurt. She didn't understand. It sounded a lot like that was fun, now what's next? And what was next didn't include her. She went out to the barn and saddled up a horse. Robb had told her not to ride a certain trail as it had been washed out by a hurricane. She didn't care. She just wanted to end her life as it wasn't going anywhere. She left the barn and headed out to the trail that Robb had warned her about. She rode for several miles and when she felt the trail winding down hill she knew it was the trail she shouldn't be on. She urged her horse to go faster and then it stumbled as the trail fell away and Jill pitched forward in the saddle and fell from the animal and rolled down the hill side. She broke her neck in the fall and was dead before she stopped rolling down the hill.

The next morning the horse came back to the barn and Jill was noticed as missing from her room. Robb was worried about her and when he looked for her in her room he found a note.

Dear Robb,

I know that I am just a joke to you and Lisa but I have been a joke to some people for a long time. I decided to just end the joke and see how you feel when someone hurts you. I took a horse and went to the trail that you said is not safe to ride on. I have always been the butt of jokes all my FAT life. Now you can just live without me as I have had enough. Tell Lisa that we could have had a good time if she and you would have just not ruined my life. So I will say good bye you FUCKERS

Love
Fatty Jill

Robb ran from her room and went for Tex. He showed him the note and they got a pair of horses and went looking for her. When they got to the trail they looked down and saw her body laying at the bottom of the sloop. Tex called for some hands to bring an ATV out to retrieve her body. He sent Robb back to the house.

When he returned Tex saw a note from Robb.

Tex,

I am going to my Moms in New Mexico. I have to have some down time. See you next week.

Love
Robb

Kitty met him at the door and they sat down in the living room. Robb told her,

"Mom I need to have you listen to what I have to say. I have had two women that I have had sex with and now they are both dead. I just can't understand why this is happening to me. Am I that bad a person? What can I do to make up for what I have done?"

Kitty called out for Trish to come and sit with them.

"Robb has a problem and he needs our help. He is worried that it is somehow his fault that Lucy got murdered and now that Jill has committed suicide. We have both been down similar paths and perhaps we can share what we had that helped us to get past our days."

Trish looked at Robb and said,

"I am so sad to hear that you lost two of your friends like this. What happened to Lucy was not your fault. It was Brad who killed her, not you. There are always going to be terrible things that happen to people that we know and there is nothing we can do about it. As far as Jill is concerned she had her own demons for a long time. She suffered at the hands of bullies that teased her about her looks. They are the ones who should be suffering, not you Robb. There are always going to be bullies and there is not much we can do to undo the damage they have done. When Kitty and I moved here we wanted to get away from the bullies and the name callers that we put up with. We ran away. They are still out there picking on other people. We raised all you kids to be respectful of others who are not the same as you. Whether skin color or language spoken or even sexual orientation you do not tease anyone about things they can't change. Maybe Jill could have changed the way she looked to others but maybe she couldn't. Hatred is a terrible thing but the worst kind is hating yourself. Jill shouldn't have listened to the bullies. Maybe she could lose some weight. Maybe she couldn't. But first she needed to love herself no matter what she did. You need to sit yourself down and look at yourself. You are basically a good person. You are going thru some of the same things that we all go thru. To love someone and then to lose that someone. Life isn't easy. But we have to learn from our mistakes and move on." Robb sat and listened and then he spoke.

"Thanks Mom's. You are the smartest people that I have ever known and now I just have to think about what you have said.

Growing up here we never had any outside influences that shaped our lives. It was you two who molded us and kept us on the right track. We have all become successful in what we do and you're still providing role models for Adam and Penny. I think I have found the one that I will spend the rest of my life with. You must meet Krissy. You are going to love her, I do."

✳ ✳ ✳

A week later Robb returned to the Ranch and sat down with Krissy and Tex. Rob told her about the things that he had done with other women and asked her forgiveness. He told Tex that he wanted to take a more responsible part in running the ranch. He said,

"I have just been having fun and letting you do the heavy lifting. That is going to change. When I was at Mom's place we talked and we listened to each other. Now I understand why they did things the way they did. It was to build the best people that we could become. Evan became an Army officer and then a CIA Agent. He died a hero. Buddy studied hard and invented some heart gadget that saves lives. Patty has a huge Grooming business and has a great partner in Tina. My little half-sister Katelyn is in college working on getting into Veterinarian school. I don't know why she is looking at Vet and not Med. Med is easier to get in. Now little brother and sister, Adam is a musician and Penny is an artist."

Tex replied,

"Yes, you come from a great family. And you do carry your weight around here. I know because I see everything."

Robb appreciated Tex's comments and now he had an idea. He told Tex,

"I want Trish and Kitty to meet Krissy, so I am going to take her out to their place so she can see the woman that I love and I want their blessing for our marriage."

Tex looked at Krissy and asked,

"Do you really love this young man for who he is or just for what he's got?"

Krissy's jaw dropped and her eyes opened wide when she told Tex,

"Yes I really do love Robb. He is the most sensitive and balanced person I have ever met. I know he loves me too. So I want to go meet those women that are responsible for making him the man he is today."

Tex looked at Robb and smiled,

"I think you are one lucky fellow to find a girl like Krissy. She is the real deal. She quit a good job in the big city to come and live on an actual ranch with you. Not just for a week or two for a getaway. But to come here to be with you. Again I think you are a lucky boy. I would like to go with you two when you head on over to New Mexico."

A few days later they got ready to leave the ranch in the capable hands of their trusted employees and head for where Robb was born and raised.

When they arrived at Trish and Kitty's home they were greeted by Adam who was sitting on the front porch playing his guitar and singing an old song that he heard Dolly Parton sing one time and he liked it.

"In the pines, in the pines, where the sun never shines
And you shiver when the cold wind blows"

He put his guitar down and walked out to greet them. He gave Robb a hug and then turned to Krissy and said,

"So you're the one who stole my brother's heart?He could have done worse. Come on in and meet our parents."

They went into the living room and found Trish sitting on a reclining chair with Kitty sitting on the couch reading a book. Kitty got up and walked over to Krissy and gave her a hug. Krissy smiled at her and said,

"Robb never told me you were so pretty. I guess I just thought that you guys would look like some old Diesel Dykes. I am sorry I even said that. It was rude of me and I apologize for having some characterization of what a lesbian looks like."Trish was the first to speak when Krissy said what she said.

"No need to apologize for anything. We are just another middle aged pair of people who are in love for over twenty years. There have been some men in our lives that did change the way we live. Kitty had a bad relationship that was nearly deadly. I rescued her and she was able to escape from him. I had several failed relationships and was really getting depressed when life happened. My dad died when I was not even thirty, But he did leave my brother and I a comfortable inheritance. I met Kitty in Bar Harbor Maine while I was satisfying my taste for Lobster. We traveled all the way across the country and settled in this spot. We thought it would be a great place to raise kids without the impact on their lives would be if they were in a town."

Kitty added,

"Yes, she rescued me, but I think I rescued her as well. Right from the start I always thought that she was looking for something in her life that was reassuring. I think that I brought that out of her when she started taking care of me. It was not long after we settled here that we adopted three kids who lost their parents in a terrible car wreck. Robb has probably told you about how our family grew with Foster kids. We just adopted these two." Motioning to Penny and Adam. "We couldn't have found any better kids then them. You heard Adam playing when you pulled up. Penny is working on a painting for a show in Taos. She has quite a talent."

Krissy was impressed at what these two women had accomplished. She looked at Robb and said,

"You sure were a lucky boy to be born into this house where loving you and teaching you the way they did without the interference from the outside world. Yet you are all not only surviving in the world, but thriving.All kids should be so lucky."

Tex added,

"I am a lucky man too from meeting Trish and Kitty here at that Rodeo. I didn't know then that our lives would end up where we are today. These two ladies have accomplished so much without braking a sweat. I am ashamed to say that I would not have been able to take in some of these youngen's that have a less than perfect background. So I have to say that it has been nothing short of a miracle that we met that day."

Meanwhile Robb stood up and took Krissy's hand and they walked up to his Mom's and said,

"I have something to say and now is as good a time as any." Robb took a knee and reached into his pocket and produced a diamond ring. He looked up at Krissy and said,

"Krissy Karr, will you be my wife?"

Her mouth dropped open and then she replied,

**YES **

He slipped the ring on her finger.

Trish and the others all clapped their hands and then Trish and Kitty hugged the engaged couple and they cried with happy tears.

That night when all of them had gone to bed Tex woke up to find Trish in bed with him. He was delighted to find her there. She put her hand on his back and rubbed it from his neck to his butt. She ran her fingers down the backs of his legs. He rolled over on the bed and exposed his engorged penis to Trish. She crawled on top of him and took her hand and pushed it into her pussy. She had not had sex with a man since the last time that she and Kitty went to get Tex to be a sperm donor so Kitty could get pregnant. Katelyn is his biological child. Even though it was Trish that inserted his sperm into Kitty. Now Trish felt the urge to have her own baby before it was too late. She was going thru perimenopause and wondered if it was even possible to still get pregnant. If it was this was the best shot she had to get it done.She and Tex had sex several times at the ranch. She even had Tex introduce Kitty to anal sex. Tex had fucked both of them back when they wanted his sperm. He ended up going with them to a clinic in Huston and just made his donation in a cup.

Trish could feel him moving under her as she rode him all the way to his explosive ejaculation. When he slipped out after a time she left a puddle on his belly. Some was his and some she knew was hers as she too had an orgasm.

Down the hallway in the room where Krissy and Robb were sleeping. Or should I just say fucking all night. It's O K, they are engaged. (Snicker, snicker)

The next morning they had breakfast on the back porch overlooking the pond. As was her usual day Penny was busy down at the boat dock with her easel and her paints.She really enjoys painting and enjoys going to the art shows where she has been able to sell her work.

She went back to the top of the hill where she had the run-in with Mike brown, the poacher, and had finished the scene that she saw there. She still had some flash backs of him coming after her. He wouldn't have tried it if he had known she was packing her mom's 40 Glock pistol.

She held him at bay until Trish got on the scene and took over. He stupidly tried to escape before she could take him to see the Game Warden for the buck Mule Deer that he shot out of season. She shot him in the leg to disable him. He is now in State prison for five years for a number of crimes. Including abuse of a corpus. It seems that when he found a young girl who was buried on the hill and he fucked her dead body and then removed it to the pond where Kitty and Adam found her.

During the autopsy the Coroner's team found sperm cells from two different men. He was one and her killer was the other.

Katelyn was a precocious young girl of fifteen and had past all the courses to graduate at that young age. Kitty had pushed her along as long as Katelyn was happy and fully understood the work. Her application to university of New Mexico was accepted and she started classes in the fall. She stayed with Patty and Tina in Nob Hill the first semester. Student housing opened up after Christmas and she was able to get housing on campus.

She was a little homesick for a couple weeks until she was able to make some friends who took her under their wings as they thought it was neat that she was so young to be in college. Her closest friend was Ashley Sweet from Santa Fe. They shared a room on the second floor of their dorm. Ash was a junior in a computer programing class. She had stared early also at seventeen.

Katelyn was fascinated by Ash who regaled her with stories of frat parties she had been to. Telling her about the guys who tried to make out with her and those who did. She especially liked the stories about when Ash lost her cherry at a party to a Black guy. Katelyn had never had any dealings with any Black people considering where she was brought up and lived her whole life. There were Indians that she saw that lived on the Reservation and her brother Buddy had married a girl from the reservation. But no Black people. There were some Mexicans who came across the border in search of work. They usually kept going north to get away from the Border patrol. So for her to see and have classes with some Black gals and guys was fascinating to her. Ash said that she could sneak Katelyn into a party sometime so she could see what it was like. This got her interest peaked.

That weekend she asked Ash,

"Do you think we can get to a party this Saturday? I will get all my class work finished up on Friday and be ready for some fun."Ashley tilted her head to the side and asked,

"Are you sure you want to do this? You are still a bit young for that crowed. I'm sure you would have fun there. I always do."

Katlyn said,

"Please Ash, take me along. I'll be good."

Ash replied,

"I'm sure you will, it's the guys that I'm not sure of. They are always on the lookout for 'fresh meat 'and you are the freshest."

Katelyn smiled and told Ash,

"Well this fresh meat is ready to grow up and have some fun." She grabbed her crotch and shook it. Ash laughed and said,

"WHOA GIRL! You are coming on to strong. You have to be more demure, like me." As she tossed her long brown hair with streaks of blue and green braided in the different colors.

Katelyn went to bed that night and fantasized about having sex with a college boy for the first time.

That Saturday they left the dorm about ten o'clock and went to a party at one of the Greek fraternity's. When they entered the room they were confronted by a crowd of young people who were dancing to a 'D J's loud tunes. Mostly heavy metal and grunge style music. Katelyn smiled at Ash and over the loud music she said,

"This is way different from back home. My Mom's didn't like this music and so we never heard much of it." Ash replied,

"I'm not a big fan of it myself. I like to slow dance so I can get my hands on a male body. Or a pretty girl sometimes."

Katelyn smiled at that and told her,

"I told you my Moms are lesbians didn't I?

Ash smiled and replied,

"That's cool with me. Some of my friends swing both ways. You'll figure it out here at school. You will have some of the wildest experiences of your life. Enjoy it while you can. My parents divorced when I was ten and I lived with my mom one week and my dad the next. It was confusing for me and I had a hard time excepting that they were not going to be together anymore. Then my dad died suddenly and I was with my mom all the time. I was twelve when that happened. My mom had a boyfriend who would come over and stay the night. He always left in the morning. I watched them doing it on different nights and saw that they did it different ways sometimes. I never did it until last year when I hooked up with Freddy Odom. He was gentle and kind when he did it. I was a little scared at first but then it felt good."

Katelyn thought about what Ash had said about Freddy. She asked,

"Is Freddy here tonight?"

Ash laughed and replied,

"Yes, he is right over there by the beer keg. Do you want to meet him?"

Katelyn thought about what Ash had said about Freddy being

gentle with her when he became her first.

She replied to Ash,

"Yes, I want to meet him. Will you introduce us?"

Ash reminded Katelyn that he is just a player and would not be any kind of regular date material.

"However if you are just interested in getting a good fuck, he's your man."

Katelyn didn't take her eyes off Freddy as she and Ash walked over to where he was talking to some of his friends. Ash touched him on his arm and when he turned to see her he smiled and said,

"Hi cupcake how you been? Haven't seen you for a while. Didn't know if you left school or somethin'."

Ashley pulled Katelyn up beside her and told Freddy,

"This is my roommate Katelyn. She was an early starter and is a bit young. She wanted to meet you as I told her that you are a gentleman and not a jerk like some of these guys are. Katelyn, this is Freddy Odom he is a premed student with a dual major, Bio and Chem."

Katelyn nodded her head in acknowledgement.

Freddy extended his hand and she held it for a moment and looked at his eyes. She saw a man with the darkest eyes she had ever seen. He didn't have a wide nose like some of the Black people that she had seen. His black hair was straightened and he wore it mullet style.

He smiled at Katelyn and she was immediately taken under his charming spell. They played a slow dance and he asked her for a dance. She went with him onto the dance floor. He held her close and ran his hands down her back until he touched her ass. She jerked when he did it and then relaxed as he gently rubbed his fingers across her. While they were dancing he asked her,

"So just what did Ash tell you about me?"

Katelyn looked at him and did a little giggle and said,

"She told me that you were her first and that you are gentle in bed." Freddy smiled and gave a little laugh,

"She actually told you that? Did she also tell you that she broke my heart? I really thought that we could have a relationship of some kind. Turns out she just wanted my body." Katelyn thought about what Ash had said about him being a player and replied,

"She told me that you are a player and you just want a girl for sex and that was all. She never told me that you had feelings for her."

He replied,

"I still do. But she just teases me by bringing you over to meet me. I don't know what she means by doing that."

Katelyn answered him,

"The truth be known she told me about you with nothing but respect. Even though she knows that I want you to be my first too. We have been roomie's for just a few months but she has been real nice to have around. She 'Mother hens' me since I am so young."

Freddy replied,

"I will be happy to take care of your desires and I hope you tell Ash that even if I were a player that she is the one I really like to play with."

Katelyn could feel his cock getting hard as they danced. She asked him,

"Is there a place we can have some privacy?"

Freddy walked her off the dance floor and to a room in the back of the house that had a single bed that was used by other couples who wanted 'privacy'.

They went in and he locked the door behind them.

While they were standing by the bed he bent down and kissed

Katelyn like she had never been kissed before. She had not. She was a total virgin in all ways. By instinct she opened her mouth and put her tongue against his.

Freddy explored her mouth with his and could feel her breathing increasing and her hands on his ass cheeks. He worked her sweater up and over her head. She raised her arms so that he could remove it. Then he unsnapped her bra to expose her small perky tits. She took his shirt off and then unbuckled his belt and helped him to drop his pants to the floor.

Freddy left the kiss and worked his way down her chest. Stopping to lick her nipples and suck on her titties. He slid her panties down her legs and she stepped out of them. He had dropped his boxers and kicked them aside.

Katelyn laid down on the bed looking up at Freddy she invited him to lay down on top of her. He did and then he continued to suck her titties and after a while he moved down her belly and licked around her navel. He reached back under her legs and pushed them up to her chest. He went down and kissed her clit. Katelyn moaned with pleasure. Freddy went down to her virgin opening and thrust his tongue inside as far as he could and licked up her juices that had started to run. Freddy was not bashful and went all the way to her anus. There he rubbed his tongue across it and up and down. He went back to her clit and sucked it and rolled his tongue on it.

As she was getting really wet he pushed a finger in her pussy. He stroked it a few times and then he used two fingers. Katelyn raised her hips to allow them to enter as far as they could. Freddy was ready. So was she. He moved up so that he could rub the tip of his cock in her wet crack. She pushed against it and she could feel it going inside her. He would stop and just stroke it before going farther. He pushed all the way in and she could feel it bottom out when it came to her cervix. She wasn't sure if it would go any farther, but she pushed against him and the tip pushed thru. She winced in pain and he pulled out.

"I'm sorry if I hurt you. I didn't mean to." She looked at him and said,

"Freddy that was the most exciting thing that ever happened to me. You really were the first one to ever fuck me and I liked it. Can we do it another way. Ash said something about cowgirl and doggie style."

Freddy knew he had a very interested student and he was happy to be her teacher. He laid on his back and told her to straddle him as he slipped it back in her now open hole. She rode him for a while and then he told her to get up and get on her hands and knees.

She did and he mounted her from behind. This was one of his favorite positions as he could reach around and touch her clit while he was stoking his cock inside her. He liked the sound of his belly slapping against her ass.

Katelyn had started to feel some strange like contractions and relaxing of her legs and her belly. She had experienced an orgasm before and knew that was what was happening.

He increased the speed of his strokes and then as he was about to ejaculate he pulled out and shot his load on her back. She felt it hit and was warm. He rubbed it on her back until it started to dry up.

Freddy got up and helped her to get off the bed. He had her sit on the edge of the bed. Then he told her that part of this was that she should lick his juice from his cock. She reached over and put her hand around it and began stroking it until it started to harden up again. She licked the tip and ran her tongue around it. She allowed more to enter her mouth and she proceeded to suck and lick him for a time and he got hard again and he spun her around and stood by the bed with her ass toward him. He had a tube of KY jelly in his pants pocket for the occasion. He smeared some on her anus. He told her,

"Now this might hurt at first so just try to relax. You will enjoy it once I get just part way in.

Katelyn wanted to experience everything she could. Ash was right he was gentle and caring with all that he did to her. Now she had to try to relax. She knew what he was going to do next.

She was right. He first put a finger in her anus and rubbed some of the KY inside her. Then he tried two fingers. It was tight at first until she relaxed again. He was able to get the two in and he worked them around so that she was well lubricated. He put a condom on and lubed it also. He pushed the head in just a bit and reminded her to relax. She did and he was able to get in another two inches. He knew from experience with some older women that he had anal sex with that they said that they could get orgasms faster and more intense this way. He hoped that Katelyn could experience this like those women. She pushed back as he pushed forward. He slid in a bit farther and began slowly stroking in and out. It was not long before she started breathing hard and he could feel her mussel's contract and relax, contract and relax. He smiled as he knew from experience that he had done a good job of breaking in another virgin. He hoped that they could hook up again sometime. Freddy was indeed a player. He was done playing for tonight.

When Katelyn next saw Ash she was waiting outside the house for her. She winked and asked,

"So did you have a good time?" Katelyn replied,

"You were right he was very gentle and he made me cum three times. It was magnificent. He knows all the right things to make a girl feel gooood!!"

✳ ✳ ✳

Brenda and Buddy were excited when the day came for their baby to be born. They went to one of the Hospitals there in Kansas City. They were welcomed into the maternity ward by two older Nurses. The one asked,

"Is this your first baby?"Brenda nodded her head and smiled. Buddy told her,

"Yes, her contractions are coming at five minutes apart so we thought we should get here."

About that time her water broke and the Nurses took over and put Brenda on a gurney and pushed her into a delivery room.

It was less than an hour later when little Evan Patrick Flick was born.

He was seven pounds six ounces. He was twenty inches long and had a head full of black hair. Showing his native genetics. His mother was full blooded Apache and Buddy was half Irish and half Apache.

He was on the phone a half hour after the birth to tell his moms that they were grandparents.

He called Patty to let her know as well.

When he told her what they named the baby Patty cried over the phone because it was just too emotional. She still missed her older brother.

Buddy told her that the name was picked to honor both their brother who died while on a mission for the CIA and also their Mother's father Patrick Malone. They had never meet their Grandparents since they were in Ireland. They lived in New Mexico all their lives. They now live in Olathe, a suburb of Kansas City. Buddy thought that when the baby was a little older they would take a trip to see the other half of their heritage.

His father was Apache and his mother was Irish. They met while he was recovering from wounds he received in Afghanistan in an Army Hospital She was a nurse there.

Brenda was full blooded Apache from the Mescalero Reservation. She and Buddy met while they were attending classes at University of New Mexico. Their childhood was somewhat different. He was adopted and raised by Trish and Kitty.

Brenda was raised by her Grandmother after her Father left and went to California. He left her and her mother behind. It was never a good marriage. When she was sixteen her mother developed ovarian cancer and died before Brenda was seventeen. It was her Grandmother on her mother side that she lived with.

When she and Buddy got married Trish saw that Brenda had a large college debt when she graduated and so she paid it off for her as a wedding present.

Trish is well known for her generosity when it comes to her kids. The inheritance that her Father left her continued to grow after she went to New Mexico and it was now worth more than it started out thanks to the Financial Adviser that worked with her Fathers former law firm.

She always had them do chores around their home so that they learned responsibility and made their education fun so they all had learned fast.

All but the youngest had gone on to higher education on her dime. Their time will come. Not having to worry about the costs allowed them to be able to concentrate on the books.

Robb was the only one who did not go on to College. He had inherited his Fathers cattle ranch in Texas. He shares ownership with Tex Duncan who was his dad's best friend since they were boys.

✳ ✳ ✳

Penny and Tina were approached by Lois Lawrence to go to a Dog show in San Francisco. Tina told Patty about what happened in Denver and said,

"I think you should go with her this time it's a lot of fun at the show to see all the beautiful Dogs and all the Pageantry. And best of all is Lois is really good in bed."

Patty snickered at this and told Tina,

"Well when you got back I could tell that you had a good time there and it was not from grooming Sparky."

Tina replied,

"You would not believe the woman is sixty years old. She has a body like a much younger Lady. Her tits are not all saggy like most old women's are, they are still a bit perky, like yours."

Patty smiled at Tina and said,

"It sounds like I am going to like going to San Francisco next weekend. Meanwhile give me a good wet kiss."

✳ ✳ ✳

Back at the Ranch Robb and Krissy were making plans for their wedding. They decided to have the service there at the ranch and have it on horseback like Lucy had envisioned. Tex said,

"Robb, your dad would be so proud of you right now. You have a beautiful bride to be and she will be an asset here at the Ranch. She is as good a horsewoman as they come. And you have learned a lot about managing the place. With the regular duties of running a cattle operation and with the Dude ranch you have a lot on your plate. You are handling it as well as I would expect you to. Since your dad is gone I guess that I will just have to be the one to be proud of you.

Robb blushed a bit and replies,

"Well, thanks Tex. I appreciate your confidence in me. I still have a lot to learn and you are the man that I will learn it from. We are more than Partners, we're friends." He went over to Tex and gave him a hug. There was a tear in his and Tex's eyes.

Trish and Kitty and the kids, Penny and Adam went to the Ranch the week of the wedding and Kitty helped Krissy with her wedding dress. It was a simple cream colored flared skirt that would be appropriate for sitting on a horse. She got a pair of white riding boots and a cream Cowgirl hat that Trish had attached a vale to the front and side. Krissy looked like she was as happy as she could be. She was a long way from home and had asked some of her friends from back in Virginia and from work in DC to come to the wedding.

Her boss, the General, that she worked for back there sent a huge bouquet of white lily's and roses that looked like the winner of the Kentucky Derby would have on that horse.

The Ranch hands all worked to get the horse barn spotless and gave a fresh coat of white paint around the outside of the barn doors so it looked like a picture frame when you looked straight in.

Robb was wearing a light brown shirt and trousers with a gray vest. He had a new pair of black boots and a light gray Cowboy hat.

On the day of their wedding they mounted a matched pair of Buckskin horses. She and her Bridesmaids, Katelyn, Penny, Patty and Tina along with Trish and Kitty were all on horseback on the back of the barn. While Robb and his best man, Tex and Harold lined up in front of the barn.

When Adam started to play the wedding march on his guitar

the entourage came around the barn and lined up with Krissy and Robb beside each other. The Minister that spoke at Robb Sr.s funeral presided over the wedding.

After the formal wedding ceremony was over and Robb leaned over and raised Krissy's vale and they kissed. Then they all went for a ride over the pasture before coming back to the house where the Caterer and Harold had set out a feast that was the best ever served on that Ranch.

Tex had a country band come out from Huston and they setup for the music that afternoon and into the evening. Everyone had a good time dancing and eating from the wonderful food that was set before them.

When all the celebrating was over and the party was winding down Robb and Krissy took leave of everybody and said that they were going to bed to the delight of the guests who laughed and thru Bird seed at them as they went in the house.

Robb had planned to do a short Honey Moon trip to Virginia so that Krissy could see some of her relatives. Aunts and uncles and Cousins who were not able to attend the wedding in Texas.

They would start out near DC and then head west to the Skyline Drive and follow the top of the Blue Ridge Mountains all the way to Tennessee. There they spent a Day at Dollywood park and enjoyed some Blue grass and country music.

From there they went to Nashville and on to Memphis. After a week on the road they arrived back at the "Acken Back Acres" Ranch where their life together would begin.

Patty packed a small suitcase for the trip to San Francisco with Lois. Tina drove her to meet Lois and Sparky at the Albuquerque Airport.

The flight was not long about three hours when they landed at the San Francisco International Airport. Lois hailed a Cab and they headed to their Hotel. It was an older building with an Art Deco style exterior.

They were holding the Dog Show at the Convention Center a block from their Hotel.Patty and Lois went in the Lobby and went to the desk to get the room card.

The got on the elevator and went to the fifth floor where their room was located. It had a view of the Golden Gate Bridge and the Bay.

Lois said,

"We can get cleaned up and go down to the Restaurant. They have an excellent menu to choose from and I'm sure you will find something that will please your pallet."Patty replied,

"I hope so. They don't feed you much on these short flights. I'm hungry.And I'm sure Sparky is ready for his supper too."

After they ate they walked down to the Center where the show was being held the next day. It was a very nice facility and they were excited to be able to get to this show.

Sparky missed it last year because Lois had the covid 19 and was laid up for three weeks. Lost her smell and taste. Lost 10 pounds. Fortunately she did not have to get on a ventilator like so many did. She feels great now and is happy to get her dog back on the circuit

They walked back to the hotel and went back to their room. Lois made the first move with Patty. She said,

"Tina was a real sweet girl. I can see why you two have hooked up. We got along great when we went to Denver. She has such a cute body when she is naked. Yes, we played some games while we were there. Are you ready to have some fun and play some games too?" Patty smiled at Lois and replied,

"She told me that you have a nice body too, for a, well older woman." Lois said,

"Would you like to see my nice body, I want to see yours dear." Patty walked over to Lois and put her arms around her and kissed her on her mouth.

Lois responded by putting her arms around Patty and pushing her tongue into Patty's waiting mouth. She rolled her tongue with Lois's and they started to remove each other's clothes. It only took them a little over a minute before they were down to their panties. Lois ran her tongue down Patty's neck and in her ears.

She continued to work her way down to her tits where she licked Patty's nipples and sucked on them on both sides. She told Patty to roll over on her belly and get on her knees. Patty did as instructed and Lois produced a strap on harness and an eight inch dildo attached to it.

She got behind Patty and licked her from anus to clit and back again before she slid the dildo into Patty's pussy hole. She held her hips as she stroked it in and out.

She was able to get Patty to a nice series of orgasms before she removed the harness and had her lay on her back and spread her legs apart. Patty did and Lois slid in between her legs with one leg over Patty's so that their clits lined up and she pressed up against Patty and bumped and rubbed their clits together. This was a new sensation to Patty. She can't wait to do it with Tina. They rubbed their pussies together until Lois was the first to get an orgasm that way.

She told Patty to mount her sixty nine style. Patty took the top position and put her hands on Lois's ass cheeks and rubbed them as she licked Lois's girl parts. She tickled her clit with her tongue and then sucked on Lois's labia and licked her open vagina. Lois raised up so that Patty could get to lick her anus. This always sent her over the top. And it did again. Patty was enjoying her experience with

Lois and had another orgasm when Lois massaged her G spot while sucking her clit.

The next morning they had their breakfast and took Sparky to the show. Right before he was to be walking around for the judges to observe him Patty gave his coat a final brushing.

He was one beautiful Dog and he knew it. After the shows he gets to screw the prettiest female water dogs in the country.

At the end of the show Lois was disappointed that Sparky did not win best in show like he has so many times. This time the winner was a Golden Retriever that had placed third in the Denver show. How did he get that much better in the eyes of the Judges? Lois was not a happy camper. She knew the owner of the dog and she went up and congratulated him on his win. He responded by saying,

"Well ole Sparky has had a good run. Now he may as well put out for stud. He has some good years in him yet. My Duke is coming into his prime and I am going to milk it for all its worth. The trophies are nice, but it's the bragging rights that are what is important to me. Now I can say two things. One, I won the San Francisco show and two, Duke beat ole Sparky." Then he turned and laughed at Lois. She glared at him and said,

"Hey ass hole. See you in San Diego next month."

She and Patty collected Sparky and headed back to the Hotel. They got their things together and headed for the Airport.

✳ ✳ ✳

Katelyn and Ashley had returned to their dorm and they heard a shout from behind them.

"Hey, wait up." It was Freddy Odom.

Ashley stopped and asked,

"What do you want?"

Freddy came up to her and Katlyn and said,

"I just wanted to thank you for introducing me to Katelyn."

Ashley looked at him and said,

"Why do you think I did that? Just so she could lose her cherry? I wanted her to be with a safe guy if she was going to get fucked here on Campus. You are the most gentlemanly of the whole college. Most of these idiots I wouldn't trust to walk my dog. Let alone fuck my roommate. She is a nice kid and I didn't want to see her get hurt."Freddy replied,

"I know what you're sayn 'and I want to be up front with you. Ever since we did it I have felt something for you. I don't know what it is. If its love it hurts. I know that I have been a player the past two years and have had a lot of casual *friends*, you know wat I'm sayin'? But you were different from all the others. They don't matter to me. Please think about what I'm sayin' and give me a chance."

Ashley was shocked at what Freddy said to her. She never would have thought that he would ever want to be anything but a player. Now that he has bared his soul to her what should she say? What should she do? She turned and went in the dorm and closed the door. Freddy stood out front for five minutes before he dropped his head and left and went back to his Fraternity house.

✳ ✳ ✳

Penny wanted to get some professional lessons to help her with her art work. She was doing a good job as it was but different people have said that if she just had that little bit of technique that is missing. She could be fantastic. Everything she draws or paints in a month all get sold. The prices have gone up some. But not like some of the other Artist's that she sees at the shows who are selling theirs for thousands while hers are selling for hundreds.

She asked Trish,

"You said I could go to Art school sometime. How old do you have to be to go?" Trish thought about it for a minute and replied,

"I'm not sure baby but we will find out. Maybe we can find some Artist who will give private lessons."

The next time they took some of Penny's pictures in to Magdalena they asked the store owner if she knew of someone who could help Penny develop her style.

The woman studied on it for a while and then said while pointing her finger and wagging it at the same time,

"You know there is a man who I know who sells his work privately. Not like your local artists who hope you can sell a few in my store. This man sells his for thousands of dollars and the people come to his house to get them. I will give you his phone number and maybe he can help her"

It was a week later when Trish got a call back from the man. His name was Giorgio Mendez and he lived out route 60 near Pie Town at the continental divide in a log cabin he built himself. He lives with his three dogs and his Maine Coon cat. The Cat, Fidel, rules the dogs.

"Hello, is this Trisha Flick?"

"Yes it is."

"This is Giorgio Mendez. You have a daughter who wants to be an Artist?"

"Yes her name is Penny and she has been doing oil paintings of Cats, dogs and scenery since she was about eight years old. She has been selling some of her work in Maggie's store in Magdalena and some up at Taos on the street."

"Yes Ms. Flick, I have seen her work and she is way ahead of her peers. I would be happy to give her lessons here at my home for sixty dollars an hour or I can come to your home and teach her for one hundred an hour. It is roughly ninety miles from me to Magdalena."

Trish replied,

"We are located near the Gallinas Mountains about fifteen miles north of Magdalena."

"I see. Well as you can see I would have a lot of travel to your home. If you would be O K with it I can have her as a live in student and stay with me when school is out."

"That would not be a problem as she is home schooled right here. Let us think about your offer."

"The sixty dollar price will include room and board as long as she likes Mexican food. We eat a lot of Torte's and Enchiladas and corn bread."

Trish said again,

"Let us talk about it and get back to you. Oh, would you like to come visit us some time? "

Giorgio thought for a short moment and replied,

"I would be honored to come visit and see the places that Penny is using as subjects for her work."

"O K, then we will look forward to seeing you on Wednesday if that suits your schedule."

He laughed and responded,

"That is no problem for my schedule. As long as my dogs and cat are fed and have water I am free to travel. Sometimes I bring them with me."

Trish laughed and said

"Bring them along we have a Golden Retriever that likes company." Giorgio laughed and said,

"My first dog was a Goldy, I named her Mandy. She was my constant companion. I was heartbroken when she got cancer and I had to have her put down. The dogs I have now are all rescued dogs from the shelter in Magdalena. Two of them are Jack Russel mixed with who knows what. But they are young and still like puppies. My older dog is Pito, he is a mix of Airedale and maybe German Shepard. "

Trish told Giorgio that his dogs were welcome to come along and visit. So the following Wednesday Giorgio came to visit along with his three dogs. Penny was delighted to see them and to meet Giorgio. He looked at her and said,

"Hello Penny. I have seen some of your paintings and I am looking forward to working with you to polish your style. You have a great natural flair. That is why you are being successful selling some of them."

Trish invited him in the house and they went to Penny's room where she had her easel with her latest work on it.

It was a scene of the pond in the background and Ginger walking up from the dock.

Giorgio looked at it from several different views and finally said,

"I don't know how you learned to paint a dog that its hair looks like it is real. You have captured the shine in her eyes and her tongue hanging out. That is a real touch that you have seen and are able to put it on the canvas. I am not sure I can do a lot to improve on what you are doing. I will set up next to you and show you how I do certain things. You are doing a good job of mixing colors to get a shade that you need for shadows and when you have mastered that you can paint anything."

He stayed for several hours and at the end of the day Kitty had the kitchen table set for supper and insisted he stay and eat with them.

They chatted while they ate. They found out that Giorgio had graduated from Stanford University with a degree in Structural Engineering and had worked for a Company in San Diego that designed and build steel framed buildings and bridges. His Family came to the United States from El Salvador when he was five years old in search of a better life. He studied hard in school and got a scholarship to Stanford.

One day he decide to walk away from his job and start to paint some pictures while set up on a street in San Diego and sold a few.

It was enough for him to leave California and go to New Mexico. He is able to make a living as an Artist.

He married a local girl when he was twenty five and they had a son who died from pneumonia when he was three years old. His wife was heartbroken and she died shortly after their son.

Trish and Kitty told him that if he could work with Penny like he did that day he was welcome to come to teach Penny on the Wednesdays for the next month. Trish told him that she would pay his price for four hours a trip. He agreed with that and took his leave and headed back to his home in the mountain.

*** *** ***

Krissy drew a picture of the March Hare from Alice in Wonderland and had him standing up and holding a pocket watch. She put a caption on the drawing that read

"I'M LATE.I'M LATE."

That night she put the picture on Rob's pillow before he got to bed. He got out of the shower and dried off before he walked over to the bed. He saw the drawing and asked,

"What's this Krissy?"

She smiled at him and said,

"What do you think it means?"

Rob scratched his head and just looked at it for a minute and the biggest grin that he ever made lit up his face like the fourth of July.

He said,

"Does this mean what I'm thinking it means? Are we going to have a baby?"

Krissy put her arms around him and kissed him. Then she said,

"I'm two months along and I think we will have our little bundle of joy in September."

Robb rolled her into the bed and gave her a long and tender kiss. She responded by spreading her legs and pulling his body up tight to hers. They made love until after midnight. She fell asleep in his arms.

The next morning he called Kitty and asked her,

"Can you guess who is going to be a Granny in September?"

She let out a holler that got everyone running to her. Penny and Adam were the first to get to her with Trish and ginger close behind. Kitty announced to them,

"Krissy and Robb are going to have a baby in September. Isn't that great?"

With Brenda and Buddy in Kansas and Robb and Krissy in Texas Trish thought,

'Too bad they are both so far away. It's been a long time since we had any little ones around here. I wish Tex had made me pregnant that night. It was a good chance. My cycle was at the best place. We did it enough times that night. Tex is not an old man yet. I sure would like to get laid again. I love Kitty. But I still have desires. She's had two kids. Why can't I have at least one of my own?'

Patty and Tina were getting ready to go to Phoenix with Lois for another show. . Lois was going to meet them at the airport.

The flight was just about an hour and they did manage to get a bag of peanuts on the plane. When they arrived they went to pick up Sparky from the baggage area where they always put the animals for the flights.

He was happy to see Lois and the girls and his tail was in full wag mode. They made their way to the Taxi stand and got a cab to take them to the Hotel downtown.

It was three o'clock when they got there and Lois suggested they go up to their room and get comfortable before they went for supper in the Hotel Restaurant.

They entered the room and Patty and Tina fell onto one of the King Size beds and sprawled out with their arms up and their legs spread out.

Lois remarked,

"Well you two look relaxed after the flight. What would you like to do before supper?"

Patty said,

"You are welcome to come and relax with us. It's a big bed and we are little girls far from home and want to experience all that we can on this big bed." Lois smiled and replied,

"You want to start early? I am O K with that. Just let me get out of this business suit. I always dress for the flights. People respect you more when they see you dressed up. While I do that why don't you two show me what you do for fun with each other? Don't be bashful."

Tina looked at Lois and said,

"I can't wait to see you out of those clothes. You have an amazing bod. I know some younger gals who would like to have a rack like yours."

Lois smiled at her and told her that she could just wait for a minute and she could see her in her entirety.

They all proceeded to remove their cloths. Patty was the first to be down to her skin. Lois looked at her with hungry eyes and wanted to just get started licking Patty's pussy. She remembered the times they had at the San Francisco show. Even though Sparky only took second, she came home with a new appreciation of Patty. While at the show they got to investigate each other's most intimate parts. Her trip to Denver with Tina was just as interesting. They are so similar in body that if you didn't see their faces you would have a hard time telling them apart. She liked that but it would be nice if one was just bit different.

"You know what girls? Lay down on the end of the bed so that your legs hang over so I can lift them up to admire your pretty pink pussies. You can kiss while I am busy giving you both a thrill."

They did as Lois instructed and looked at each other and smiled. They held hands and kissed as Lois first raised Tina's legs up to her chest so that she had total access to her crotch. Lois went down on her and licked Tina's crack from her clit to her anus. She licked all parts in between. She kept it up and hoped that she could give Tina a good wet orgasm. She was not disappointed. After about ten minutes her vagina leaked her girl juice in copious amounts. Lois licked up every drop and then went and kissed them both sharing Tina's gift.

She had Patty take the same position and she ate her pussy until she too had a wet orgasm. She found not much difference between the two girls. They both tasted good to her.

Lois told Patty to go down on her and lick her the same way she did her.

She wanted Tina to sit on her face at the same time as she liked the way her parts felt on her. With the two of them servicing Lois she had a great orgasm herself. She knew that Patty was getting some of the juice that she was exuding from her mature lady parts. It felt good.

Tina had another climax while she had her pussy covering Lois's mouth. Patty and Tina swapped sides and Tina went down on Lois and with two fingers in her to tickle her G spot while she licked and sucked on her clit she knew that Lois would have another orgasm. She was right. The next thing they knew it was time to go for supper. It was a very satisfying afternoon and Lois hoped they would have a good meal and return to the room for some evening fun.

The next day they ran into the man with the Golden at San Francisco. He sneered at Sparky and then gave Lois the one finger salute. She returned it to him.

He said,

"I'll tell you what if your dog beats mine I will eat your pussy in the lobby of the Hotel. If mine beats yours out, I want you to suck my cock in the same lobby."

Lois squinted her eyes and replied,

"My panties are wet already Mother fucker. I have two of the best Groomers along to make Sparky shine."

He replied,

"Well my cock is growing already."

Tina interjected,

"Do you two always trash mouth each other at these shows?"

The man looked at her and said,

"This is not just idle trash talk. We are serious. We have done this for the past several years. She has gotten to like my cum, right Lois?"

She replied,

"O K, after the show we will go back to the room and we can settle the bet, work for you? Or don't you want to have two other girls watching you kiss my ass?"

He looked at Tina and Penny and he countered,

"If Sparky beats out my dog I'll even lick your groomer's pussys. Now how's that for a bet?"

Patty and Tina looked at each other and said,

"What have we gotten ourselves into here?"

The next day Sparky won Best in Show again and the man was good to his word when he met the women at their room to pay off his bet.

Patty didn't mind his five o'clock shadow when it scratched the inside of her legs. Lois and Tina stood and watched and clapped when Patty finished with a real wet climax. She got off the man's wet face and told him,

"Now if you would like a good blow job before you leave I think Tina would like to see just what kind of rascal you're hiding in those pants."

Tina's mouth dropped when Patty volunteered her services when she really didn't have too. She decided to be a good sport about it and got on her knees in front of him. He dropped his pants and displayed a nice eight inch un-clipped boner. Tina looked at it and put her hand on it and slid the skin up and down. It slipped over the head when she did this and then slid back to display his wet pink glans. She licked it along the length and then put the tip in her mouth. He pushed it into her cheek and placed his hands on each side of her head just to keep her focused straight ahead. She sucked it and stroked it for nearly a half hour before he finally came in her mouth. She stood up and planted a kiss on him and returned his gift.

All three of the women clapped their hands and he raised his hands in victory.

When they all were headed for the Airport, Lois said good bye to the man and asked if he was going go to the show in Dallas. He told her,

"I don't know. You are a real formidable adversary. And if you have these top of the line Groomers along how can I win?" He smiled and reached over to give Lois a kiss before he left for his plane.

✳ ✳ ✳

Back in the State Prison Mike Brown was doing his time for poaching and for the disgusting crime of having sex with a corpse. He was just counting the days until he would be released from this place where he was raped by Black guys and Mexicans.

He was too small to defend himself and almost from the first day he was in here someone was after a piece of his ass. Literally, some of these degenerates carried some kind of lube with them in case they could catch him when he was in a safe place where the guards couldn't see what they were doing.Either they would fuck him in the ass or make him suck them off. They told him that if he EVER bit one of them they would cut his throat.

He tried to make friends with some Skin heads who he thought would protect him from the Blacks and Mexicans who were raping him on a regular basis.

Instead he found himself being raped by the skin heads. There was just no one he could trust until a new prisoner showed up. It was a guy who Mike couldn't believe could have such big muscels. He was some kind of body builder who was convicted of attempted murder because he lifted his girlfriend off the ground while strangling her.

She barely survived to testify in Court. He got a sentence of three to ten years for it.His name was Sam Rodgers. He was from the Santa Fe area and had a long criminal rap sheet. From the time he was fourteen he was in trouble for beating some other kid up. He was expelled from school when he was sixteen.

He became Mike's cell mate and they came to an agreement. Mike would give Sam blow jobs for Sam protecting him from being raped by others.

They were both within a month of being released and Mike had gotten to be real antsy about getting out so he could go after the bitch who shot him in the leg. He wanted Sam to help him to get his revenge.

CHAPTER FIVE

Love & Vengeance

Mike Brown counted the days until he would be released from prison. His cell mate Sam Rodgers was going to be released next week. Mike was not getting out until the end on the month. There was only five days different but it felt like a year as he waited for their release dates.

Sam had asked his sister to get him a car that he could leave prison like a normal person. Not ride away in a fucking Gray Hound. He would come back to get Mike who had been not only his cell mat, but his lover as well.

Sam provided protection for Mike from the other prisoners who were raping him before Sam arrived. Now he was the only one who was fucking Mike or getting a blow job from him. Sam liked the arraignment.

It was less than a week until Mike would be getting out so Sam hung around the area until he walked out the door. Sam gave Mike a hug and a kiss before they got in his sisters blue Ford sedan.

They headed for Santa Fe where Sam was from. There they could plan how they would murder Trish for shooting Mike in the leg. They were both felons so they were prohibited from getting a gun.

That would be too easy to suit him. He wanted suffering.

***

Kitty and Trish have to accept that their kids are becoming adults and are starting their own futures.

Evan is the first to leave the nest. He decides to join the Army. His biological father was a Soldier. He wanted to honor his memory by signing up as well.

His entrance exams showed that he was above intelligence for the average Recruit and offered him a list of possible occupations that he was qualified for. He saw that he could go into Military Intelligence. It included the opportunity to learn different languages to be able to operate in foreign countries in the local tongue. Among those were Chinese, Russian, German and Arabic.

He signed up for a six year enlistment. That was needed to get into these opportunities.

He went thru basic training and at the end of that he was told that he was going to be assigned to the advanced training course and then on to the Intel building to begin his language training.

He enjoyed the chance to read and wright in other languages and to speak it as well. Evan excelled at all levels of the training and was enlisted in the Officer Training corp. This was the ranks that he need to get for the advanced intelligence work that he would be responsible for.

He finished the training and was promoted to Second Lieutenant. Over the next six years he not only learned four languages but was going up the Ranks to become a Major. He was recruited by the CIA and was killed while on a mission to stop some computer hackers.

His ashes were returned to Trish and Kitty for placement in their memorial garden.

✳✳✳

Back home Luke and Lilly decided to get married after they finished their College experience. He was going on to M I T for his Master's degree in Mining Engineering.

Lilly went to nursing school and became a Registered nurse with a specialty in surgery. She landed a job in a Hospital in Huston. This was nice because Luke had a job working for an Oil company that was also based in Huston.

Rob had moved to the Ranch in Texas. He and Tex decided to start a Dude ranch. They had a bunkhouse built and an addition added to the kitchen area. He meets Lucy. She was a homeless girl that came to the ranch for a cooking job. She was the one who showed Rob how much fun they could have in bed.

He kind of got addicted to having sex with Lucy and wondered what it would feel like to fuck a fat girl. He got the chance. Jill had a long term problem with her weight and committed suicide. Lucy was killed by one of the Dude ranch guests.

Rob felt he was responsible for her and Lucy's deaths. He took a break and went to see Trish and Kitty. They helped him get past his depression.

Patty and Tina were doing well with the grooming Spa. They had been going to Dog shows with Lois Lawrence. She has been a long time owner of a Portuguese water dog named 'Sparky', who was a serious contender at most of the shows that she entered him in.

She hired the girls to go to the shows to do his grooming before the competition. She also enjoyed their company in bed.

Lois's late husband was a banker who had amassed a fortune managing banks in New Mexico, Arizona and California. He left Lois with more money than anyone can spend in a lifetime. She liked to spend money on them and Sparky.

Rob's and Krissy were having a good time with their son, Robert Evan Harris, they called him Skippy. He was a happy child and had fun playing around the ranch. The Dude ranch visitor's thought he was the cutest little Cowboy they ever saw. He kept Krissy busy teaching him about the horses, the cattle and the other wildlife that abounded on the Ranch. It was a great place for a little boy to grow up.

Penny was now seventeen and had grown into a beautiful young woman. Her art talent had really blossomed when she started to get some art training from a man named Giorgio. He took her under his wing and showed her some technique's that really made a difference that could be seen in her art work.

Rob was really excited when Krissy told him they were expecting another baby. Little Skippy was now five and he was excited to find out he was going to be a big brother.

Krissy had nursed him for nearly a year and he grew like a weed on her milk. She planned to nurse the new baby as well. Rob liked a little taste himself. Krissy would teasingly admonish him'

"You have to leave some for the baby."

Rod would lick the dripping milk from her nipples and then say,

Babies sure are lucky. They get to suck on their mom's every three hours. I just get the left overs. Still tastes good."

Patty rolled over in bed and put her hand on Tina's pussy while she slept. It felt so nice and warm to her hand. She gently rubbed her clit and knew that she would wake up soon when she felt the touch. Tina smiled and kept her eyes closed while Patty continued to rub her crotch. Her legs splayed open and her labia parted so that her vagina was on display. Patty went down and licked and kissed Tina's legs from her knees to her shaved mound. She ran her finger up and down her crack and felt the wetness growing. She licked her fingers and then put them into Tina's hole. She moved in and out for a minute and then started to work her G spot with her finger tips. While she had her finger in her Patty licked her clit. Tina finally aroused from her sleep and placed her hands on Patty's head. She ran her fingers thru the long dark hair that glistened when the moon light hit it. She was fully aroused now and wanted Patty to get her to her orgasm. It was not long before she had the first. She pushed Patty away from her so that she could do the same for her. Patty rolled onto her back and allowed Tina to take control. After they each had at least one good finish they would go into sixty nine position and continue to pleasure one another.

Sam and Mike went to Sam's place in Santa Fe and Mike went about planning how they would do their dirty deed and kill Trish. Since they did not have a gun they thought about kidnaping her and torturing her for a while. Maybe even fucking her double penetration. Sam in her cunt and Mike in her ass at the same time. It made Mike Horney just talking about it. He fantasized him on the bottom with his cock in her pussy and fucking away while Sam lubed up her ass hole before he pushed his cock in her as far as he could go. They could both feel their balls slapping against each other. While they were doing this Mike said,

"Now would be a good time to strangle her or put a plastic bag over her head and smother her that way. What do you think Sam, huh? Is that a good way to do It.?"

Sam replied,

"You have a fucked up mind. You know it? You can have her ass I want her wet cunt."

They decide to plan a kidnapping.

***

Buddy and Brenda came to visit Trish and Kitty for a long weekend. Friday until Monday. They flew into the Albuquerque airport from Kansas City. The flight only took about two and a half hours. It take longer to get to Trish and Kitty place by car then for the flight. Their son was now nearly six years old and he was always excited to go to his Grandmother's house. He could swim in the pond and just play outside as he wished. His name is Jessy Lee Flick, they call him Jess.

***

Penny and Giorgio were up on the hill behind the house on a beautiful clear sky day. He wanted to watch how she was doing some of the things that he showed her.

She had been taking lessons from him for the past five years and she was making progress that he couldn't believe. Her work looked like some of the work put out by Artist's who had been at it for twenty years.

He put his arms around her and gave her a squeeze. He said,

"I have to say Penny that you have matured quite nicely these past years. You were a little twelve year old girl when we met. Now you are a full grown woman. I have always wanted to hold you in my arms like this and feel your body close to mine. If you don't want me to do this let me know."

Penny leaned back against him and put her hands on his as he held her. She knew that what she was thinking was wrong and she shouldn't want him to make love to her. But she really did want to experience this if it was going to happen. Giorgio was a man of fifty and had enough experience with women in his lifetime that he knew how to seduce and make love. She thought more about it and decided she would let him de-flower her this day. She turned around and faced him and said,

"Giorgio, I want you to make me a woman. I want to feel your naked body against me. We have known each other for these five years and I have felt something from that first day. Please let me know if this is too much to ask of you. I think you feel the same, don't you?"

Giorgio looked down at her sweet face and bent down and kissed her.

Penny responded by parting her lips and pushing her tongue against his lips and then into his warm mouth. He held her gently in his arms and pushed her blouse up over her head and unsnapped her bra. She took his shirt off and unbuckled her belt on her pants. She smiled and asked,

"Am I doing this right? I want to make it special as I have never done it before but I want to do it with you."

Giorgio smiled at her and unbuttoned her pants and zipped the fly down. She slipped her pants down her legs to expose her crotch thru her pastel panties. He dropped his pants and removed his shoes.

There was a picnic table at the place where they came to paint. He laid her down on the table and proceeded to run his fingers up her bare legs. She shuddered and then grinned at him.

Penny said,

"That feels so good."

Giorgio asked,

"Can I take your panties off so I can see your pretty pussy?"

Penny lifted her hips and allowed him to slip them off. After he did he said,

"Now I will show you how I like to make love. First I will kiss your sweet lips down there and lick your little love bump to make you feel ecstatic. I will hold your butt in my palms while I do this and give them a gentle squeeze.

Penny was panting and could hardly wait for him to begin teaching her the ways of love. He did as he said he was going to do and he cupped her ass cheeks in his hands and put his mouth between her legs. She felt his warm breath on her girl parts and it made her quiver with expectation. Then she felt his tongue on her crack and felt it push into her hole. He lifted up and licked her clit. He continued to give her the bet feelings of her life. He moved his under pants down his legs and pulled her up to the edge of the table. Then he gave her another good wet lick and then he pressed his cock slowly into her. He told her,

"Try to relax. It won't hurt if you relax."

She tried to relax and enjoy this first time. She knew that it was not going to be the last time that she gets him to make love to her on this hillside.

Giorgio had a lot of life experiences to know how to prolong his climax. He would pull out and go down and lick her clit and lick up some of her girl juices. He would go back inside her and pump some more. He did this about ten times and then he pulled out and shot his load onto her belly. She watched in amazement at how much came out of him. She reached down and touched it between her thumb and fingers. She felt its stickiness and then wondered what it may taste like. Penny put her fingers in her mouth and licked his seed from them. She looked at him and smiled and asked him,

"So now are we done for today or is there something else we can do?"

Giorgio looked at her and asked,

"Did you like the taste of me? I liked the taste of you and I want more."

Penny stood up by the table and got on her knees. She put her hand on his cock and stroked it a bit then she put the wet tip in her mouth. She licked his semen from the length of it and then put it in and sucked on it.

Giorgio leaned his head back and marveled at how well she did it. For a young girl who led a sheltered life she could really make him a happy man. He gave her a small amount of his juice. He went down on her again and licked and sucked until she gave him a wet face. He licked up all of her juice from her legs and down her crack.

They finally got dressed and headed back to the house. He would be back next Wednesday.

✳✳✳

At the College dorm Katelyn and her roommate Ashley were getting ready for bed and before they turned the light out Ash gave Katelyn a kiss on the lips and said,

"Good night. I will be thinking of you when I fall asleep." Katelyn smiled and then wondered what she meant by that. *'She would be thinking of me', Where is this going?"*

She closed her eyes and tried to sleep. But that kiss still lingered on her lips. Ash was a really pretty girl and she didn't mind getting kissed by her. She wondered if she should return it. She tossed and turned until she finally got out of bed and went over to Ashley's. She bent down and touched her cheek. Ash woke up and looked at Katelyn. She told Ash,

"I think this belongs to you."

And kissed her back on the mouth and they opened their mouths to let their tongues wonder and enjoy each other.

Ashley moved over in the bed and let Katelyn lie down beside her. They laid on their sides and held each other in their arms. They both found it arousing and let their fingers wander about their bodies. Ash found Katelyn's ass first and she squeezed it and rubbed it with both hands. She pulled her up against her and they kissed again.

Now Katelyn got adventurous and felt down between them and found Ash's pubic mound. It was as smooth as a baby's behind as she shaved it several times a week. Ash got on her knees and got in front of Katelyn. She said in a low voice,

"Will you do mine? And then I will do yours?"

Katelyn had never done anything with a girl before so she needed a little bit of instruction first. Ashley pushed herself up against Katelyn and told her,

"Lick my clit first and then you can get go down on me later. No hurry is there?" Katelyn did as she was told and held Ash's ass checks and pushed her face into her crotch. The smooth pubes felt good on her cheeks as she wiggled her tongue in to lick Ash's clit. It felt good to be able to pleasure her knowing that she was going to have it done to her. She thought,

'I guess that we are more than just roommates now'.

Sam looked at Mike and thought to himself,

'This motherfucker really wants to kidnap and murder this woman. He is really a nut case. I don't really want to go back to prison for helping him. I think I will just fuck him in the ass one more time before I just really disappear.'

Mike rattled on about how,

'We can just show up at night and break in while the women were sleeping and have our way with them. You're stronger than they are and we can tie their legs with zip ties and then use duct tape to tie their hands. They wouldn't be able to move and me and you can just take our time raping and then murdering both of them. That sound like a plan Buddy? Huh?"

Sam just nodded his head yes and then he walked over to Mike and told him,

"Before we do anything, **'Buddy'**, I want you to bend over and let me have your skinny ass again. I'm getting horney just thinking about those two cunts we're going fuck."

Mike was afraid of Sam and did whatever he wanted him to do. He dropped his pants and pulled his underpants down to his knees.

Sam always carried a tube of lube with him so he can be ready to fuck Mike whenever he wanted. Mike got down on his hands and knees. He bit his lip when he knew it was coming. Sam kneeled down behind him and rubbed some lube on Mikes butt hole. Then he moved up to him and with his hands on Mikes hips he inserted his hard cock in about four inches the first shove. He pulled out part way and shoved again. This time he managed to get his full ten inches all the way in. He reached around and found Mikes cock. It was soft. Sam could feel it getting harder as he moved in and out. At last it was hard enough for Mike to stroke himself until Sam fired his load in Mikes ass, Mike would ejaculate at the same time. They learned how to do this while in prison.

Sam backed out of Mike and got up. He told Mike,

"How was that you crazy motherfucker? I hope you liked it because that's the last time for you crazy shit. Did you really think I was going to go with you on this crazy kidnap fantasy you have?"

He turned around as he pulled his pants up and while his back was turned Mike took a long hunting knife with serrated blades and thrusted it into Sam's back right where the kidneys are located and gave it a twist. A gusher of blood poured from the wound and Sam faced Mike and went to punch him only to find Mike ready to give another thrust into Sam's' chest severing his aorta.

Sam had his blood coming from both wounds and succumbed in a matter of minutes.

Mike had killed enough wild animals that he knew the right places to inflict a fatal wound that would bleed out quickly.

As Sam lay dying on the floor Mike stood over him and sprayed him with his urine. He told Sam,

"You know what? I was afraid of you and was scared shittless when you fucked me, but I hoped you would help me. Instead you turned on me and after you fucked me one last time you say you are leaving me. How did that work out you asshole." Mike saw Sam's eyes roll back and his mouth opened as he struggle against the pain and finally died.

***

Trish had bought Penny a car for her seventeenth birthday. Now she could take her paintings into town to the store where they were sold herself.

She was proud of how her work improved with the guidance that Giorgio had given her the past several years. He had become a regular guest at their home and they fixed up a bedroom for him so he could stay the nights when his lessons ran long. It was over a hundred miles to his house in the far mountains.

Penny liked it when he stayed over. She hoped that he would come and share her bed. Most of the time he would visit Kitty and Trish. Pleasuring one and then the other on his next trip. They were both happy to have a man that they could share, even if it was just for fun. Sometimes they would pleasure each other and let him watch. When he did he would sit in a chair and masturbate.

On this trip when he went back to his bedroom he was surprised to find a naked Penny in his bed. He walked over and laid down beside her. She reached her arms around him and pulled him on top. He smiled and pushed his bathrobe aside and was naked with her. It was this trip that he taught her how to ride a man Cowgirl style and reverse Cowgirl. They both liked it Doggy style. Then they tried it standing with Penny bent over the back of a chair. When they got to this position Giorgio told her,

"Some time women like to do it anal. With the man's cock in her backside hole. "

Penny studied on that for a bit and then she asked,

"Can we try that sometime? It sounds like it would feel different. Does it?"

Giorgio replied,

"It can give a woman a faster orgasm than in the vagina. To do it the woman has to understand that she must relax her backside muscles and push back while the man is pushing in. It goes better that way. We can try it sometime if you want to."

She said,

"Maybe the next time you are here. I'm going back to bed now." She gave him a kiss before she left. *He smiled and thought,*

'I must be the luckiest man alive to have found this family. Unlimited sex for the taking.'

Their oral skills improved with time and they both learned what the other liked to do the best.

Giorgio found that most women like to have their anus's licked or at least around the area so the tip of their partners tongue just touches them. This is best after a bath. Of course it works both ways for a man.

Tex told Robb that he was going into Huston to pick up some mineral blocks that they needed. They put the blocks out where the cattle can lick them to get a mineral supplement to stay healthy. It is mostly salt with other trace minerals.

While he was there he planned to stop by his Lawyer's office and see if his secretary was free for lunch.

They had met when she came along with her Boss to finalize the Ranch Partnership between Tex and Robb. Tex had been fantasying about what he would do if he ever got the chance. She was looking good when she was at the ranch and Tex wondered if she would accept an invitation to come and visit. She could play Cow girl for a week for free if she wanted.

He went onto the Lawyer's office and was surprised to find a new girl at the front desk. Her name is Ellen Bare. She was another knockout like the former secretary was. Tex stepped up and introduced himself.

"Howdy, my name is Tex Duncan. I am a client of your boss. I just wanted to drop by and chat with him a bit. I haven't seen him for a while."

She replied,

"I am so sorry. He is not here at this time. He took off for a couple days to go deep sea fishing with a friend. He will be back on Monday."

Tex said,

"That's too bad I was hoping to take him out for lunch. Would you care to join me instead?"

Ellen smiled at Tex and replied,

"Let me get my jacket and we can go. I will lock up for now. Where do you want to go?"

Tex came back with,

"Do you like Chinese? We can go to Bennie Wong's place down the street."

Ellen smiled and said,

"That's one of my favorite places to eat. We go there at least one or two times a week. There or the Panda Palace. Both have great Buffets."

They went out and got in his pickup and went to the restaurant. On the way she asked,

"It looks like you are a Rancher. Are you?"

Tex told her,

"Yes, we have a large Dude ranch operation about 30 miles or so west of here. You should come out sometime and ride one of our horses. You can have a good time out there on the trails."

Her eyes lit up and she bubbled,

"WOW that would be a lot of fun. I haven't ridden since I was a teenager. I had an Uncle in Oklahoma that had some horses that I rode when I went to visit him and my Aunt. Can I come out this weekend?"

Tex grinned at her and replied,

"This weekend will be good. We have a nice Bunkhouse and the food is great. I'll write down the directions to the place for you."

They went to the Panda Palace and had a buffet and talked for an hour. Ellen said,

"Well it's been fun talking but I better get back to work for now. I look forward to my visit."

Tex took her back to her office and walked her to the door. She turned and gave him a kiss on the cheek.

On the trip back to the ranch Tex sang as he drove along. He just knew he was going to get laid this weekend.

✳✳✳

Mike used his hunting knife to sever Sam's arms and legs from his torso and then disemboweled him to remove some of the weight from the chest and abdominal cavity. He cut the knees loose from the calves. Then he cut off the head. He put each of the pieces in separate plastic bags along with the viscera. He loaded the bags in the back of Sam's car and drove out into the hills. He found an overlook that was at the top of a high cliff. He pulled over and parked. He checked to be sure no one was in sight. Then he took some of the bags out and dumped them over the cliff. He drove on until he found another good place to discard Sam's remains. He figured the scavengers would find the bags when they started to rot.

He went back to the house and cleaned up all the blood and random pieces of meat from the sawing that he did on some joints that the knife wouldn't cut. When he finished he called Sam's sister and asked her,

"Did you see Sam? He got mad at me and took off. I don't know where he went. Do you have any idea where he might have gone?"

She answered,

"Why no. I thought you two were real tight and took care of each other. When he got out of Prison I washed my hands of him. I don't give a rat's ass what he does or where he goes."

Mike answered,

"Thanks. I'll tell him you said that if I see him."

He hung up the phone and smiled. No one was going to be looking for Sam.

***

Giorgio was having a good time with Penny and the women of the house. They have accepted him as a house guest with benefits. Unaware that he was having sex with Penny, Trish was getting her own satisfaction when he was there. She looked forward to his visits to help Penny with her art work.

After they would retire to their bedrooms at night Trish and Kitty would allow Giorgio to come into their room and pleasure Trish while Kitty watched. Somehow it fascinated her to see her getting straight intercourse and even anal which Trish enjoyed. Kitty had only done it once with Tex and she didn't really care for it. Trish on the other hand had been doing it ever since she was in her early twenty's. She learned how to do it from a teenage friend who lived nearby named Jeff. When his cousin Vicky invited Trish to come and go swimming. They ended the day going up to his bedroom where he demonstrated on his cousin first how he did anal. She was up for it and Trish really enjoyed doing it. She had shown Tex how to do it in the shower with soap bubbles for lube. While Giorgio was in Trish she looked at Kitty and asked.

"Are you sure you don't want to participate with us. We would love to have you join in." Kitty smiled at Trish and said,

"Maybe, I like to see you two going at it and I think about how we had some wild times with the lady's from Connecticut on the way out here that time. It was neat how we played swap partners and got to have fun with each other. Now that I am thinking about it I am starting to feel "loveable". "

Trish said,

"Well why don't you lay down here and let Giorgio lick you while he is fucking me. Then when he is done with me we can go sixty nine. He likes to watch us do that. Maybe if we give him a little rest he can even get in you while I watch. It's not often we have a man to service our needs. So come on lets have some fun."

* * *

Patty was working on a Standard Poodle at her shop when she got a certified letter from a Lawyer's office. She didn't know why she would be getting this.

She opened and read with disbelief. Lois had a heart attack and passed away. Before she did she had made a will leaving the bulk of her estate to Patty and Tina. With the rest going to the Animal Rescue in Albuquerque.

Penny was stunned. She called out for Tina to come to her.

Tina asked,

"What is it Babe?"

"Lois died from a heart attack and left us some money or something. We need to call this Law office to find out what's up."

They made the call and were told to come to the office the next day to review what was in the will.

When they arrived they were escorted to a small conference room on the second floor. There they met with several other lawyers and Clerks who had a lot of paper work to review.

Dan Bolton, the Attorney who represented Mrs. Lawrence spoke first,

"Thank you for coming in this morning. I want to extend our condolences for your loss. I understand that she had you go with her to a number of dog shows over the past year. She really developed a love for you two and to show her appreciation she has left you with an inheritance of two and a half million dollars and her home and cars. She also asked that you continue to keep Sparky healthy and allow him to keep going to the shows. He so enjoyed going."

✳ ✳ ✳

Penny was shocked. Tina's mouth dropped open and she turned a bit lighter. When they both came around they asked the Lawyers,

"So how do we go about getting this money and everything else?"

He replied,

"Here are the Bank checking accounts and savings pass books to her other accounts. They have been transferred to your names jointly. The keys to the cars and the house are in this envelope. I hope you know how much you meant to Lois. She was a very generous woman and had many friends on the rescue boards here in the County. You have made a lot of friends as well from your grooming business. We can only wish you a safe and comfortable future."

With that he handed them the envelope with the keys and the folder with all the banking information.

Patty could hardly wait to call Trish and Kitty to tell them what happened.

* * *

Tex waited for Ellen to arrive that Friday afternoon.

He watched as she drove up the winding lane and parked by the Bunkhouse. She got out as Tex walked over to greet her. She looked great in a pair of tight blue jeans and a yellow halter top. She was sporting a pink Cow girl hat and neckerchief.

"Howdy again Ms. Ellen. Have a good trip out here?"

She smiled at tex and replied,

"I sure did Mr. Tex. I am sure lookin' forward to sittin' my cute ass on top of one of your darlin' horses. But first, where should I put my things?"

Tex motioned her towards the Bunkhouse and said,

"Right thru that door and then to your left to the door marked #3 on the right. It is a private room to yourself right next to the bathroom. When you get settled in come on over to the Chuck Wagon and I will get you checked in. Did you have lunch yet? I'm sure we can 'rassel you up something fit to eat. Harold is the cook right now and he has a way with peanut butter and jelly."

Ellen laughed and said,

"I am so hungry I could eat a Rattlesnake if he held still a minute. But a PB & J would be good with chocolate milk."

Tex chuckled at that and said,

"We do have a few rattlers here now and then so be careful, I don't want you to be eaten' 'em all up."

He couldn't stop looking at her figure. She had an ass that he would just like to get his teeth into and he was looking forward to spending some quality time with her in the evening.

Rob's wife Krissy was coming back up to the house when she spied Ellen coming out of the Bunkhouse and starting up the walk to the Chuck Wagon. She hollered to her.

"Hey girl! How are you? Mind if I walk with you?"

Ellen looked at Krissy and said,

"Not at all. My name is Ellen, I work for Tex's Lawyer in Huston and he invited me to come out for the weekend. I just got here a few minutes ago. He said to go up to the Chuck Wagon for lunch. Want to join me?"

Krissy caught up with her and they walked together to the building where they went inside for lunch.

Harold welcomes them and asked,

"Would you like some chicken salad or ham and cheese for sandwiches?"

Ellen told him,

"Tex said you only had PB &J's for lunch. He lied right? I would love to have a chicken salad. Do you have an iced tea to go with that?"

Harold replied,

"Coming right up mam. What would you like Krissy?"

She replied,

"The same sounds good Harold. We will take them out on a

table, O K ?"

"Be right out with them. Want some chips too?"

Ellen said,

"What's lunch without potato chips? So Krissy is your name?"

Krissy responded,

"Yes, I am married to Rob Harris. He is Tex's partner in the Ranch. I moved here from D C when we got married. We have a little boy running around here somewhere. He's name is Rob too, but we call him Skipper. As you can see he is going to be a big brother soon. "As she patted her stomach.

Ellen looked at her and said,

"I hope I have some kids too someday. I'm not getting any younger. Will turn thirty next month."

Krissy replied,

"Heck thirty ain't old yet. I'm thirty five."

Tex came out and joined them at the table as they finished their lunch. He asked Ellen,

"Would you like to take a ride out to see some of the Ranch? We can grab a couple of horses and go."

Ellen hopped up and said,

"Let's go."

Rob came by then and asked Krissy,

"Who's that Kris? She a new 'Dudette'?"

"Yes she is a friend of Tex's from Huston. She works for his Lawyer."

Rob said,

"She must be new there. I never saw her before. Looks like Tex is going to show her around personally."

"Yeah, Tex looks like he is quite taken with her. I never have seen him take so much interest in a client before."

"Can you blame him? She sure is a looker, right?"

Krissy looked at Rob and said,

"He needs someone to take care of."

Rob told her,

"She looks like she can take care of herself."

✳ ✳ ✳

Patty and Tina were still in a state of disbelief when they arrived at Lois's former home. Sparky was at a boarding kennel after Lois died and they had stopped by to get him. When they got out of the car and went in the house he looked all over for Lois and couldn't find her. He whined and looked and when he couldn't find her he cried. Tina held him close to her chest and cried with him. She missed Lois too.

After he got resigned to his new mistresses he settled down. They took him for a walk in the back yard of the house. It was completely fenced in so he could run free and be a dog.

The girls moved their belongings from Patty's apartment to the new house and got settled in. They found the house to be larger than they were used to but not enormous. It had four bedrooms and two full baths and a powder room downstairs. A formal living room and dining room. The house sat on a full acre lot and was in a nice but not pretentious neighborhood. It was about two miles from their shop.

Sparky liked to go with them to work every day and when they found out where the next show was scheduled to be held they entered him in it. It was in Oklahoma City.

✳✳✳

Penny knew what was going on with Giorgio and her Moms. She was a little jealous but was still happy when he spent time with her in his bed and on a blanket out on the mountain. They were pretty sure of what Penny and he were doing and realized that it was their fault that it had gotten out of hand. They also knew that he was no fool and was enjoying every minute of having sex with both the women and Penny. They just hoped that Penny was not going to get pregnant.

Kitty took her aside one day and told her that she knew that she was having sex with Giorgio and that she must play safe. She gave Penny a pack of condoms and told her.

"You give these to him and tell him there are more where these came from and to use them. We don't want you to be getting in trouble."

Patty blushed and then asked,

"Do you use them when he fucks you and Trish?"

Kitty looked at her and asked,

"What makes you think he is doing that with us?"

Penny retorted,

"OH PLEASE, I am not a child I know what is going on behind closed doors at night. I know it's not just me he is having fun with. So admit it. I listened at your door and could hear what was being said. I just don't want you to not think I know about it."

Kitty pushed her tongue into her cheek and thought what Penny said. Then she put her arms around Penny and said,

"He sure is gentle isn't he? I know he is with us. If you are alright with the arrangement then we will let you and him continue to make love, just don't get pregnant. At least not yet."

*** ✳✳✳

When Ellen and Tex got back from their ride it was about time to eat and Harold had made some Rib eye steaks for supper that night. Several of the other guests joined them at the table and they enjoyed a round of drinks and then apple pie for desert.

After they had finished eating and the conversations were winding down they drifted over to the bunkhouse to get to bed. Tex escorted Ellen back to her room and left her at the door. Before he could turn to leave she took him by his arm and pulled him inside and closed the door. She turned a lamp on next to the bed and then asked Tex if he would like to hang out with her for a while. He agreed and sat down on the edge of the bed. Ellen sat down beside him. She turned and reached up to kiss him. He bent down slightly to meet her lips. He put his arms around her and held her close. They opened their mouths as they kissed and allowed their tongues to meet. They moved from her mouth to his and back again. They swirled around each other and as they did Ellen and Tex became more motivated toward each other. She took off his shirt and moved to open his belt. He removed her shirt and bra. She stood to remove her jeans and shoes and socks. Tex stood too and dropped his pants to the floor. Her arms encircled him and she put her hands on his butt checks. She gently rubbed her hands over them and reached around and touched his cock. He had gotten hard before they had their pants off. He pulled her up close and fondled her soft ass. He laid her down on the bed and with her legs spread he went down and kissed her pubic mound thru her panties. She slipped them down and kicked them off. Tex then started to lick her thighs and moved up to her girl parts. He licked her clit and up and down her wet pussy crack. Making it wider with every stroke of his warm tongue. She laid her head back and put her hands on his head. She held him so that he was at just the right spot to make her cum. She had her first release and then opened up her vagina to welcome his hardness to her wet and hungry place. He slipped it in slowly inch by inch. He enjoyed the warmth of her body. He pulled out slightly before pushing in more. After a few minutes of this he had his whole ten inch's inside her. She wrapped her legs around him and rubbed her heels against his back. They continued to fuck for a while longer and then she asked,

"Will you let me get on top?"

Tex smiled and got up and laid on his back. She climbed up and straddled his hips. Slowly she lowered her self-back down onto his still stiff member. She let herself slid all the way down until he had again reached bottom. She moved front and back and up and down moving from side to side and back and front again. Tex thought,

'this girl sure does like to ride cowgirl alright. She's the best one I ever had. I hope she's up for some good fanny fucking to. She has a nice ass and I'd like to get in some of that.'

Ellen could feel another orgasm coming and she squeezed her vagina muscles tight on him as she rode up and down and released again. This time Tex met her stroke for stroke as he too released his load inside her.

They laid on the bed and relaxed in the afterglow of their union and after awile she reached over and touched his soft cock and stroked it a bit and then she raised up and moved so she could put her mouth on it. Tex relaxed as best he could and let her suck him back up hard again. He asked,

"Ever take it in the back door?"

Ellen took her mouth off and replied,

"Do you want to try it? I think I can if we have some lube. I have a tube in my purse. Never know when a girl may need some, right?"

She got up and went for her purse. She soon returned and gave it to Tex.

"Here, you do the honors Cowboy."

Tex opened the tube and squeezed some onto his hand. He rubbed it up and down his hard cock and after she got on her hands and knees he wiped some on her opening. He got behind her and ran the tip up and down her crack and then pushed the tip gently into her anal opening. It slid in easily and it was not long before he was in about half way. He started to stroke in and out as it went in farther. When it was all the way in she tightened her anal sphincter around him and opened and closed it and repeated that motion as he slowly pulled back out. When he was all but out he slid it back into her tight hole. He fucked this way for what seemed like a half hour. More likely ten minutes. Tex could feel another load about to release and he held her around the waist as he shot into her again.

He had hoped that he would be able to get her in bed sometime but didn't expect to have her fuck his ass off the first night. She was good.

✳ ✳ ✳

Mike Brown watched from up on the hill that he had climbed last night so that he could see a clear view of the back of the house. As he watched he saw an older man walk out onto the porch. He thought,

'What the fuck? Who is this guy? What's he doing here?'

As he watched he saw a young girl come out of the house and walk over to the man and put her arms around him. The man responded by holding her to him and kissing her.

Mike recognized her as the girl who held the gun on him. She had grown into a full sized woman with tits and a nice ass and all. He sure would like to fuck her. Maybe he would. But first he had to figure out how he was going to get the woman who shot him.

Trish noticed Ginger acting strange. Her ears perked up and she tilted her head to the side. She gave a low growl.

Trish knew there was a stranger nearby and it was not someone that was familiar to Ginger.

She went to the gun safe in the bed room and retrieved her Glock 40 that she had used before when she had too. She hoped it was not needed again.

She went up to the second floor where she had a pair of binoculars that she could scan the hillside behind the house. She watched over the hill and slowly moved from one spot to the next. She stopped to analyze every view she had until she was satisfied there was nothing there. Then move on, overlaying each view with the last. She had become very proficient doing this and there was not much that she missed. Ever since the incident with Newt she didn't trust to chance. She had been alerted that Mike Brown had been released from prison so she had taken precautions in case he showed up.

Mike watched as the man and the girl went to his truck and got in and headed toward town. So they were gone. That left the two women.

An hour later he saw the one that didn't shoot him come out of the house and walk down to the boat dock. She got the sail boat ready to take a morning ride on the pond. After she left and was out of sight he decided that the only one left in the house was the one who shot him and caused him to go to prison where he was raped by Mexicans and black guys. They did it every day to him until he got Sam as a cell mate.

Sam was a big and tough guy. They didn't mess with him. Problem was that Sam was now raping him. This worked out o k as Sam protected him from the others.

Mike thought that now was his best chance to go in after her and slash her throat for shooting him.

He was not permitted to have any guns anymore as a felon so he has resorted to knives. He had killed Sam and got rid of his body. Now he was ready to kill again.

He crept up to the house and walked onto the back porch. He approached the back door and listened inside the house. He could hear a radio or something playing inside. He pushed the screen door open and stepped inside the kitchen. He walked in the direction of the radio sound. He thought she would be close by. It sounded like it was coming from up the steps. He crossed the living room and started up the steps when suddenly he was attacked from behind by Ginger who sank her canines into his pants and into his ass cheek.

He let out a frightened shout and tried to turn to get at the dog. He lost his balance on the step and fell over onto his side. The knife that he held was lost when he fell. The dog continued to hold on and started to growl. Trish heard the commotion and raced for the steps. When she saw what was happening she raised her gun and when she fired this time it was not his leg that was hit.

Ginger let go of him and watched as he laid dead on the floor. She licked up some of the blood from his head.

Trish saw who it was and saw the knife on the floor. It didn't take her long to figure out what he was doing in her house. Cold shivers ran down her back and she gripped the gun tightly in her hand.

She went to the telephone and dialed 911.

*** ✳ ✳ ✳

Back in Albuquerque Patty and Tina were getting ready to take Sparky
to Oklahoma City for the show. They had groomed his considerable
hair and painted his toenails in preparation for the show.

Tina asked Patty,

"How long will it take us to get to Oklahoma City from here?"

Patty replied,

"I did a Bing search and it is about 543 miles and will take us
about 8 hours to get there. So we can leave here at 8 am and be there
at 4 pm in time for supper at the hotel. Hope they have Surf and
Turf."

Tina agreed,

"That was good when we had it with Lois on that trip. Well every
trip with her was a fun trip. I miss her. She sure did treat us nice."

When Sparky heard Lois's name he perked up. It had been several
months since her death and he still misses her.

They decide to take Lois's Range Rover to the show. After they
were all packed up to go and had Sparky in his crate in the back they
headed out. It was a clear sky and just a beautiful day to travel.

They stopped for lunch at a Denny's at Tucumcari. This felt like
a good time to take a break. Sparky got out and stretched his legs and
did his business before they continued on toward Oklahoma City.

When they arrived they checked in and went up to their room
on the second floor. They carried Sparky's crate up to the room and
walked him thru the lobby to the elevator. He was used to this routine
after going to so many shows all over the country. After getting him
settled in they went back down to the Hotel restaurant for supper.

Patty recognized some of the other dog owners that she had

met at other shows. She smiled and nodded her head at one young woman who shows her female Miniature Poodle in the Toy class. She was a consistent winner like Sparky.

She and Tina struck up a conversation with her.

Patty said,

"Nice to see you again, Tracy is it?"

The woman smiled at Patty and replied,

"You have a pretty good memory. Traci is correct, changed the y to I, so Tracy is now Traci. You do know that I am Trans Gender?"

Patty's jaw dropped when she heard this. This person is a very pretty woman. She had never met a Tran's person that she knew for sure. She replied,

"No I didn't know that. You're in good hands here. Tina and I are domestic partners so we know some of the prejudice that you must face as well. Our Grooming Salon was vandalized by some bigot who hated Lesbians. Bashed in the front door and wrote with blue paint some anti lesbian graffiti. He went to jail for five years for a hate crime and vandalism. After we are done with supper would you like to hang out with us?"

Traci gleamed and said,

"I would love to hang out with you guys. Some of these people here are not very social. What's your room number? I'll stop up after I take my little girl for a walk outside."

Patty told Traci,

"Our room is 208 on the second floor. See you then."

Tina grinned at Patty and whispered to her,

"I wonder if she has had the operation yet?"

Patty looked at Tina for a second and then her eye brows went up as she realized what Tina was referring to.

She said,

"We can ask, I guess. She offered to share her gender identity with us. And we with her. So why not. It is something of interest."

Tina chuckled a bit and replied,

"It sure is interesting. Show me more." She waggled her eye brows up and down several times and then she winked.

*** ✳ ✳ ✳ ***

They took Sparky out of his crate and took him for a walk before putting him up for the night. Shortly after they got back there came a knock on their door. It was Traci.

"Hi guys." She said as she walked in the room. She was wearing the same skirt and blouse that she had on when they met her in the restaurant. It was a nice combination of blue top and light green skirt.

Tina opened the door and welcomed her in. Their room had a couch and two chairs plus the double bed. It was a large room compared with where they had stayed before.

Traci sat on the couch with Tina seated beside her. Patty sat on one of the chairs closest to the couch. They all looked at each other and just smiled at each other. Patty opened the conversation by asking Traci,

How old were you when you knew that your birth sex was not right for you? Did you have any idea of what you were in for when you decided to change? How far are you along with the change?"

Traci smiled at Patty and told her,

"Well I think I was about 12 when I started to wonder why I was feeling these feminine feelings. I didn't want to hang out with boys my age. I preferred to be with girls. Not to be girlfriends. Just to be with girls. When I was 16 when I found out that a person could change their sex from a boy to a girl or a girl to a boy. But as they say it's easier to dig a hole then to build a pole. I started taking the hormone shots to develop breasts and change the shape of my body. I didn't know how doing this could happen. After several years of this therapy I had blossomed up top and I had been letting my hair grow long. I started to fashion my hair with bangs in front and long to my shoulders. Do you like it?"

Tina moved over and ran her fingers thru Traci's blond hair.

Traci responded by putting her hand on Tina's knee.

Patty watched as they played with each other's hair and fondled their breasts.

Traci asked,

"Would you like to see my tits? I am pretty happy the way they came out. Not real big and not at all small."

She opened her blouse and loosened her bra straps so that she could pop her breasts out over the top of her bra.

Patty and Tina admired Traci's titty's and Traci asked,

"You can feel them if you want to. Everybody does when they see how they look. Aren't the nipples nice and pointy?"

The girls were fascinated with Traci's openness about her change. They felt them and admired how they felt when they gave them a gentle squeeze. Finally Tina could not resist any longer and she went down on Traci's left tit and sucked it. She ran her tongue over the nipple and it got hard to her touch. Traci put her hand on the back of her head and held it as Tina continued to nurse between both of Traci's breasts. Tina could not resist the urge to investigate farther and ran her hand up Traci's skirt. She found that Traci had no panties on and Tina found her soft cock. She pulled away and then put her hand back on it. This was different. She looked at Traci and she looked like any other girl that she had ever seen and then to be holding a cock amazed Tina. She asked,

"Traci, when do you get your final surgery? Can you still get hard now? Or do the hormones block it somehow? If I sucked you off would you still cum like when you were all boy?"

Traci looked Tina in the eye and asked,

"Why don't you find out?"

Tina went down and started to suck Traci's cock. Patty watched and waited to see the expression on Tina's face when she got Traci's load. She was sure she would by the look on Traci's expression.

Yes, Patty was right and Tina got a mouth full of Traci's gissim. She swallowed it like she does with any other man that she ever sucked off.

Traci told them that she was going to have the final surgery later that year. Then she would have a vagina when they turned her penis inside out. She just hoped that if she could get fucked that it would somehow feel good.

Then next day they went to the show and at the end of the day Sparky didn't disappoint. He took his class but failed to win Best in Show. That went to a Cocker Spaniel from Kansas that they never saw in the shows before. It was a beautiful animal and the way he presented himself was nothing short of perfection.

Up in Maine Evelyn and Jack took her Lobster boat out on the Bay and were having a great catch of Lobsters. Best part they were nearly all mature and only a few small ones to put back. The live box was getting full and she decided to head back to the dock and sell their catch.

After they got back to the dock and sold the catch they headed back to her house. They had been getting more and more familiar with each other's bodies and she was finally getting what she had been missing for all these years.

Jack had had a number of sexual encounters in his life but this was different with Evelyn. He didn't know if this was love or just some passion that would go away and she would be forgotten like the rest. No, this was different alright. He was convinced that this was the real thing. He had never been as happy as he was now. Evelyn felt the same way. She didn't know if another man would treat her like Jack does but she didn't care she just wanted him to be her man.

The following day the sky was overcast and a north east wind was starting to raise some white caps on the bay. They went out anyway because they felt they would have another big catch like yesterday.

Jack headed the bow into the wind and headed for the first pots. They hauled them up and sure enough it had a good catch. They dumped the catch into the live well and rebaited the trap. They continued on and got to around the fiftieth trap when the wind turned to a gale and the wave's turned from little white caps to huge waves that broke over the sides of the boat. Jack kept trying to keep the bow into the wind but now it seemed to be coming from all directions. Evelyn was in the wheelhouse with Jack and they both held on for dear life as the boat shuttered from the pounding that the waves were battering it from all sides. The waves were higher then she had ever seen them before She heard of rogue waves that were up to

50 feet high and there was no way to survive the harsh pounding that they wreaked on a small boat like hers. The back of the boat bobbed up and down for a beat and then it turned down and the bow turned up and the Kitty Kat sank below the waves. Jack and Evelyn had their life jackets on and then the sea finally lost its anger at the world and relented. They were able to stay on top of the water. They had no idea where they were or how they would be found.

She had activated their locater beacon before the boat sank and now she had lost it when a wave hit her and she lost her grip on it. She didn't even know if it was in the water near where they were. The Coast guard would answer the beacon and come looking for it If the weather was favorable they would dispatch a helicopter to do search and rescue. But the weather was still not settled down. They were in the water for what seemed like hours when she thought she heard an airplane. She hoped it was from the Coast Guard and rescue was eminent.

Jack had been hit on the head by something in the wind and had been nearly knocked out. He revived quickly and kept his wits about him. He had a terrible head ache and figured he had a concussion from the blow to the head. They had a rope tied to each life jacket so they wouldn't be pulled apart and get lost from each other.

The sound of the airplane went away and their hearts sank. It was several hours later that they heard it again. This time it was closer. Jack looked up and saw the plane bank over and circle their location. It circled twice and then they saw a Jumper come out and his parachute opened. He landed in the water about a hundred feet from them and swam over to where they were. Evelyn reached out and grabbed onto the man and cried. She was sure she was going to die that day .Jack held onto her jacket.

The man told them that the coast guard had picked up their

Locator beacon and dispatched their plane to do a wide search for them and when they found the location it was sent back for a rescue boat to come and get them out of the water and back to safety.

✳ ✳ ✳

Tex and Rob took Krissy into Huston to the Hospital

for the birth of Rob's second child. A girl. She weighed 6 pounds 4 ounces and was 17 inches long. They named her Roberta Kristine.

They had his son, Skippy along with them and he was so excited to meet his baby sister. Right from the start he was to be her protector.

Krissy came thru the delivery with no problems. She was released a few days later and went back to the Ranch.

Tex's girlfriend Ellen from Huston took a weeks' vacation and came to help Krissy with the baby and take care of Krissy.

She didn't stay in the bunkhouse anymore. She slept in Tex's room. They were getting serious with their romance and all the Ranch hands saw it coming even if old Tex didn't. When her birthday came around they were gathered around the table in the Chuck Wagon and they had just sang, **Happy Birthday sweet Ellen**, and then they cut the birthday cake. When everyone had a piece of the cake Tex said that he has something important to say. They all got quiet. Tex walked over to Ellen and knelt down in front of her and asked,

"My sweet, sweet Ellen will you be my wife?"

She smiled and said,

"YES"

Tex slipped the two caret diamond ring onto her finger and they kissed. The crowd around the table whistled and clapped their hands.

Tex was getting married.

Was this the smartest thing he has ever done? Time will tell
Meanwhile they all danced until late that night.

✳ ✳ ✳

Trish called 911 to report the incident at her home with Mike brown.
She told the dispatcher that they could take their time getting there
because he was dead.

By the time the Police got there Giorgio and Penny had returned
and Kitty was back with the sail boat. They were all gathered on
the back porch when the Officers arrived. The first thing they did
was to check out the body and the crime scene. Trish explained how
he had entered her house and was coming up the stairs when her
dog attacked him from behind and bit his ass. He hollered and fell
backward down the steps the knife flying from his hand. When he
went to try to punch the dog she fired one shot from the top of the
steps. The bullet hit Brown in the head. He died instantly. The lead
Detective reviewed all the information that she gave him and then
he asked,

"This is the same Mike Brown that you shot before isn't it?"

She replied,

"Yes Sir it is. I helped to put him in prison for five years. He got
out recently and I guess that he came looking for me. I'm glad my
dog was here to stop him."

The Detective smiled and replied,

"Me too. How is it you are so proficient with that hand gun?"

"I'll show you. They went out to the end of the yard where she
showed him the target range.

"When we moved here one of the first things we did was to build this range. As our Kids grew up we taught all of them how to safely handle firearms. I got that gun on my 18th birthday from my Father. He had my brother and I practice every day with it. We both became sharp shooters. I was still better then him. But that doesn't matter. What matters is when the chips are down what can you do?"

The Detective thought about it for a few seconds and replied,

"You know what? I think I am going to get my Daughter's a handgun and get them started like you have done. Like I tell people, 'A protection from abuse' or a 'Restraining order', is just a piece of paper'. "

"And as this fellow learned to late, "Don't take a knife to a gun fight."

"Every things in order and the Coroner is on the way to pick up the body. Or as I sometimes say off the record, to take out the trash. Have a better day Ms. Trisha Flick."

✳ ✳ ✳

Back in New York State Trish's brother Tommy and his wife Vicky and their twins were all packed up and ready to go to the airport in Albany. They were flying down to New Mexico to visit his sister after many years apart. They talk on the phone a few time a month when they find time in their busy lives.

Their kids were on break from College and they all agreed to go visit their Aunt Trisha who they have never seen except for pictures. They knew she was married to another woman and they had adopted several foster children. They all went to College too.

Tommy's kids were Darla and Tim. They were both 20 years old and in their junior year at SUNY in Syracuse.

(State University of New York)

They were both pursuing degrees in Business management so they could manage the family fortune. Since their grandfather passed away and left his estate to their Dad and his sister, Aunt Trisha, they were encouraged to prepare to make wise decisions with regards to how the money was invested. Their father had managed it well and what he inherited had more than doubled in 20 years. They had watched as they were growing up how he had always made them have summer jobs and shovel snow for the neighbors in the winter to grow an appreciation for their lives.

Darla had grown up to be a beautiful young woman who had lots of young mem pursuing her hand. She didn't know if they were interested in her or her dad's fortune. Everyone in town knew that he was one of the wealthiest men in the county. She was very cautious when dating. She didn't let on that her family had any means that were above the normal. When asked what her parents did she answered that her Dad was a handyman and fixed up houses. Her mom was a house keeper both answers were true. Her Dad did do some handyman stuff on the dozens of rental houses that he owned in the two county area. Her mom did stay at home and keep the books for the several different Real Estate operations they had.

The flight to Albuquerque was smooth and only took a little over 5 hours from Albany.

When they went out the gate Trish and Kitty were waiting for them. They loaded all their luggage and stuff into the back of the large Dodge pickup. It was a big Dodge Ram with 4 wheel drive and all the options the factory could think of to tack on. What do you want for $80,000.00? It was there.

They headed down the road toward their home. It was the first time that the twins had met their Aunts. When they arrived at the

Ranch they all got out and stretched. Tommy looked out over the pond and commented to Trish,

"Not quite like at home, but still a nice setting. I see you have a Sunfish. Do you get to do some sailing on the pond?" She replied,

"We sure do. All the Kids learned to tie knots and how to tack. As soon as they are old enough they learn how to shoot like Dad taught us. At the end of the yard is our target range if you want to burn off a few rounds while you are here I have that Glock that Dad gave me when I turned 18. It has come in handy a time or two, or three." She gave a little smile at Kitty.

✱✱✱

Adam showed up and was introduced to his extended family from New York. He was playing Guitar at a family gathering for background music while the people were eating and talking. He kept the volume down so that the people could talk comfortably. He was in demand for these settings and they paid well. If they wanted to have him play louder he would do whatever the Host wanted him to do. He had a Booking Agent from the City who called him when he had a client. Adam was doing well as a Free Lance musician.

His Sister was an Artist who had come into her own at a young age.

Penny was now 17 and had been learning some advanced techniques from a man named Giorgio Mendez. He was a very talented Artist himself and was also in love with Penny. He is 50 years old and Trish was against it at the beginning but gave in to Penny when she found that she loved him too.

While Trish's family from New York and her gang from New

Mexico were all there she called them all together for a celebration of family.

On the day of the party Giorgio showed up with a picture frame under his arm. He set up an easel in the yard between the pond and the house. He told Trish to have them all gather around so he could show them a painting he had been working on for six months. When they all had assembled he called Penny to come and stand by him when he unveiled what he had on the easel.

He looked out over all the faces and then at Trish and Kitty. He said,

"My dear friends and family I want all of you to see what it is that I treasure more than life its self and here it is."

He pulled the cloth that was covering the painting and revealed a picture of Penny walking up from the dock with Ginger beside her. It was so lifelike that you would think it was a photograph. They all gasped at its realistic quality. Then he said,

"My dearest friends, Trisha and Kitty, I want to ask you if you would make me the happiest man in the world and allow me to marry Penny, your beautiful sweet Daughter. I know this is sudden and I want you to truly think what it would mean to both Penny and I. There are more than a few years difference in our ages but love doesn't care about years. Our love for each other has grown over these past five years and we do love each other."

The whole group was stunned at what he had to say. They were all silent and then Trish said,

"Giorgio, you came here as a teacher of art so that Penny could improve her painting. I never thought that it would ever turn into what it has. I know that you love her and that she loves you. I am also aware that there are a lot of year's difference in your ages. You say Love doesn't care about years. In twenty five years you will be seventy-five and she will be forty two. If you are still alive. What would she do with an old man like that? Still love him or would she be looking for a younger man who would still be able to keep her satisfied. I am not doubting your love for her or her love for you. I'm just saying that I think it would be a bad match. We love you Giorgio and you have made all of our lives more alive than before you came into them. You are both of age of consent so if you both wish to marry that is your choice. You have heard my side now."

All were silent and finally Penny said,

"I love you Giorgio. But like my Mom said, what about when you are old and I am still young what will we do? Will our love still be strong enough to withstand the temptations in life? I can't honestly say that I would still have a love strong enough to stay loyal and to give all my love to you alone my sweet."

Giorgio answered,

"Penny, darling Penny, if you have needs that I can no longer satisfy then I will let you go to find a lover who can take care of your needs. But I will still love you."

He walked away from the painting and there were tears in his eyes. He was heartbroken.

He had bared his very soul out there in front of everyone. Now they probably thought of him as some old fool who had the misfortune to fall in love with a young girl who was just too young for him. He had thought that himself. But he told himself that his heart would triumph over all and they would be happy together. She had professed her love for him and they made tender love together. Was it all over now? Did he make a fool of himself? He got in his truck and headed back out to his cabin on top of the mountain with his dogs.

A week later a friend stopped by when they saw his truck was back. They knocked on the door. There was no answer. They knocked again. Then they pushed the door open and saw him seated at the kitchen table with his head on it. He had indeed died of a broken heart. His friend took the dogs along with him and called the Sherriff to report Giorgio's death.

***

Patty and Tina talked as they drove the Range Rover back home. Tina said,

"I really like Traci and it is a shame that some people just can't understand what it must be like to grow up knowing your sex is wrong for you and when you finally are able to 'come out' you are persecuted. Some States even ban Trans gender kids from playing girls sport. They claim they have an unfair difference in body strength being born as a male. They say it is simple biology. Men are stronger then women."

Patty replied,

"Do you remember the Tennis match of the century between Bobby Riggs and Billy Jean King?"

Tina said,

"Yeah, Riggs claimed that men could beat women because they are stronger than they are. We know how that ended. Well years later Billy Jean came out as a lesbian. So was that HER strength that helped her beat him?"

Patty told her,

"Yes I like to think that. But it just pisses me off that a certain political party is the one who proposes these human rights be legislated so they become a solution with no problem. An answer to no question. I don't want to talk about it."

They rode in silence the rest of the way back home.

An Independent Church in Albuquerque has had rocks thrown thru their windows so often because they were openly known as welcoming to LGBTQ people looking for a spiritual home. It happened so many times that they just piled up the rocks on a table as you walk in the front door. The Pastor of the Church is a Lesbian herself and has done what is said in the Bible.

Turn the other cheek.

Patty and Tina started to attend services there.

After another year passed they decided to make the leap. They were going to get married.

CHAPTER SIX

Still in Love

Trish and Kitty are still in love after all these years. Their children are the kind of kids that make you proud.

Their oldest son, Evan died a hero while on a mission for the CIA. His ashes are in a memorial garden at his New Mexico home where he grew up.

Their second oldest, Buddy, is a successful medical device engineer and lives near Kansas City. His wife, Brenda is a full blooded Apache from the Reservation in southern New Mexico. They met in College. They have a Son.

Their youngest adopted child is Patty. She opened a Dog grooming salon near Albuquerque. She has recently married her business partner and lover, Tina Frost.

They inherited a large fortune including a house and several cars from one of their Grooming clients. They had accompanied her to Dog shows to do grooming on her dog. They also inherited her Dog, Sparky.

Kitty's son, Rob, has moved to the Ranch that his biological Father owned. He shared ownership with his father's best friend, Tex Duncan who was at the Rodeo when he died after being thrown from a bull. He and Tex have opened a Dude ranch operation and host people for a week or two week stay. It has proven o be a profitable idea.

One of the guests was Krissy Karr from Washington DC who came to the Ranch and she and Rob fell in love and got married on horseback. They now have two children. The oldest is called Skipper. His name is Robert Evan Harris. His little sister is called, Sunshine. Because she always seems to be smiling. Her given name is Roberta Kristine Harris.

✳ ✳ ✳

Back in New Mexico at Trish and Kitty's little 30 acre Ranch, they call it. They still have two adopted children. They were nine and seven when they lost their parents to drugs. They have grown up to be talented in music and art.

Adam, the older has become a semi professional Musician. He has self-taught himself on the Guitar and gets some small jobs playing solo at parties.

His sister, Penny, has been able to produce works of art that the public likes and has been paying increasing prices for her work. She had an art teacher, Giorgio, for five years who was able to greatly increase her skill level.

They fell in love over time and when he asked for her hand in marriage Penny decided to end the relationship when she realized the age difference was too great to last. Giorgio died of a broken heart.

Trish thought about how her kids had grown up and left their home to start their lives. It was just her and Kitty at the ranch now.

Adam left for Nashville to pursue his music. He has a love interest now. She is from Viet Nam. Her name is Jenni. Her grandparents came to Texas following the fall of their homeland to the communist's.

They made their living working from a Shrimp boat. They were successful in spite of the harassment they took from the white shrimpers and fishermen.

After these people saw that her grandparents were good, friendly folks that would be willing to help them out in a pinch they relented and became friends with them.

Her father "Tommy", was a teenager when they arrived from Vietnam and growing up in south Texas he had to watch his eye for the local white girls that fascinated him.

He was an outsider and the white boys didn't like the idea of one of their girls being with a "Gook" as he was called. This to him was the same as a black man being called a "nigger". He hated it.

In spite of the racial differences he found a girl who fell in love with this young man. Her name was Darlene Minnich.

She was descended from immigrants from Germany who came here before the Second World War to escape the Nazi's. Her Great grand parents came into the States by way of New York City.

They soon left for the Midwest settling in Indiana for a few years before going south to Texarkana Texas. Their son, Franz, married a light skinned black girl from there named Patsy Mae Wilson. Her mother was white and her father was a black man named Jonny Odom.

Patsy took her mother's maiden name when her parents split up. Patsy married Frans Minnich and they had a daughter, Darlene.

She married Tommy and they have a daughter, Jenni.

Jenni and Adam met on the sidewalk in downtown Nashville one day and when she smiled at him with those brown eyes and long straightened brown hair that she wore down to her mid back he knew then and there that he had met his soulmate.

They went for coffee at a Starbucks. While sitting there he asked her,

"What's your name? Mine is Adam Flick and I am a musician. What brings you to Nashville?'"

Jenni replied,

"I came here from the Gulf coast of Texas to study at Vanderbilt. My name is Jenni."

Adam looked at her and said,

"You know what? You have the most beautiful eyes I have ever seen. Your lips just make me want to kiss them and your hair? I would love to run my fingers thru it."

Jenni laughed at that and said,

"You know what "Cowboy"? If you play your cards right you just might get a chance to do those things.'

They finished their drinks and left hand in hand. When they were outside, he asked,

"Where are you staying?"

She replied,

"I have an apartment off campus. Would you like to see it?"

Adam grinned and said,

"My, my, the lady asks, 'Would you like to see it?' He answered,

"In a New York minute."

They hailed a Cab and she directed the driver to her address. It was just short distance, maybe a mile. When they arrived she invited Adam to come in with her to see the apartment.

She went to the kitchen and got a pair of sodas from her refrigerator. They sat in the living room on her couch beside each other. They started with some small talk about where they came from and what they planned for their futures. Jenni told Adam,

"Like I said I grew up on the Coast. My parents are living there and he operates his Shrimping business that his father started when they came from Vietnam. My mother is a melato black with some German thrown in. So you see I am a mix of the whole world."

Adam replied,

"My parents both died when I was young from a bad batch of drugs. I and my sister were adopted by a Lesbian couple in New Mexico. They are both white and from the east coast. New York and Maine. They moved to New Mexico to start over as a couple. We lived way out in the mountains and had a pond in the back that we would swim, fish and go sail boating. We have several older step siblings that are half white and half Apache. The oldest died while in the CIA. His brother is a medical device designer in Kansas City. Their younger sister has a dog grooming place outside of Albuquerque. She has a wife too like our moms. They have been together for a long time. I don't know if they will adopt any kids like our mom's did. I think it would be a cool thing to do."

"WOW, you shared a lot more than me." Jenni said.

"Tell me about your sister. What's her name? And what's she do?"

Adam took a deep breath and let it out before he spoke,

"MY sister, Penny went thru a traumatic shock and she ended up in a facility to treat her depression. She has been there in treatment for the past two years. She will be getting out soon."

Jenni sat up and asked,

"What happened to her to cause this condition?"

He answered,

"She had a man who was older then her with whom she fell in love. He asked our Moms if they could get married. After they talked, Penny decided to call it off. He left that day and she never saw him again. He had gone home and died there. She felt that she caused his death somehow and she went into that deep depression that we were afraid she would be suicidal."

Jenni put her arms around Adam to comfort him because she could see a tear forming in his eyes. She responded,

"Oh, Adam that is so sad. I hope that she gets well and can restart her life. What did she do?"

Adam told Jenni,

"Penny is one of the most gifted Artist's that I have ever been around. The paintings she does look like they are alive. I hope she is able to continue to paint. The man who she loved was also her teacher for five years."

They sat for a while and then Jenni took Adams chin and tilted it toward her. She kissed him on the lips gently and then she leaned back on the couch so as to lay down. Adam followed her lead and laid down beside her. She was small next to him and they both fit on the couch. They continued to kiss and hold their body's close. Adam asked,

"Would you like to get more comfortable on your bed?"

Jenni got up and took him by the hand and led him back a hallway to her room. When they walked in they both started to remove their cloths.

Jenni could feel the heat on her face growing as she watched him finish the last of his cloths. They laid down on the bed and kissed again. This time they both had their tongues exploring their warm mouths. She reached down and touched his growing manhood. She sighed an approval of what she felt. She gently squeezed it as it got harder.

Adam rolled her over on top of him and squeezed her small ass checks with both hands. She pulled herself up and with her hand she directed his cock into her warm wet pussy.

He let out a moan as he slid into her. She was tight even with as wet as she was. He laid and watched as she moved up and down slowly and rode back and forth. He hoped that he could last for a long time. He looked into her eyes as she rode him and saw her looking back at him. She picked up the pace and then when she was sure that he was about to cum too she had her release along with him.

They laid beside each other and cuddled. After a time she moved down Adams chest and sucked on his nipples. Biting them gently and licking them. She went down and licked his navel before getting closer to his now soft cock. She licked the end of it and put her hand on it to start stroking it back to a nice erection. She liked to lick the tip and gently suck it into her mouth. She could still taste a bit of his juice that had dried up after being wiped on the sheets. She didn't care about the sheets. He could leave "pecker tracks" anywhere at all. This beautiful hunk of man that she wanted so much to pleasure and make happy. She needed to be careful with what she was doing as she just wanted to get him hard again. Not to make him lose his load in her mouth. Not that she would mind. It was just that she still wanted and needed to get fucked again.

Adam got up and mounted her from behind, doggy style, his favorite and hers. They both liked to hear the slap of belly to ass cheek. It was like music to their ears.

Before he did he went down behind her and licked her pussy and ass to get her ready for when he pushed his now hard as a rock cock into her again and again and again untillll POP!

Jenni rolled over on her back, parted her legs and beckoned him to go down on her wet pussy and lick up all of their mixed juices. He gladly did. He licked the back of her smooth tan legs and worked his way up to her crotch. He moved his tongue along the legs until they became the edge of her pubes. He licked them on both sides and finally up to her clit. Adam sucked and licked her little pleasure spot and then thrust his tongue into her wet pussy. He rolled it around and around and Jenni enjoyed another orgasm while holding his head tight to her crotch.

✳ ✳ ✳

Penny had just returned to her room from group sessions when she was called to the front desk. They told her that she had a visitor and she could meet them in the lounge area of the hospital. When she arrived there she saw Kitty had brought Ginger their Golden Retriever to visit today.

Penny was so happy to see the dog that she got down on the floor and hugged Ginger all the while the big dog's tail wagged up a storm. She was so happy to see her again. And Penny to see Ginger. It had been a long recovery that Penny had gone thru.

The depression that she suffered after the death of Giorgio was so severe that she had even considered taking her life. The combination of the medicines and the counseling that she received had been an alleviating force and has helped to bring her back from a self-destructive path.

Trish and Kitty first noticed when she started cutting herself on her thighs and arms.

They were told by the councilors that she did this to punish herself for Giorgio's death. That she felt the need to cause herself pain for his pain.

The day was coming that she was being released from the Hospital and going home. She felt that she had been given the tools of recovery by the councilors to be able to get herself back to her life before depression. She would still need to take an anti-depressive but nothing so strong that would make her a Zombie.

On the way home she told Kitty,

"I want to get back to doing my art again. I do truly enjoy and need to get back. I know it will remind me of Giorgio, but I have learned how to control my anxieties and I am confident I can manage."

Kitty told her,

"We will take small steps at a time. There is no reason to jump Willy Nilly back into things. Just relax and get to know yourself again. The mountains and the trees are still waiting for you to get better. We know you can do it. Trish wants you to go visit Rob and Krissy at the Ranch for a little while before you come home. That alright with you. You can play with the little kids there. Skipper and Sun shine will warm your heart. They are both little sweeties."

Penny smiled and replied,

"I can't wait to see them again. It has been so long."

When they got back to the ranch, Penny and Kitty went in to the house and when Trish saw her she beamed and said,

"Welcome home baby. Did the trip go well coming back?"

Penny replied,

"Yes it was as long as usual, but I knew that when I got here I would feel safe with the two of you. Kitty said I can go visit Rob, Krissy and the kids. I would love to do that."

Trish smiled at Kitty and asked,

"When do you want to leave? Do I have time to pack a bag?"

They all laughed and the room sounded like it did in the past when everyone was happy.

✳ ✳ ✳

Rob got the call from Trish that evening and was happy to hear that they were coming for a visit. He told Krissy, Tex and Ellen at supper that evening that they were getting guests.

Tex was happy to hear that Penny was released from the mental hospital. He said,

"That poor girl has been thru a lot and I hope she continues to get better. I was not all that happy when I heard about that man, Giorgio, getting involved with her. It really got me angered when he died and poor Penny thought it was her fault. I think she thought he committed suicide. The autopsy showed he died from a heart attack. Poor girl. Pass me the potatoes please."

✳ ✳ ✳

Trish and family arrived on Friday afternoon and got settled into their rooms. After they all ate supper Rob suggested a short trail ride under the full moon. They all enjoyed the rides in the evening when the sky had just fallen from bright red sunset to the gray of twilight. To hear the lonesome call of the Coyotes as they called to each other let you know that you were in the West.

When they got back to the Ranch it was getting late so they all said their good nights and headed for bed.

Trish and Kitty laid awake for a while talking. Kitty said,

"Penny seems to be her old self again. Doesn't she?"

Trish replied,

"God I hope so. She really had me worried there before she went away. Giorgio was a mixed blessing in a way. He did make her a better Artist. But then when they got involved romantically I cringed. I saw how much he meant to Penny. But I didn't want to see her get hurt. She was anyway."

Kitty replied,

"Yes, but we probably made a mistake of taking him into our beds too. You know?" Trish looked at her and then said,

"It was fun while it lasted. You have to admit you enjoyed it as much as I did. Even if we both knew it was wrong. He was an amazing lover. Wasn't he Kitten?" Kitty sighed and replied,

"You're right as usual. He did take the edge off of my sexual frustration. I'm not saying I am frustrated with our relationship. That is far from true. We have been in love ever since Maine all those years ago. We have stayed together and raised all our kids to be good people. And now the best is still out there. Kiss me my sweet."

Trish put her arms around Kitty and held her as she gave her a warm passionate kiss. They held their bodies close together and began to touch each other all over from shoulders to butts. Kitty could feel herself getting very wet and lovable as she sucked on Trish's warm tongue. Trish responded by reaching between Kitty's legs and giving her pussy a gentle squeeze. Kitty took a big breath and spread her legs as an invitation to Trish to give her some tongue pleasure. That was when Trish slid her hands down to Kitty's ass cheeks and while holding them she moved her face into Kitty's warm place between her legs. Trish put her tongue in Kitty's vagina and licked it fervently until she moved up to her clit. She licked and sucked on it all the while Kitty played with Trish's hair. She loved to feel Kitty's fingers going thru it while she was pleasuring her. Kitty experienced several orgasms before she let Trish go and moved over in the bed to let Trish lay down so she could be pleasured. After more than twenty years they both knew what they liked best. It was over an hour when they released their hold on each other during a sixty nine session that resulted in several more good orgasms for both. They kissed and went to sleep.

✳ ✳ ✳

Tex and Ellen laid down in his bed and he stared at the ceiling for some time before she asked,

"What are you thinking about sweetie?" Tex put his arm around her and said,

"You know I think I am the most fortunate man in Texas right now. You want to know why?" She looked at Tex and asked,

"Why do you think that?" Tex replied,

"Because I am the only man in Texas that is going to make love to you tonight. Do you think that is why?"

Ellen parted her legs and let him place his big hands down on her pussy and run his fingers up and down her crack and in and out of her warm, wet hole. She gave him a kiss and then motioned him to lay on his back. Tex rolled over and Ellen moved over on top of him. She kissed him again and then moved down to take his cock in her mouth. She liked to suck Tex until he got really hard. She would then move up to ride cowgirl after lowering herself down on his cock so that it slid slowly inside her. He took a deep breath and let it out slowly as he glided inside her. She liked to rock back and forth and up and down while squeezing him with her vaginal mussels. They would do this position for a while and then she would lay on her side with him spooning her as he again slid it in. They could fuck like this for over an hour until they felt the urge to finish with an orgasm and ejaculation of his seed into her wetness.

When they were satisfied for the night they went to sleep with him still spooning her in his arms.

Rob and Krissy were up early with their kids. Skippy liked to run down to the horse barn and play with the pony that they still had from when their Aunt Katelyn came to visit. The Pony was her favorite until she out grew it. Then she liked to ride Rosie. She was Rob's favorite too. Sunshine was trailing after him as usual. He played nice with her, but was sometimes a little too fast for her to keep up.

Katelyn was soon to graduate from the University of New Mexico with her degree in Social Science. She wanted to become a Councilor so she could help kids like her sister, Penny. She saw how Giorgio's death had hurt her so much. She was sure there were other kids like Penny.

Her best friend Ashley Sweet had graduated the year before and Katelyn was asked to be her Maid of Honor when she and Freddy Odom got married. They all were close friends in college and she loved Freddy as much as she loved Ash.

They were getting married in Texarkana Texas so that Freddy's elderly Great Grandfather could attend. Jonny Odom lived nearby. His wife, Nancy passed away two years ago.

Freddy's Grandmother, Jonny's daughter Rita Moore lived near

Biloxi Mississippi and she was coming to see her Grandson who was now a University Graduate with honors and he was getting married to this pretty white girl. She just knew they would make some pretty babies.

His mother Rose, lived near Clarksville Texas with a friend that Freddy never met but once who was a Preacher. She kept the Odom name as her mother had done when Rita's drunken husband ran off with her best friend.

Rose had Freddy out of wedlock and she too kept the Odom name for her son. She swore that he was going to be the best young man she could raise. She made damn sure he stayed away from the gang's that were around and kept him close so he studied hard and got straight "A's" all the way thru school.

He got an Academic scholarship to the University Of New Mexico. She was so proud of him she thought her chest was just goona "bust."

Rose asked Freddy,

"Would you like to have Preacher Dave to officiate at you all's wedding?" Freddy had only met her "Preacher Dave" one time. He seemed like a nice enough man so he told her,

"Sure Momma, if he would be able and you approve that will be O K. with me."

Rose was delighted.

Katelyn went to visit her brother Rob at the Dude Ranch. It had been a while since she had been there with school in Albuquerque. Now she had some time before she started grad school to get her masters as

the next step towards her goal of being a Counselor. Having started college when she was only seventeen she was a bit younger than the others that were in her Masters Study group. Some were already working in the field.

When she arrived she saw Trish, Kitty and Penny were there too. She ran to Penny and put her arms around her and gave her a hug and a kiss on the cheek. Penny was excited to see her half-sister as well.

Katelyn had never met Tex's wife, Ellen and was happy to see that she was a good fit into their extended family. Katelyn had two weeks before her classes started so she just wanted to relax and have some fun on the Ranch. She went out horseback riding every day for several hours at a time. She really enjoyed her half-brothers property and could ride for hours and still be on his ranch. She got to know his kids too and was still new at being called "Aunt Kate".

✳ ✳ ✳

Matt Frey was twenty seven and had graduated from UCLA. He was also in search of his Masters. He hailed from northern California near the Oregon border. He had gotten an athletic scholarship to UCLA for wrestling. Unfortunately during his first match he received a separated shoulder that shut him out from the wrestling program. The Coach told him that as a student athlete he would retain the scholarship grant.

"When we offered it to you we were after more than your muscles. We were after your brain as well. So just keep the grades up. You can come visit the wrestling room, but you will not be able to participate. Especially on the team. Good luck to you Matt."

At first he was disappointed, but he did as the coach told him. He buckled down and started to see his name on the Dean's list. His attitude brightened up a lot. He finished his senior year with a 4.0 GPA. The highest in the class.

He came from a Military family so he decide to enlist in the Marines for four years. They took him even though he had had surgery on his shoulder. He came thru the physical abuse of Boot Camp at Fort Pendleton in good shape.

He finished his enlistment and decided it was time to go back to school. He had a degree in Social Science and thought about getting a job working with troubled kids from the LA projects. He applied at University of New Mexico for his Masters. He arrived there on August first and the heat was worse than in California if that is even possible. He had an apartment just off campus and he could walk to class.

As he was walking in the class room he noticed a young girl who was in the same class as he. He looked her over and thought,

'How I wish I could just go over and touch her hand. It would be amazing.'

✳ ✳ ✳

Katlyn picked out a seat in the room where she felt she could hear the Professor well enough and still be able to look out the window when it got too boring. She had just taken her seat when she looked across the room and saw this gorgeous hunk of muscle and good look's. It was Matt Frey.

He took a seat in the next row over from her so that he could see her whenever she turned his way. He already knew what infatuation felt like and he knew this was it. He just had to have her.

It was two weeks into the class that he finally got up the nerve to asking her out sometime. He was blown away. She said "yes" to a coffee break that afternoon.

Katelyn couldn't believe that an actual full grown man had asked her out. It was one of the greatest things that had ever happened to her.

They met at the local Starbucks for a Cappuccino and a Scone. She asked him,

"So, what is your goal from this class? I am looking at a career in School Counseling. I was home schooled up until college of course. One of my Mom's always had a shoulder for me to cry on if I needed it. I know there are a lot of kids who don't have a shoulder they can cry on. I want to be that shoulder. I have a sister that we were afraid was going to be suicidal before she got the care she needed.

He replied,

"WOW, there have been sometimes I wish I had a shoulder to cry on. As it is I have one good shoulder and one not so good. Wrestling injury in College. It didn't keep me out of the Marines for four year's though. There are no crying shoulders there I guarantee you. You mentioned, Moms, plural. How's that?"

Katelyn replied,

"Yes, I have two mothers. They have been together over twenty years and they are still in love. If you want to call them Lesbians, well that's what they are."

Matt replied,

"I see. I have no problem with that. How they want to live their lives is their business."

Katelyn told Matt,

"Well, all of us kids, and there are seven of us that grew up in that house and all went to college if we wanted to. We were home schooled and I started college when I was seventeen. My Brother, Rob inherited a five thousand acre Ranch in Texas from his Dad. One of my sisters started a Dog grooming salon with only a year of a business course. A brother was in the CIA and got killed overseas. His brother invented some kind of heart valve and lives in Kansas City. My youngest siblings are Adam, a musician in Nashville and his sister Penny is a very talented Artist."

Matt pondered what she said and then told Katelyn his story.

"My parents have a Vineyard in California and a winery too. My mother had inherited it from her father who had gotten it from his father. So the business has been in the family for three generations. I had to work hard all the time that I was growing up. There is always something that must be done on a vineyard. From pruning the vines to picking the grapes. We hired Mexicans to do most of the work, but I was out there toe to toe with them every day that I was not at school. I grew to hate the business even if it could make a lot of money. It was first and foremost a lot of work. Don't get me wrong, I am not afraid to work. I just decided to be my own man and not just inherit all the work that was there."

Katelyn said,

"I don't blame you Matt. That is a lot of work and I think you are right to leave it behind."

Matt replied,

"After seeing what I have seen in Las Angeles I know that I have a calling to go help those kids that are being forced into gangs and drugs and other bad stuff. If I can make a difference I want to do it."

When they left Starbucks Matt asked her,

"Where are you staying?"

She replied,

"My Mom, bought me a Town house here in town for while I am here and then I can sell it and use the money to do whatever I need to do. Or keep it for a Rental."

Matt thought about that for a moment and then asked,

"Where is your house?"

Katelyn replied,

"I am on my way there now. Would you like to ride along?" Matt said,

"Maybe next time. I have to get back to my apartment to feed my dog."

Katlyn asked,

"What kind of dog do you have?"

He answered,

"It's just a mutt that I picked up along the street. It had no collar and it looked hungry. So what was I to do? Just walk away? Not my style. So now Sly is my constant companion when I am not at classes. Or soaking up coffee at Starbucks. See you tomorrow."

Katelyn's heart was racing when she got to Patty's Grooming salon. She pushed the door open and announced,

"I'M IN LOVE!!"

Patty and Tina looked up at her and asked at the same time,

"WHO's the lucky girl? Or is it a real guy this time?"

Katelyn told them about Matt and how they had coffee together. Patty pushed the Cavalier St Charles that she was working on away and got up to hug Katelyn. Tina kept working on the Afghan hound that she was occupied with. He was a show dog like their Sparky. Patty took Katelyn by the hand and led her into the office. When they got there she told Katelyn,

"Take a seat sweetie and tell me all about him."

Katelyn started be saying,

"His name is Matt Frey from California and he was in the Marines for four years. He lived on a vineyard up north. Hated it and decided to go to college to get into the same line of work that I want to do. He is in my class at the University. We went out for coffee at Starbucks and spilled our guts about family.

I offered to take him over to my house but he had to go feed his dog. Isn't that sweet?"

Patty nodded and said,

"He does sound like a keeper. Couldn't be seduced, A? Well that's nice. Says something about him. Maybe he's gay. Hate to see you take his pants off on the first date."

Katelyn laughed at her and replied,

"Now that's something you might do. Especially if Tina could hold his arms to keep him from fighting you two off. Don't tell me you wouldn't bring some poor soul in off the street and have your way with him. I'm not even going to bring him over here to be introduced. HE'S MINE!"

✳ ✳ ✳

Donnie Brill had just gotten off the Bus that brought him back to Albuquerque from the State prison where he has been housed for the past five years for just messing up some lesbian's Dog grooming place. He mused to himself.

'They want to see a hate crime. I'll show them what a real hate crime looks like next time. While I was in there I got raped or beat up by Niggers or Spicks every other day. I'm gonna get me some of them too. I hate them Spooks and Spicks. They will pay for my pain. I will pay a visit to my favorite Gay church again. This time it won't be rocks. I know about Molotov Cocktails now.'

✳✳✳

Ellen told Kitty,

"I'm not going to be as cute like Krissy was with her pregnancy announcement. You remember, The March Hare from Alice with the pocket watch and saying, "IM LATE IM LATE". Instead I am going to just say, 'Everyone put your arms up. Now anyone who is not pregnant put your hands down.' Then I will be the only one with my hands up. Won't that be fun?"

 Kitty laughed and said,

"MAYBE, you will be the only one with your hands up. Who else do you think it might be if there if another pair of hands stays up?"

Ellen replied,

"It's not you is it? I know that Trish was hoping that she could have a baby. But I don't think it is her."

Then Ellen said,

"I guess we will see when we all get together. Are all your girls from Albuquerque coming here for the Fourth of July party? I'll bet it's one of them."

✳✳✳

Donny Brill watched as the Bus dropped off some more people in front of the African American cultural center where there was going to be a celebration of the signing of the Civil Rights Bill in 1964. There were a good number of White and Black and Hispanic families who had already entered the building. He watched as the last ones entered. He waited for about a half hour before he carried out his attack.

He walked up to the front door and lit the rag that was stuffed into the neck of the wine bottle that he had filed with gasoline. He watched as people milled around tables of food and listened to a local band playing.

Then he tossed the bottle into the air and watched as it came down and broke open spuing flaming gasoline on the floor and on several people who were standing near where it broke.

Pandemonium broke out and people started screaming and running for the doors.

Donny ran across the street and watched as the fire spread to anything in the way. There were several fire extinguishers in the building and some of those inside managed to get them and proceeded to fight the flames. In a few minutes they had the fire out.

Someone had called 911 and both Fire and Police arrived at the same time. They questioned the people to see if anyone saw who tossed the fire bomb. A little eight year old boy who was standing at the front of the room saw Donny come in and toss the Molotov cocktail. He was able to give the Police a pretty good description. He noted that it was strange that someone was wearing a hoody that time of year. He also had a mask on so that he could only see enough of the man's face to tell he was white.

Katelyn went to class that day and was happy to see Matt standing by the door to the class room. He smiled at her and said,

"Hi Katelyn. Are you ready for the big test today? I studied all weekend and my brain is fried. I didn't think this was going to be this difficult." Katelyn replied,

"I studied for it too and it all just seemed to come fairly easy. Maybe we should study together next time."

Matt thought about it for a second and replied,

"That sounds like a plan. Want to hit the Starbucks after class? We can talk about getting together for a study date."

Katelyn almost turned inside out with glee at hearing Matt suggest a DATE. Even if it was just to study,

"We can go to my place. I have a lot of room to spread out papers and books. It has a nice kitchen to make something to eat. I had two great cooks to learn from growing up. So I can make us a meal when we get there and we can study in the evening."

Matt said,

"I am looking forward to it. For now let's just get past this test today."

Katelyn smiled at him and they walked in the room together.

✳ ✳ ✳

Patty and Tina had just finished up the last of the dogs they had scheduled for the day and the last owner had arrived to pick up their pet.

They closed the shop and headed for home. They were tired and in need of a shower.

Sparky enjoyed going to the shop every day with them. He liked meeting the dogs that came in for grooming service.

When they arrived home they took him out in their enclosed

yard to do his business before going in the house. He ran around the yard a few times to stretch his legs and then he pooped and peed. Now for his supper.

Tina was the first to hit the shower and Patty was not far behind. With the water running as hot as they could stand it they proceeded to lather each other up as they always did.

Patty liked the feel of Tina's hands working all over her body. When she reached between her legs Patty parted them so that she could get all her girl parts as clean as a girl can be. She did the same for Tina.

Patty asked Tina,

"Shall we go to bed and play for a while or should we eat first?" Tina replied,

"If we eat now we will have all evening to play. I would like that if you agree to it."

Patty said,

"How about we play now and have supper and play again?"

Tina agreed. She took Patty's hand when they got out of the shower and toweled her off and powdered her dry skin with baby powder so she smelled good. Patty did the same for Tina. They headed for the bed adjacent to the bathroom.

When they laid down Tina had her head on a pillow and Patty put her hand on Tina's leg and ran her fingers up and down it until Tina put her hand on Patty's and guided it toward her center. With her hand embracing Tina's pubic mound they kissed and Tina pulled Patty over on top of her. She said,

"Let's do what Lois showed me that time. Remember? We cross our legs so that our pussies are touching and then rub them together and push in and out."

Patty replied with a smile,

"O K, I like that. Then we can do what we like the best. You can be on top to start and then the next time I will take top."

They got in position with Tina's left leg over Patty's right leg. Patty had her left leg over Tina's right so that they were in a scissors position. They could see their clits and vaginal openings matched up and ready to move. They did some bumping and then they rubbed their pussies across each other. I t felt good and they knew from experience they could both attain an orgasm from rubbing their wet parts together.

They played like this for fifteen minutes or so and then switched to sixty nine with Tina on top and Patty on the bottom. Patty liked to be able to hold Tina's ass while she licked her pussy. She could use her hand to run it across Tina's opening and make her squirt sometimes. Patty liked it when she did, even if it made a little mess in the bed. It was worth it.

✳✳✳

Donny watched for a while and then walked a block over and got in his car and went home. He was disappointed that no one was killed and only a few suffered burns. He thought,

'Next time I will have to plan ahead and make sure there are no fire extinguishers for them to use. When I do the Lesbians this time I will just fire bomb them like the Niggers. Only I won't fail like I did with them.'

Katelyn and Matt left the campus and headed toward her house that was only a mile or so up the road. When they arrived she parked in the driveway and they walked around back and entered the back door. She liked to go in this way better then thru the formal Livingroom. It just seemed cozier to her. It went right into the kitchen. Alongside the kitchen was a dining room that went to a staircase that went to the second floor where the bed rooms were located. They stopped along the way and picked up a Pizza to have for supper.

After supper they worked on some of the things they had been assigned by their professor. They were told that there were some things in that material that would be helpful for when they had to put together their Thesis.

Katelyn said,

"I don't think I will have much of a problem putting mine together. I am just going to use my own experiences growing up in a blended family of Natural, Foster and Adopted kids. How that dynamic shaped who I am and how it will help me in my career in social work."

Matt replied,

"You do have a lot to draw on. I have a dysfunctional family in some ways. In other ways it all seemed normal. I guess that it was my fault that it seemed dysfunctional. I rebelled at working on the vineyard when I was fourteen and didn't like the way my father and mother treated me afterwards. That was why when I left College I joined the Marines. I have a couple Uncles who were Marines. Anything to keep from going home."

They ate the Pizza and talked for a while when out of the blue Matt asked,

"Katelyn, would you mind if I gave you a kiss? I know I am being a bit forward but I can't stand seeing you and not showing my affection for you." She replied by moving over to him and putting her arms around him. He kissed her on the lips and she was receptive to his warm tongue in her mouth.

They kissed like that for a short time when he reached around her back and under her sweater and unhooked her bra. She raised her arms so he could remove the sweater. Then she took off his sweatshirt and then they kissed as they found a way to remove their pants.

They were down to their under pants and panties. She took his hand and led him to her bed. He laid her down gently on her back and pulled her panties down her legs. He dropped his to the floor. He got down on his knees at the side of the bed and pushed her legs up so he could kiss and lick the back of her legs. He did this to both legs and licked his way up to her crotch.

She remembered the first time Freddy Odom did that. It felt good then and it did now. She liked it when Ashley did it too. Right now she was just going to focus on how Matt was doing it. He was so slow and deliberate when he licked her clit and went down slowly until the tip of his tongue was just at her opening.

He slowly pushed his tongue in her and put one of his fingers inside her vagina. He pushed it in and rubbed her "G" spot while he was sucking on her clit. The more he rubbed it and sucked it the stronger she felt her orgasm happening.

When the first one past she pulled Matt up so that she could have him enter her with his stiff cock. He obliged and when the tip had entered he stopped and pulled out and then pushed back in. Little by little he went deeper until he had pushed all the way in.

Katelyn squeezed her vaginal muscles tight around him and then relaxed. She liked to do this as she knew it would give him a good feeling. When they had done it missionary for a time she pushed him off and said,

"My turn on top, O K?"

Matt rolled onto his back and she mounted him cowgirl style and held his cock so that she could guide it directly into her wet pussy again.

This time she rode him slowly pulling up so the tip was just inside and then slowly lowering herself back down. She kept this up until she could see in his face that the end was coming soon.

She picked up her speed and it was not long before she felt the warmth of his release inside her. She laid down on top of him and he held her in his arms. They fell asleep.

✳ ✳ ✳

Freddy Odom was so excited to be getting married to Ashley that he was beside himself. He had invited all his Frat House Brothers to the wedding. Only a few could accept as they lived too far away to attend.

His Mother, Rose Odom was excited too. Her son had not only graduated from the University, but had a job offer in Dallas. Only a few hours away from her.

Her Mother, his Grandmother was excited also but for another reason. She wanted a Great grandchild and she just knew that it wouldn't be long before she could be holding him or her in her arms. She was not the least bit concerned that the baby's mother was white.

She had seen the result of inter-racial mating's before and she thought they were the prettiest children around. Her own Grand Daddy, Jonny Odom had a girl child with his white wife Barbara Wilson. Her Mother Rita was from his black wife, Nancy.

Rita always wanted to have a white mother. But she was just

black on black and that was who she was. She was just as happy as could be when Freddy announced that he was marrying a white girl from college.

✳ ✳ ✳

Donny waited for the women to leave the grooming salon that evening and he followed them to where they lived. He watched as they got out and went in the house. He waited around until it got dark.

He watched as the upstairs lights went on and then a half hour later they went out. The only light then was from a TV in the bedroom. After the eleven o'clock news was over that went out. He waited until midnight so that he was sure they were asleep.

He got out the Molotov cocktail he had made and walked up to the front door. He peered in and with a flashlight he searched for the stairway to the second floor. His idea was to set the fire in the living room where the stairs were so that they couldn't get out that way and would be forced to jump from the upstairs if they even woke up before the flames reached them.

He turned the bottle upside down to allow the gas to run down into the rag that was the wick.

When he did some of the gas spilled on the sleeve of his hoody. Some splashed on his pant leg as well. He stood at the front door and as he lit the rag the vapors from his pant leg and sleeve reached the flame at the same time.

He dropped the bottle and it broke on the porch and engulfed him.

His screams woke the girls and they smelled the gasoline and saw the flames on the porch.

Patty called 911 to report the fire. Then they ran down and went out the back door with Sparky.

The Fire Department got there in fifteen minutes and were able to extinguish the fire on the porch and found a scorched body there with a broken wine bottle nearby.

There was still some fingers left on its left hand that allowed identification of Donny Brill. They linked him to the other fire-bombing the week before.

Patty was relieved when she found that it was him that had vandalized her shop before. She thought that it was sad that he had to lose his life because he was so hateful of some other groups.

She and Tina went to Church that Sunday and prayed for his poor soul.

✻ ✻ ✻

Kitty took her new Grandchildren back up to the Ranch in New Mexico for a couple weeks so that she could have them close to her and Trish while they were still very young. It seems that kids are born and the next thing they are off to College.

While there they took them out on the sail boat every day and Skipper liked to catch fish. Sunshine liked to play with the old Golden Retriever, Ginger. The dog liked the attention and enjoyed chasing the ball when it was thrown.

While they were there Kitty got a call from her brother Jack. He told her that Evelyn and he were lucky to have survived a boating accident on the high seas. They decide to take the Insurance money for the lost Lobster boat and start over in something that had a solid footing instead of a rocking deck.

The cold snowy winters in Maine were catching up with them and they decide to move south and open a Bait and Fishing Tackle shop along the Gulf coast and wondered what Kitty thought about the idea. She said,

"You ever hear about something called a Hurricane? They happen pretty frequently along that coast. You know Texas has a lot of inland lakes that are not totally immune to storms but they are usually a lot less damaging. And I'm sure there are places for a Bait shop." Jack thought about what she said and then replied,

"You know what little sister? You are still pretty smart about some things. This is one of them. I am going to look at Texas and find a place to call home. It will be hard leaving Maine with some family still there but Evelyn and I have had enough."

Kitty replied,

"Why don't you two come on down and stay here for a while until you find a spot. My son Rob and his Partner know a lot of people over that way and can probably hook you up with a good deal. There are a lot of large lakes out west of Austin. Like Lake Buchannan and Lake Travis."

Jack said,

"We'll think about your offer to stay with you guys until we can get settled somewhere. Talk to you later, love you sister, Bye now."

Kitty replied, "Love you to. Talk again later."

When she hung up the phone she turned to Trish and said,

"That was Brother Jack. He and Evey are abandoning Maine for a warmer place. They lost their boat in a storm and with the insurance money they are looking to open a bait shop somewhere warm. I told him there are a lot of lakes in Texas that would probably have room for another bait shop. I told him they should come here to stay until they find a place to settle."

Trish replied,

"That sounds fantastic. I have never met your Brother but I know he cares a lot for you and you for him. Of course they can stay here. Love to have them."

✳ ✳ ✳

Penny loved to watch the sunset up on the mountain as the colors changed from blue to red to a golden orange mixed with yellows. She liked to try to match those colors in her work. She had done a series of paintings where she would do one and then turn her vision so that the next one was at the edge of the first. Making a panoramic series from the one place where she set up. She did this at different times of the year to pick up on the different colors that prevailed.

In late winter when there was still snow on the high places and the Aspin were still bare skeletons of themselves. The rocks and fallen logs were able to be seen on the ground.

One day as she was working on a painting a young woman walked up the mountain with her little dog. She stopped to watch and chat with Penny. She was an attractive Apache about thirty years old. As they chatted she told Penny,

"My Sister is an Artist too. She likes to do portraits of our old people on the Mescalero Reservation. She has sold a number of them down in Santa Fe." Penny replied,

"Oh really? My adoptive Brother married a girl from that reservation. They live up in Kansas now. I don't get to see them very often. They come down maybe once a month for a weekend. That's about it. Her name is Brenda. She lived with her Grandmother on the reservation after her mom died. What's your name?"

The woman replied,

"My name is Ronnie Davis. I moved from the reservation when I went to College in Santa Fe. I went to Saint John's College for my bachelors, a liberal Arts degree. I applied and was accepted to Southwestern College for my Masters. It was in Counseling and Art Therapy. I heard about you in my travels and wanted to meet you. I understand you suffered a loss in your life and it left you in a world of hurt. I understand it took a while for you to recover from it. Can I ask you about your recovery? I know we have just met, but your Mom's said I could talk with you if you are willing."

Penny looked at Ronnie and after a bit she asked,

"What would you like to know?"

Ronnie replied,

"Has your Art helped you to stay focused away from the pain you experienced?" Penny responded,

"I have been home now for some time and I feel that it does help me. The man who helped me to fully develop my talent was the cause of my problem. We fell in love and when the romance dissolved and he left I was heartbroken. He died shortly after that and I felt responsible for his death. Which was ridiculous. He just had a heart attack, not my fault. Let's move on, please." Ronnie looked at Penny and then asked,

"Do you still have feelings for him?" Penny replied,

"NO, I have recovered from the hurt and I have moved on. I do not have an active love life at this time and I am alright with that. I live here with my mom's and I enjoy painting and then taking my work to town to display it for sale."

Ronnie asked,

"Would you go with me to Santa Fe to meet my Professor and

tell her how your recovery and life are doing with your Art as a means of copping with your grief?"

Penny looked at her and without hesitation said,

"When would you like to go? I can pack up a few things and we can be on our way today if you like."

Ronnie smiled at Penny and told her,

"You sure are an enthusiastic girl if I do say so. Let's go talk to your Moms and let them know what we are doing. O K?"

Penny packed up her supplies and easel and headed down to the house. When they arrived she told Trish and Kitty that Ronnie wanted her to go with her to Santa Fe to visit her professor so that she could ask her about how her Art has helped her to return from the dark place she was in following Giorgio's death. The women thought about it for a moment and then Trish asked Ronnie,

"This isn't something that is going to possibly set her back is it?"

Ronnie told her,

"No, I think she has enough recovery time to be past any loss of progress. I wouldn't ask her to do this if I thought it would."

Kitty asked,

"How long will she be there?"

Ronnie said,

"Only a day or two. I want to have her visit the Campus in case she ever wants to pursue a career in counseling herself."

Trish told Ronnie,

"She doesn't even have a bachelor's degree to be able to attend a Masters course. I don't know if she wants to do that. She got a lot of help from the professionals at the Hospital she was at and has a deep respect for them."

Penny said that she did indeed respect them, but really did not want to pursue that as a career. With that she looked at her moms and said,

"So can I go with Ronnie?"

They agreed that it would be alright for her to visit Southwestern College for a few days.

She packed up a few changes of clothes and they were on their way by noon after a light lunch with Trish and Kitty. Ronnie was very interested in how Penny came about being raised by two women.

On the way she asked her and Penny replied,

"When my Brother and I were young our parents both died from a drug overdose. We became wards of the state as we had no other relatives to go to. Kitty and Trish were contacted by Children's Services and we were placed in their care as Foster kids. They later adopted Adam, my Brother and I. We have been here ever since. We couldn't have found a better home to live in."

"Has the fact that they are Lesbians had any effect on you or your brother?"

Penny said,

"We get that a lot. No, we have had a very happy home to live in and they have been the most loving parents that we could ever ask for. I do have an older sister who is married to another woman. They are happy together and have a dog grooming shop near Albuquerque. So I guess that a girl can fall in love with whoever they want. Whether it's a man or another woman."

She asked Ronnie,

"Do you have a boyfriend or do you have a girlfriend. I am going to guess the latter. Am I right?"

Ronnie replied,

"Guilty as guessed. Your "gaydar" is pretty well tuned. We have been together for over a year now. She was from Dallas and came to the College for her Masters too. Her name is Jamey and she is twenty six. She is a mixed race girl whose father was Black and her mother was Asian. They met in College too. Jamie is a very sweet girl who is 5'-6" tall and has a lighter shade of skin, kind of like bronze. I guess. You will meet her at our house."

The rest of the trip was made up of small talk. When they got to Santa Fe they stopped for supper at a Red lobster. Penny enjoyed the trip and the meal. They headed over to the house that Ronnie and Jamie shared. It was about two miles from the Campus.

Jamie met Ronnie at the door with a kiss. Penny followed her in and smiled at Jamie. She looked Penny up and down and then told Ronnie,

"This is the prettiest girl that you have brought home in a long while. That last one was the super model from San Angelo Texas. She was a doll, but this gal is no slouch. Hi my name to Jamie. Pardon me if I gush. That's just my personality. Ronnie probably already warned you about me."

Penny laughed and said,

"That's alright. I am usually on the quiet side until I get to know someone. She failed to tell me that you are so pretty. I love the color of your skin. I am an Artist and I take notice of skin colors of people. She told me you are mixed race. I have three siblings who are half Apache and white. They tend to be a shade lighter than bronze. So when their parents were killed in a car wreck they were shunned on the reservation for having a white mother. That's how they got to be in my family. My Mom's adopted five of us. There are two more who just happened to get born into the family."

Jamie and Ronnie took all this in and then Jamie remarked,'

"She has an interesting past. Makes you wonder where she may go."

Ronnie asked,

"Do you mean career wise or orientation wise?"

Jamie looked at Penny and then just asked her,

"You are a big girl. Which way do you think you will want to swing?"

Penny looked up at the ceiling before she answered.

"Is this what this is about? To see if I am interested in your lifestyle choice? Perhaps I am. I have never been kissed or done anything else with a girl." Jamie asked,

"Would you like to try it?"

Penny looked at her and without any warning she grabbed Jamie and kissed her on the lips. Jamie pushed her away and said,

"Ronnie and I are a couple and although I would like to bed you sometime I don't think it is appropriate to just up and kiss me like that."

Penny was embarrassed and replied,

"I'm sorry I just had to do that. I wanted to feel what it was like to kiss a girl. I am sorry if I offended you or acted out of place."

Ronnie told Penny,

"That's O K. I like to watch when Jamie is making love with another woman. She likes to watch me too. So don't be embarrassed for what you did. It happens all the time. When you meet my Professor you will be amazed at how beautiful she is for a Tran's woman."

Penny's eyes went wide and her mouth dropped open.

"Are you serious? I have never met a Tran's person before."

Ronnie told her,

"You are in the big city now country mouse. You may see and hear things you have never encountered before. Let's sit down and talk for a while about things."

Penny nodded and took a seat at their dining room table. Jamie sat across from her and Ronnie sat at the end. Ronnie started the conversation by asking Jamie,

"Tell us how you lost your virginity. I know the story but I think Penny will like to hear it.

Jamie looked at the other two and then she said,

"It happened a long time ago. I was twelve at the time. There was an older man who lived next door and we would visit back and forth. One day when my parents were away he came over and asked me if I would like to play a game with him. I asked what the game was and he said, here I'll show you. With that he pulled out his cock and told me to lick it and watch it grow. I trusted him and so I did as he asked. While I was licking it he pushed it into my mouth. I pulled away from him and told him I didn't want to play his game anymore. He grabbed me and pulled my pants down and slipped my panties off. He then picked me up and while he was sitting on the couch he sat my naked butt down on top of him. It hurt when he tried to put it in me. I wiggled around to try to keep it from going in. He did manage to get the tip in and then he worked it around in there until I was wet enough for it to slip in. He rocked me front and back so that it went in and out of my pussy. After while it started to feel good and then I felt something warm in my belly as he ejaculated inside me. When he was done he asked,

'Now didn't that feel good like I told you it would? Next time we'll try to get in the back door. But before I do it I will lick your pretty little pussy and your ass hole to make you really feel good before we do it the back way. OK?'

Penny sat spell bound as Jamie related how she lost her virginity. Ronnie said

"O K, now I will tell you my story. I was thirteen when my older Brother came in my bed room while our parents were asleep and he asked me if he could lick my pussy. I told him to go away that no

I didn't want him to do that to me. He insisted and got in my bed and pulled my nighty up and pulled my panties down. He pushed my legs apart and buried his head in my crotch. The next thing I know he is pushing his tongue into my crack. It felt weird but I kind of liked it. He found my clit and as he licked it and stuck his finger inside me I felt a strange thing happening to me. I never felt it before but now I know it was my first orgasm. He slid up my belly and I felt him pushing his cock inside me. It went in slowly and when he had the whole thing in I felt him let go with his load. He didn't know then how to control his ejaculation back then. Believe me he knows now. He told me that he just thinks about something else. Sometimes he can just think about mowing the yard and trimming the edges. Doing this he said he can last for a half hour or more. Depending on who he is fucking. She looked at Penny and said,

"Your turn Country Mouse. Tell us how it happened."

Penny sat there with her hands in her lap thinking about when Giorgio had first taken her virginity up on the mountain side in the daytime on top of the table. As she thought about it the feelings came flooding back. The sensation of his hands on her naked skin. The feeling of his tongue on her girl parts. How wonderful it felt when he did it. Then the feeling of his cock sliding inside her. Finally she spoke,

"It was the most amazing thing that ever happened to me and I do truly miss him. "

Ronnie and Jamie sat and looked at Penny and then Ronnie said,

"That is precious Country Mouse. Tell me about you're feeling about girls. Have you ever had any thought about how it would feel to be in the arms of another female?"

Before Penny could reply Jamie asked,

"Do you ever taste your own juices down there? You know when you masturbate."

Now Penny said,

"Yes I do fanaticize how it would feel to be with another girl. They are so much softer than boys and men. Yes, Jamie I do masturbate like all girls do and boys to. I have seen my Brothers bed sheets. The answer is yes I have tasted my juices and I like them. I suppose that most all girls taste alike."

Jamie asked

"Would you like to find out? There are two of us that you can do a taste test on if you want to find out." Penny looked at Jamie and said,

"I have never done this before so you will have to guide me so I do it right, OK?"

With that all three got up from the table and Jamie led the way to their bed room.

When they got there Ronnie was the first one naked. Jamie was not far behind.

Penny started to remove her cloths. She looked at the two naked women laying on the bed in front of her and she could feel herself getting very turned on.

They started kissing and fondling each other's breasts. Penny watched with interest while she removed the last of her cloths. She got up on the end of the bed and watched as the other two laid on their backs and parted their legs.

Penny could see both of their open and wet pussies. She moved up closer and put her finger on Ronnie's clit and watched her face as she gently rubbed it. She put a finger on Jamie's clit and worked both of them at the same time it brought a smile to all three of them.

Penny moved closer to Jamie and touched her tongue to Jamie's leg where it touches her pubes. She licked there for a minute before moving into her vagina.

She licked it and pushed her tongue in as far as it would reach. She went back up to her clit and sucked and licked it until she felt Jamie having an orgasm. She decided it was time to service Ronnie. She did the same treatment that she gave Jamie. Then Ronnie told her,

"O K you did good. Now it's our turn to pleasure you Country Mouse."

Penny moved over to let the others get up off the bed. She moved over front and center.

Ronnie went first and pushed Penny's legs up to her chest. She went down on her pussy and followed on down to lick her anus. She spent a lot of time there as she knew how good it felt.

She let Penny's legs go back down as Jamie climbed on to get a face job. Penny was amazed at how these woman could give her some of the most amazing orgasms of her life.

The other two let her sit on their faces as well so that she could get as much experience as they could deliver.

Before the night was over they introduced her to scissoring or 'tribbing' as it is also called.

It is where the two women cross their legs so that they can rub their wet pussies together. Rubbing their clits and feeling their wetness can bring them to an orgasm sometimes if not every time. This comes from reliable sources.

✳ ✳ ✳

The next day Ronnie took Penny over to the College to meet her Professor. When they entered her office Penny was amazed at how everything looked. The Professor walked in a minute later and shook Penny's hand.

It took a minute for it to register what Ronnie had told her yesterday that this is a Tran's woman. Penny looked her over and noticed her breasts. They were a nice size and shape. Her hair was brown and hung down below her shoulders.

She had a nice figure thanks to the hormones that she had been taking for several years. She was in her forties, but could pass for thirty. Penny wondered if she had the final surgery.

Ronnie introduced her to Penny,

"Penny, this is Ms. Donna Dixson, she is the Department Head. She has been here for the past fifteen years and knows more about Art Therapy then anyone on the planet. She has several PHD's in phycology and Social Science. Ms. Dixson I want you to meet Penny Flick from up north around Magdalena in the mountains. She had been in treatment for deep depression with suicidal tendencies for nearly two years. She has been discharged for some time and she is an excellent Artist who has sold many of her paintings in Magdalena as well as up in Taos. After watching Ms. Frick for the past several days at her home and then in my home. I truly feel that her Art work is helping with her depression. My Partner and I have seen that she can be made happy and contented by Lesbian activity, which she says is a new thing in her life. Whether she ops for the lifestyle or not is up to her. We have shown her that she can be happy on that side of the street, meaning being a Lesbian. She has two Lesbians as her parents since she was seven years old. It is not a life style that is foreign to her.

The Professor looked at Penny and then asked,

"Are you happy with your life right now or is there something that you would like to do that would make you happier or more contented?" Penny looked from Ronnie to the Professor. Then she replied.

"Yes there is something that I would like to do that will make me more contented and happy. That thing is to have my own Art Studio and teach the techniques that Giorgio taught me to younger student so they can have similar success like me."

✳ ✳ ✳

Brother Adam in Nashville has met a girl who he has fallen for. Her name is Jenni. She comes from the Gulf Coast and is the daughter of a Vietnamese immigrant and a mixed race woman. She is drop dead beautiful and it is not wasted on Adam.

He has invited her to come and hear him play at a Club in Nashville. A local band picked him up to replace their Guitar player who left town suddenly and left the band short a key player.

Adam auditioned for the spot and got it. The pay was not too bad either. The Head of the band told Adam that he had bookings in town for the next five weeks and then he was heading to Dollywood for a week. He was able to give Adam work for six weeks. He hoped that there would be more gigs coming. Adam liked the guy and enjoyed playing with a band. He mostly played on the street or for parties as back ground noise.

Jenni showed up at the Club with a couple of friends from College that liked Country music. After all this is Nashville. They arrived shortly before the band was to start playing and Adam saw them in the audience. He smiled and waved to Jenni and her friends.

They started playing and the band was known to do a lot of Garth Brooks songs.

Everyone enjoyed them and when they played "I've got friends in low Places" the whole room went wild. The girls had a lot of fun and decide to become "Groupies" and follow the band around town while they were playing here.

Maybe even get lucky some night when the band was Horney.

Jenni was waiting when the evening came to an end at two a.m. Adam packed up his Guitar and they walked out to her car. They loaded it up and headed for her place.

They got there and went inside. Jenni poured them each a cold Ice Tea. Adam liked that better than sodas. Sodas made him burp.

Jenni had some news to tell Adam. Her parents were coming up from Corpus Christi to visit for a couple days. She wanted him to meet them.

Her Mom and Dad liked country music and was sure that they would like to hear Adam play. She was right.

They arrived at her Place on Friday afternoon and Adam had a gig that evening.

She took them out for supper and then to the Club to hear him play in the band.

They enjoyed the evening and then they headed back to her apartment after the club closed. They were impressed with Adam and thought that Jenni had found a nice young man.

He came over to meet them the next day when they could spend more time in a quieter environment than the Club. He told them his family history and how he and Penny were adopted and grew up in New Mexico.

Jenni's mother asked him,

"Did you have any harassment growing up with having Lesbian mothers? It was probably good that you were away from the town or cities at that time."

Adam replied,

"No, it was never a problem. They are very independent women who took no disrespect from anyone. They have been the most loving and supportive parents any child could want. There were seven of us kids in the family and we all got along together. Most have gone on to College and have been successful in life. My brother Rob has a big Ranch west of Huston."

Jenni's Dad asked,

"What happened to your parents?"

Adam told him,

"They both died from a drug overdose we were told. We went to Trish and Kitty at first as foster care and then they adopted us. Best thing that could ever happen."

Her dad said,

"It sounds like you are right. Jenni should bring you down to our home some time. I will take you out on one of our shrimp boats. You like shrimp?"

Adam smiled and replied,

"I sure do Sir. Right up there with Barbequed Pork ribs."

Her Dad laughed and said,

"A man after my own heart. My wife here can do up some of the finest ribs you will ever eat. She grew up in a mixed up family like ours, except her mom was a half black and her dad was from German emigrants and was as white as could be. I am from Vietnam so Jenni has a varied racial background. But ribs are a favorite at our house.

Adam replied,

"Yeah, my Moms were raised in the Northeast and they learned how to cook Pot roasts at a young age. My mom, Trish lived in New York and had a Nanny that taught her how to cook. Mom Kitty, was from Maine and knew how to do sea food."

They continued to chat into the evening and about ten o'clock

Jenni's mom and dad said that it was their bed time.

Her dad said,

"We'll see you two in the morning. Our long trip and the time at the club is catching up with us."

Jenni and Adam said good night to her parents and they all went to bed.

After she and Adam were in her bed they talked for a while about how her parents seemed to like Adam. He said,

"They are really nice people. You picked a good pair to be your parents."

She laughed at that and said,

"Luck of the sperm I guess. I could have been a boy and ended up on the shrimp boat from the time I was six years old like my Dad. Instead I didn't go on the boat until I was twelve. That was when I decided to go to College instead so that I didn't have to work on the deck of a boat."

Adam asked her,

"You never have told me what your major is at Vanderbilt."

Jenni told Adam,

"I am in my senior year of an Accounting program using computer science to generate profit and loss generations that can predict the future of a business and how that business can get to that level. It bases that projection on past performance and the local market."

Adam said,

"That sounds complicated. Why not just go into brain surgery or something simple like that?"

Jenni looked at him and smiled,

"Let's just forget about it and just make love."

With that she kissed Adam and put her arms around him. Adam responded by putting his hand on her pussy and giving it a gentle squeeze. Jenni gave a little moan as she continued to give him her tongue. He could feel his cock getting harder. She reached down and held it in her hand. Stroking it gently she asked,

"Would you like me to suck you off a little bit before you get inside me?"

Adam grinned and said,

"Only if you let me lick your pussy for a bit more than a bit. Like until you cum. Will that be alright with you?"

She replied,

"How about if you let me suck you all the way until you come too. Would you like to cum in my mouth or between my tits?

Adam was really getting Horney with her talking dirty to him.

He suggested,

"Why don't we just do it sixty nine? I'll let you be the top that way when I cum you can decide what to do. Spit or swallow."

She replied,

"You know I always swallow unless you want me to share it with you in a kiss."

Adam let her turn around and put her crotch over his face with her legs parted so he could get right where he needed to be. He put his hands on her small ass checks and massaged them while he licked her small girl parts. She shaved her pubic hair so the she really did look like a twelve year old girl except for her tits. She must have gotten that gene from her mother's black background. Surely not from her father's Vietnamese genetic factor.

Adam enjoyed having sex with Jenni and thought that he just might be falling in love. He had not ever felt what he was feeling now. He was also feeling that he was about to squirt his load. She had the gentlest way of using her tongue on him and it was working. He felt like his ass was turning to stone as it got nearer and nearer to the finish line. He grabbed her pussy in his mouth and shook it back and forth and he muttered,

"I love you Jenni."

As he felt his ejaculation happen. She moved up and down on him as she sucked every last drop of essence from him.

They both laid there as their passion waned and they decide to go to sleep and finish what they have started in the morning.

In their minds they both knew that this was a special time and it was going to be a life changing moment.

In the morning Adam had her mount him cowgirl way and she rode him to another warm planting of his seed. He watched her eyes as he flowed into her. They both knew that they had just started a family of their own.

Her parents left for home that afternoon and promised Adam that they would love to have him and their Daughter come to visit them in Corpus Christi.

✳ ✳ ✳

The day of Freddy and Ashley's wedding was getting near. She invited Katelyn to come down to stay with her at Freddy's Mom's house to get ready for the big day. Ash was going to be wearing a beautiful off white dress that had a train that was ten feet long. It had poufy shoulders and a conservative neckline. Katelyn's dress was a pastel green and was floor length.

Rob and Krissy and the kids were coming for the wedding and staying at a local motel. Tex and Ellen came along with them. Trish and Kitty came with Patty and Tina.

Katelyn thought,

'Wow, that's most of my extended family. I wonder who all will come to my wedding. Probably have to have a partner first. Which way should I swing? I really like a man, but I kind of like girls too. OH, Ash, you have confused my mind.'

✳ ✳ ✳

It was the night before the wedding and she, Krissy, Ellen, Trish and Kitty had a bachelorette party for Ash.

Kitty and Ellen went to a Liquor store and got several bottles of Yellow Tail Wine. They had a local Caterer come with a mix of snacks and sweet treats. Fancy cheese and crackers.

They had a good time and made fun of Ashley. Fitting condoms on a bratwurst and laying it between a pair of wrinkled up prunes. They put a hole in a large peach and stuck the Brat in it. The women drank all the wine and it was after midnight when they called it a night.

Ash and Katelyn went to bed. They had shared a bed on many occasions in College. They thought that after tonight they would not be sleeping together again.

They would go their separate ways in life and possibly not see one another again. Oh no, they would still be able to visit some times.

Katelyn did have deep feeling for Ashley. She had feelings for Freddy too. He had been their first time and he had made a bond with both of them. Perhaps they should explore Polyamory. She turned over in the bed and asked Ashley,

"I am thinking about something that I don't know how you will take it."

Ash asked,

"What's on your mind?"

Katlyn replied,

"I am thinking about having a Polyamorous relationship with you and Freddy. Do you think he would be up for it?"

Ashly's eyes went wide and she replied,

"We can ask him and I'm sure he would love to have you as his side girl. You can be my side girl too. Wouldn't that be great?"

Katelyn kissed Ash and said,

"We would be a "Throuple". Even if we live apart we can get together when we can and share our love for each other. I like the idea. Let's propose it to Freddy tomorrow after the wedding. Or, do you think we should break it to him now?"

Ash looked at her and asked,

"What's his number? I'll call him now."

Katlyn said,

"It's only two thirty. You think he is still awake?"

Ash said,

"I don't know if he had as much to drink as we have but if he did he is probably asleep like we should be. Now give me a good kiss this time."

She did and with their mouths open they had their tongues exploring each other. Ashley put her hands on Katelyn's ass and squeezed it. Katlyn responded by putting her hand down on Ash's pussy. She wiggled her middle finger in her hole and bent her finger to rub her "G" spot. Ash said,

"Let's move over so we can sixty-nine."

Katelyn smiled and said,

"I was just going to suggest that myself. You want top or bottom?"

Ash told her,

"You can take top this time. I'll do it next time."

***

The next day the wedding went off with no problem. The bride and the groom both had a slight hangover from the Bachler parties the night before.

Rob had a couple beers but Tex had a diet coke. He has been sober for over thirty years and attends AA meetings on a monthly basis. It has helped him to stay sober.

He fell off the wagon a time or two right after his best friend, Rob Harris, Rob's Father was killed at the rodeo when thrown from a bull.

He had told Rob that he needed to watch his drinking. He even told him that if he wanted to he would take him to a meeting.

Rob said that he only drank beer and he didn't drink to get drunk. He could also leave it alone if he wanted to.

Tex never pressed the issue with him. He had told him a long time ago about losing a close friend to whiskey. His friend was driving drunk when he had a car wreck that killed his girlfriend. He committed suicide shortly after. Tex was crushed.

***

Freddy and Ashley headed for New Orleans for their Honeymoon. They stayed at a bed and breakfast in the French quarter and fucked their asses off. She asked him about including Katelyn in their relationship. They both love her.

Freddy thought about it for a while and then told Ash,

"You know what? That's a good idea. And you are right, I do love her as much as I do you and if she was here right now I would let you watch as I fucked her right here in this bed."

They both laughed and Ash got back on top to ride him like a horse.

Freddy said,

"Then I can watch you two go at it with that kissin' and pussy licken'. It would make my old cock stand up and want to join in."

Ashley laughed and told him,

"Yeah, you would like to watch wouldn't you? If we saw that you were hard again we would both jump your bones. You got the sweetest cock around. I would sit on your face awhile she would suck your sweet cock until you pop your load."

Freddy grinned and asked,

"Do you want to sit on my face right now?" Ash moved up in the bed and straddled his face while she placed her hands on the head board to hold on. Freddy did a good job on her and he had her getting one orgasm after another for a half hour. He reached back and jerked off while she kept him busy with his tongue. They were both ready to go back to the real world after a week in the City. The food is great and the sex was magnificent.

✳ ✳ ✳

Patty and Tina asked Trish and Kitty about how they went about adopting a child. They felt they were ready to be parents.

They were told to see the children's service office in Albuquerque. They were sure they could help.

They would do an investigation of them first before they would recommend an adoption. Their best way would be to get a child thru

Foster parenting. That was the way they got Adam and Penny.

Tina told them,

"I have not told you my back story. I have not even told Patty. I was in the "system", foster care that is, for most of my life. My mother was a meth head and she gave me up when I was three. I was starting to be a problem when she brought the Johns home. She didn't want me to see what she did to support her drug habit. My dad was a drunk and left her right after I was born. He went back to the Reservation and he was never seen again. I was in one home after another. I didn't get along with some of the other kids there so they just kept pushing me along to another town and another house. Finally when I aged out of the system at eighteen I hit the streets. It was not long after that when Patty found me. She gave me a job that I love and now we have a beautiful house that we can raise a child in."

Kitty looked at Tina and said,

"I am sorry to hear that you had a bad experience with the system. It is broken in some places but the people there do try to do their best for the kids. Sometimes I guess that some just fall thru the cracks. We adopted Patty and her brothers when they were orphaned. We will do everything we can to help you get a child."

Trish looked at Patty and told her,

"You have really made me a happy mom. Being able to start your business and expand it like you have. Your unexpected good fortune to have met Lois Lawrence when you did. And her kindness to bequeath to you all her stuff. House, cars and her sweet dog Sparky. I just know he would like to have a playmate in the house."

✳ ✳ ✳

Ellen told Tex that she was ready to go to the hospital. If they didn't get there soon she was going to have this little girl there in the ranch house.

He told her that would not be a problem. He and Harold and the other cowboys had helped birth calves and foals so they could probably handle some little girl child.

Ellen said,

"That's O K, I still want to be somewhere that I know that they know what they are doing."

Tex smiled at her and said,

"Get in the car and we will be there in fifteen minutes or so, it's only thirty some miles to North Cypress Hospital.'

"You think I want to go a hundred twenty miles an hour your wrong. I can hold her in a little bit longer if you just drive sensibly."

Tex was O K with that. She was in a hurry to get there. He was just trying to help. It took about forty minutes to get there to Ellen's satisfaction. They went in and it was only fifteen minutes until Tex was Daddy to a six pound four ounce daughter. He didn't smoke, but he handed out cigars to everyone he met.

To be a father when other men his age were sending their kids to College was O K with him and Ellen. She was a lot younger then Tex.

✳ ✳ ✳

While Trish and Kitty were up to visit Patty they decided it was time to go to the Hospital and get their annual mammograms. They have been consciences about getting them as Trish's mother died young from breast cancer. They had made appointments earlier that week so they could just walk in at the appointed time. Kitty went first and with the three dimensional X-Ray machine it could find the very earliest signs of a tumor.

Then Trish got her's done. They waited for the results of the X-rays. The Dr. came out to the waiting room and called Trish to follow him in to see the pictures that were taken of her right breast. It showed a spot about the size of a pea. He explained that at that size they would do a biopsy to determine if it was malignant. She asked him if it could be done that day as they had traveled a long distance to get there. He said the best he could do was that afternoon about four o'clock. Trish told him that was fine. They waited at Patty's shop until it was time to return to the Hospital for the biopsy.

After the biopsy was done the Dr. reported to Trish that it was indeed malignant.

He said that they would do a "lumpectomy" to determine how far it had spread. They did that the next day and they found that it was a type of cancer that was confined to the one breast and it was not likely to be in both.

They discussed the next option. The cancer cells were found on the edges of the sample that they removed. They would have to do another lumpectomy.

That also showed more cancer cells. They conferred with Trish and Kitty and together they decided to have a bilateral mastectomy in case the cancer would eventually spread.

They scheduled the surgery to be done in two days so they made arrangement to stay at Patty's house.

Trish would be in the Hospital for about five days until the healing was starting and the stitches could come out. She had to admit they had done a magnificent job of making them almost invisible. Now she wanted to schedule a restoration surgery. To do this they told her that they take fat from the belly and move it up to where the breasts were. It is a major surgery and has its risks.

Tex and Ellen came home with the new baby. Robs kids were excited to see their new 'cousin'. She was named Rachel Gloria Duncan. They gave her their grandmothers' names from both sides of the family. She is being breast fed and Ellen is a good source of milk.